A Burnt Child

Shereen Pandit

Published in 2012 by FeedARead.com Publishing – Arts Council funded

First Edition

A CIP catalogue record for this title is available from the British
Library.

DEDICATION

For Bahir, my very own "patron of the arts" without whose moral and financial support this book would never have been written.

CHAPTER ONE

Lily came back into our lives much as she had left it – without so much as a word of warning. She left it to Viv to do her dirty work, as usual.

"You gave her my contact details?" I said into the phone. I took a deep breath to contain my anger. It didn't work. "What the hell did you think you were doing? And without asking me first?"

"She asked," Viv said calmly. I envisaged her smooth round face, six thousand miles away, totally unruffled by my rage. "I gave it. No point in saying I didn't know. She'd guessed you'd be in touch with me, once everything blew up and I wasn't untouchable any longer."

"Well, as far as I'm concerned, Lily is."

Viv said, "I could hardly tell her that."

"You're good at keeping secrets. You could have kept my details secret, if you'd wanted to. Secrets is what we do, right?"

Viv laughed. "Did," she corrected. "Did. I'm out of practice. I thought she'd see through any excuses."

"Still an expert at making people give up secrets, then, is she?" I said. "As long as they're not hers, of course." Viv said nothing. "You're a shrink these days," I raged on. "Why didn't you just tell her the truth? Don't you tell your patients it's better to face reality and all that? So, let Lily face the reality of me not being available to do whatever it is she wants from me. Because you can bet she wants something. Nobody suddenly pops up in someone else's life years after they've left it. She doesn't just want a hello over a latte."

"No. I agree. She probably does want something." A pause.

"And you wouldn't happen to know what that is."

A sigh, like she was doing something she didn't want to but thought she had to. "Listen, Yazz, why don't you see her? Talk to her? You're still so angry. It would help you to move on."

"I'm not one of your fucking patients!" I hated being told what I felt, especially being told I was angry, when to my mind I felt as calm as was possible in the circumstances. "I *have* moved on," I said through gritted teeth. "I've got a life now. And there's no room for Lily and her crap in it. You call her up, Viv. Try telling her I've gone trekking overland to Timbuktu. I've gone to the moon. I've died and you've only just heard. I don't care. Just keep her away from me."

Viv was suddenly angry herself, "For god's sake, Yazz. Listen to yourself! A lot of people lost out in the struggle. People lost their lives, remember? And Lily," she paused. "You seem to forget that Lily lost a child. Not a foetus, like you did. A living little girl."

That was so way below the belt that I gasped, as though she'd punched me. I took a deep breath to steady myself. "That," I finally said, my voice sounding shaky even in my own ears, "was *not* my fault. And I wasn't aware we were grading losses these days, to validate feelings."

"I'm sorry, Yazz," said Viv, calm and gentle once more, "I wasn't suggesting any of that. I know how much you did for Heather. I know how badly you still feel about…It's just…don't you feel any sympathy for Lily at all? How did we come to this?

"Are you asking seriously?"

"No." She paused. "Alright. I'll call Lily and tell her you'd rather not see her."

"You do that," I said, hanging up.

I went into the kitchen and took out the packet of cigarettes from under the sink, behind all the cleaning stuff, where I'd hidden them from myself. I lit one, poured some coffee, thought about whether my need for his calming voice was a good enough reason to call my husband Adam at work. Deciding it probably wasn't, I reached for the phone anyway. It rang before I could make the call. Half-expecting Lily

6

herself, I let it ring, go to answer-phone. It was only Viv, calling again to say that Lily'd already left Cape Town, first for a stop in Jo'burg, then for London. She didn't know where Lily would be staying, probably at one of the big hotels. She was some kind of executive in a big company these days. All part of black economic empowerment. Apparently she was on a business trip, not just coming to see me. So maybe it was just coffee and catch-up she wanted, Viv said unconvincingly before hanging up. "One couldn't tell with Lily these days."

Yes, I thought. One couldn't tell. Which Lily would turn up, I wondered. The Lily I'd last seen, reluctantly showing the bruises that brute Al had left her with? Lily as she'd been the day she'd arrived from Cape Town with him, the unexpected sixth member of the Cadre Group in Exile, inexplicably, at the time, surly and uncommunicative? Or had she reverted to the Lily I'd first encountered, hippy chick Lily, on campus, registration day, back in the late seventies. I picked up the cigarettes, purse, mobile. Jammed it all into a bag and hurried out, as if Lily might show up on my doorstep at any moment, despite what Viv had said about her first going to Jo'burg. I sat in a coffee shop by the Thames for a while, letting the slow moving boats on the brown-grey water restore the peace in my mind that Viv had disturbed. Watching the endless flow of people and traffic over Waterloo Bridge, trying to concentrate on conversations around me, snatches of other lives that might block off the memories – of Lily, of the struggle, of the Party we'd all built, devoted our youth to, then destroyed. That other life. That other country. Whichever Lily turned up, whatever she wanted, I wanted none of it. And this time there was no Party to discipline me for uncomradeliness. I called Adam on my mobile.

"Let's go away," I said.

"We *are* going away, remember?" I could see his bemused smile in my mind. Leaning back in his desk chair, the way he did when he was working at home, running fingers through overlong brown hair beginning to get a hint of grey. "I've put in for leave the last week of your Summer holidays."

"Let's go tonight."

"What's brought this on? Thought you had to put the journal to bed before we could go. You haven't finished already?"

I taught part-time at the local college, edited a journal for it during the summer holidays. "I just feel like I could use a break right now. It's mostly done. The rest can wait until we get back."

"Sorry, Sweetheart. I can't just up and go. Plus there's the end of the year. You wanted me to book a few weeks to go home, remember? Visit the folks? See in the New Year in Cape Town as usual? That's about all the leave I've got left." There was a pause, then, "What is it, Yazz? What's going on?"

It was great to have a partner on the same wavelength in most aspects of life, but sometimes I wished it could stop short of reading my mind on the telephone. "Lily's coming. Viv called, said Lily's coming to see me. I thought we could run away and hide." I tried a laugh. It didn't work.

"Why bother?" he asked. "You don't have to see her if you don't want to." Measured tones now. "We're not kids any longer, Yazz. You could just say no."

How am I supposed to do that? I thought. If I couldn't say no to her back then, to all of them, when it was so important, how will I say no now, about such a little thing? Yes, I'll abort my child on party instructions Comrade, but no, I won't have coffee with you. "Alright then. I'll hide by myself. Work in the library every day. Leave the phone off the hook every night."

Adam didn't sigh or tell me to move on as Viv had. He simply said, as he always did, "You must please yourself, Yazz."

"Yes," I agreed. "I will."

I got up and walked along the South Bank of the river, mingling with the crowds of Summer tourists, trying to shake off thoughts of Lily and the past. The problem was that walking here in itself brought the memories back. Lily, ex-best friend, ex-comrade in the leftwing political party we'd all belonged to in our youth, in South Africa, Viv,

Lily I. When we'd first got to Britain – minus Viv who was persona non grata in the Party then - walking here had been the only recreation we could afford.

The rule at home in Cape Town had been that we handed over ten percent of our income to the Party. Being in good jobs, we'd done so willingly, given that and more because we could afford it. Because we believed that the struggle could only be waged through a Marxist Party. Then we'd been sent from South Africa to London, a small band of cadres with a mission to set up the party in exile, establish links with international left organisations, build support for the party at home. Our leader Ben and his partner Gladys, Adam and I, Lily and Al, the man she'd married after her dreams of a life with Zac and their daughter Heather had fallen through.

The Exiled Cadres –EC - had been nothing like the Party at home. It had demanded blind faith and obedience – to supposed instructions from home. One way to get that was to make us totally financially dependent. We were told to hand over every cent we had, together with a sheet justifying every penny we needed-to live on. Money for recreation wasn't a necessity. Gladys, our treasurer had pronounced upon the virtues of walking which would keep us fit and cost the party nothing. Without money for shoes, I'd given up running. In time, walking had become my favourite pastime. Every cloud and all that. Walking the streets of London, crowds for company and amusement, sometimes with Adam, more often without.

Our different jobs in the Party didn't allow for much time alone together. But he'd been with me when we'd discovered the South Bank of the Thames. The Southbank Centre with its cardboard city of homeless people living below the theatres, bars and restaurants. I'd watch the interaction between well-heeled and homeless, just for amusement, not for drawing affirmation of political theory from the "tree of life". One bloke used to sit on his sleeping bag, surrounded by his possessions. When he caught tourists looking at him, he'd point to the cardboard sign he'd made: A fiver for a photo. For the mad tourists prepared to pay the price, he'd run his fingers through his filthy tangled long hair and look in a small pocket mirror to ensure he was at his best for his fans before letting the paparazzi take their snaps. I wondered what he'd charge me if he knew how much free fun I was

9

getting. Then our "leader" Ben found another means to control us. He introduced "time and motion sheets" on which we recorded what we did every hour of every day, every day of every week. No more long lingering walks. No more democratic centralism. Just centralism. Ben, Al and Gladys hadn't succeeded in stifling all creative thought, though. Lily'd been adept at manipulating their rules and shown me the way, so that Adam and I could occasionally live like real human beings. Steal time for walks, for sanity.

Well, the Party was dead and gone. These days I could walk for miles on a single walkway to Tower Bridge, without having to go up and down steps of bridges along the way. I could stop for a frappe at one of the bars or a latte at one of the coffee shops, linger at one of the galleries or shops set up in the new buildings that had been part of the facelift in progress when I'd first come down here. Cardboard city was gone, a casualty of the gentrification of the South Bank. An odd beggar plus dog, chin sunk into chest, not looking at the tourists, allowing his bit of scribbled placard to speak for him, was all that remained of the large group of homeless that once lived under the theatre complex. I stopped to put a couple of pounds in the tin between his outstretched legs. I didn't need the muttered thanks. I got more pleasure out of being able to do that, than the beggar could imagine. There was nothing altruistic about my giving.

Today there was no sign of the skateboarding kids who'd succeeded the homeless people as colonizers of the area beneath the theatre complex, amusing tourists with their amazing contortions. Where had they gone, I wondered. Where, did all the homeless, all the beggars, end up eventually? Where had the man who'd charged tourists for his photo gone when, driven out of area after area as up went the blocks of flats for the rich, offices of glass and chrome, restaurants serving food they'd never heard of and throwing away more in a night that they'd see in a week? All these disappeared people. The light breeze of morning had become a cloud-stirring wind. I shivered and looked at my watch. I at least had a home. And it was time I went there.

And there was Lily. Not in Jo'burg, not in the air on the way to Heathrow. Getting out of a taxi outside our front door. Lily, leaning through the window to say something to indiscernible to the taxi-driver, before going up to our front door. The taxi waited.

I watched from the corner as she rang the bell, then lifted the knocker and let it drop. She turned to scan the streets and I ducked round the corner, walked swiftly to a nearby park gate. One side of the park faced our house. I crossed the park to that side. From behind the park fence, sheltered by the line of bordering trees, I could watch her without her seeing me. This was not a Lily I'd seen before. The pink tiger lily had long gone, but so too, it seemed, had the pale white arum of our last encounter. She glanced at her watch expectantly, then stood with hands on the hips of chocolate tailored slacks that showed no signs of travel. The expensive looking pants were topped by a cream blouse and brown jacket and the foot she tapped impatiently, as though she were waiting for someone who was late, was shod in cream high-heels. Heels! Lily! I almost laughed. The head she swung from side to side was shorn of the long blonde hair, which she'd taken to wearing in a single plait down her back in the last years I'd known her. In its place was a smooth shiny bob.

She looked like she was doing well, I thought bitterly. Viv was probably right, she'd be staying in a five star hotel, like everyone who came from home "on business" these days, whether it was the business of an erstwhile NGO, or a government department of some company. The South African taxpayer had to pay for the training of its new government, its new – and not so new – ruling class. So much for the hippy chick and the stern comrade incarnations. No more insisting on the right of all comrades to occupy the homes of all others. No more sleeping on my couch, leaving a trail of dirty tissues, underwear, newspapers and leftovers all over the house for me to clear up when Adam and I had our home back again. Though, to be fair, Lily was the one person of the lot who'd always been scrupulous about leaving a place the way she'd found it, or better. She never could stand mess.

That was what had made me notice her, my first day on a campus in Cape Town in the late seventies. That, and the fact that she was wearing a shocking pink dress as loud as her mouth. Tiger Lily. At first she'd looked like just another of the unfamiliar students, emerging from the cool dim interior of the massive hall where I'd just registered. I'd stood scanning the steps and lawns in front of me for familiar faces, suddenly aware of being in a minority on this campus, despite being the majority off it. This new world loomed more than just

11

physically over the townships below it, over the factories in the distance where people like my father worked, over the farms far away in the distant valleys of the dimly outlined mountain range that cut the peninsula off from the interior. I'd felt in desperate need of a friend.

Then I'd spotted Viv, a girl who'd finished at our school the year before me, standing with a few other black students. I'd made my way towards them, moving round the girl I'd noticed a moment before, standing in front of them. Just another apparently white girl amongst so many of them with their long , loose, blonde hair, golden summer tans, some in long hippy dresses, others in the ubiquitous student uniform of jeans or shorts and t-shirts. The only difference was that in her case, the dress was a bright pink. When I reached Viv and the others, I felt confident again. Confident enough to jab a finger in the direction of the pink dress with raised eyebrows and a mocking grin. We started picking our way through the students lying about on the steps and lawns. Plates of half-eaten food, drinks cans, cigarette stubs, food wrappers were everywhere. The students seemed to be resting on a bed of litter. In a short while, seeing this accumulate every day, cleaned away every day after lunch and again in the evening by an army of cleaners, I became inured to the refusal of even the most loudly declared liberal to put his or her rubbish in a bin, still expecting servants to clean up after the young masters and madams. That first day, I'd found it shocking.

Almost without thinking, I said "Jesus Christ! It looks like liberals still expect blacks to clean up after their filthy arses."

I'd forgotten how my voice carried, even without effort, until I heard someone clap and exclaim equally loudly, "You tell them, girl! Bunch of fucking varke!"

I whipped round to see where the spontaneous support was coming from. The girl in the pink dress was clapping her hands and nodding approvingly. "Bunch of fuckin' *varke!*" she repeated, more loudly and with emphasis.

I stared at her, stunned, It wasn't the deep husky voice coming from that slender girl, nor hearing what my mum would have called gutter language from the soft, wide-lipped red mouth in that angelic looking face. It was hearing the broad Cape Flats township accent in which the words of support were spoken. Born and brought up in a country where how white one's arse was didn't necessarily determine your racial classification, I shouldn't have been surprised that no matter how white she looked, she was a township kid like us. Lily would always have that effect on me. Surprise. Shock. And this was her pattern, letting me take the first step, but there to support. That day it had been the mess of white students she'd abhorred.

When we moved to London, it was the mess of our comrades. We'd shared a lot of post-meeting moans and mockery about the filthy habits of other comrades. The thing was, she wasn't that good at cleaning up after herself when it came to other kinds of messes. Looking at her now, so different on the outside, I had no doubt that she was still the same Lily inside, coming to me with yet another mess she wanted my help in clearing up. I'd been through the fact that I didn't want to see her with Viv and with Adam. I didn't have to go through it with her. Let Viv do my dirty work for me as well. Let *her* tell Lily. I didn't hate Lily any more. No matter what Viv had said, I wasn't really angry at her either. I really couldn't be bothered, that's all. I didn't want her in my life again.

I walked to the far side of the park, took out a cigarette and found space on one of the benches among all the workers enjoying unhurried fags after guiltily ducking out for a quick one the rest of the day. I watched some kids kicking a ball around, then taking turns at doing different moves with the ball, each trying to outdo the last. I laughed with the rest when one of them dropped the ball. It was good to be able to watch kids play without constantly thinking of what might have been. After a while I went back to the trees to make sure Lily had gone. Both taxi and Lily were still there. In fact, the taxi driver was carrying Lily's bag to our front door. Lily smiled widely, handed him several notes. The driver grinned back, eyes on the front of her blouse, not bothering to check the money. It was probably way over what was owed to him. Back home Lily had always tipped generously, even when she couldn't afford to. In London, it had embarrassed her terribly when Ben insisted that we couldn't afford to tip. In those days we'd met in cafes, holding meetings while we took turns ordering coffees which we nursed for hours so we couldn't be thrown out.

13

The taxi driver got into his taxi and drove off. Lily sat on the suitcase, slender body balancing easily, one leg crossed over the other, studying her nails. That much hadn't changed about her then. Why read a newspaper, Lily, when you can do your nails? I thought. I'd always been puzzled how Lily'd gotten into the best university in Cape Town.

"Shit!" I said. Turning away, I collided with a woman holding a small girl by the hand. "Sorry."

The little girl smiled, dimples forming in her round cheeks. "You said a naughty word!" she exclaimed gleefully.

The woman glared at me. Hell, I thought. I said sorry, didn't I? I smiled and winked at the little girl, returned the mother's glare and headed home.

Lily was sitting with her head down staring at her hands in her lap. I was almost upon her before she looked up. "Yazz!" She uncrossed her long legs, rising smoothly to her feet, arms out, making as if to hug me. "There you are!"

I stepped back and felt a fleeting childish pleasure in seeing her stumble and catch the rail beside the steps to steady herself.

"Gosh I've missed you," she gushed. She looked me up and down. "You look great!"

I knew that the years of eating properly, getting enough rest and exercise after I'd got my life back from the Party, had done me good. My hair had the odd grey in it, but had remained thick and healthy, though I wore it tied back instead of showing off my one good feature. My teeth had taken a beating from the smoking but were still my own and my mirror told me that my skin was fairly unlined. Today, in my loose-fitting mid-calf Summer pants, my plain t-shirt and flat sandals, I looked fit and healthy, but I would never look anything like Lily. To me, looking great was looking like Lily, but I didn't return her compliment. "What's this? What are you doing here?"

"I know." She pulled a little face. "Just popping up suddenly out of the blue-" She paused. I said nothing. "I'm sorry, I would have been in

14

touch but….." She raised her hands, palms up, in a pleading gesture. "You know what a state I was in. I had to pick myself up, put my life together! I was living in Scotland for years, did you know that?"

I'd heard of course. Lily had disappeared into the Highlands with some Scottish bloke she'd met after the Party's implosion. Part of me had been furious, thinking that was Lily all over. Zac dumped her, she slept around madly until she'd found Al. Al beat her, sending shock waves through the Party, so she slept around madly until she'd found the Scottish bloke. I'd waited, expecting a phone call, expecting a tearful Lily on my doorstep, hand out as usual for me to hold. But no Lily had appeared. Then relief had crept in, that she was off our hands. When I'd heard that she'd gone home to South Africa, I'd wondered what this last bloke had done to her.

After all, there was nothing for her back home. Her grandmother and Heather, both dead. The struggle – well, that was dead too, at least as far as she was concerned. Whatever he'd done to send her home, Viv had never told me, though I was sure that Viv knew. When I read the Party papers, the ones we ordinary cadres had never gotten to see, I was beyond caring about whatever the hell happened to Lily.

"Then I got homesick," Lily continued. "I saw this job, thought I'd go home, look everybody up." The words were a wild waterfall, rushing to fill the abyss of silence between us, or maybe just trying to drown out any possible censure. "I said to Viv," she plunged on, hands fluttering, eyes beseeching. "I knew you wouldn't hold it against me. I knew you'd understand."

I laughed. Lily didn't seem to realise that there was anything else to forgive, besides her long absence. Had what she'd done to me been so insignificant , that she'd just forgotten? She was like a child, unaware that having broken the house rule by playing with matches, it was now in serious trouble for setting fire to the house.

"Why are you here, Lily?" I repeated.

"Didn't Viv call you?" she asked, the green eyes widening. She all but fluttered her long lashes at me.

15

"She called." I stared at her, noting that the eyes had acquired fine lines at the corners which the makeup – Lily wearing makeup? – wasn't able to cover up. Her cheekbones stood out sharply in a face that, always narrow, was now seriously thin, depending for the youthful appearance on those sparkling green eyes and that soft mobile mouth. The scar on the left cheek, a remnant of Al's mistake, the cut that Lily couldn't deny had come from him, was either well-disguised, or had faded with time.

"She told you I was coming to visit?" she said, her bright smile still unwavering. The once perfect teeth, I noticed, had yellowed and one canine was slightly chipped. Too much coffee, too many "accidents".

"She said you were coming to London on business." I stressed the last word.

"Well, that too, but it's really you I wanted to see, Yazz." She shook her head at Viv's apparent laxness. "I specially told Viv to tell you that."

God. Did she imagine that I couldn't still read her, even after all this time? She *hadn't* told Viv to call me. She knew there'd have been no need to. Of course Viv would have called me. "She told me," I said, shifting her suitcase out of the way so I could reach my front door. "If that's all you wanted, Lily, to satisfy yourself I'm in perfect health, I'm doing just fine, thank you very much, I've been fine for years." I unlocked the door, opening it just a crack and slipping in as she tried to follow me. "There really is no need to come in."

"Oh Yazz." She put her hand in the door. "You're not really mad at me, are you? Come on, stop joking." Her tone was teasing. "You've made me suffer enough, standing out here for hours. Make some coffee and we'll catch up. Then I've got something really important to show you. I see you've got a bigger place." She waved her hand over the house front and up to encompass the two stories and attic. "Won't be the same as sleeping on your sofa but everyone moves onwards and upwards!" She laughed. "Even hardcore commies like you and Adam, right?"

16

I refused to be guilt-tripped. We'd bought the big old house because we'd hoped to have a family to house in it. It was hardly our fault that hadn't happened. When we'd bought the house, it had consisted of four flats, two bed-sits on the ground floor divided by the staircase, a two bed-roomed flat on the first floor, with sitting room, dining room and kitchen and another studio flat in the attic. We'd moved into the first floor flat, where we still lived. When the students on the ground-floor and in the attic had moved out, Adam and I had kept a bed-sit each as a study and converted the attic into a large guest room. There was always plenty of room for guests – but not for Lily. "You can't stay here, Lily."

"But Yazz," she wailed, "I *told* Viv to tell you I was coming to stay. It's really important."

She was priceless. I knew what she'd done. She'd asked Viv at the last minute for my address, said nothing about wanting to stay with me, then just turned up hoping I wouldn't be able to turn her away. Hah, I thought. Watch me. I've learnt to say no.

"Look, Lily, if you walk a couple of streets over, you'll be able to get a cab. It can take you and your Gucci bag to a nice hotel."

I wasn't aware of having raised my voice, but I'd spoken loudly enough for the woman next door to come to her window, lift her net curtain and stare. Not that it ever took much. Mostly I didn't mind her letting her eavesdrop on as much of my conversations and movements as would make her happy, whilst being compatible with reasonable privacy. Sometimes I'd even smile and wave and say hello. This time, I glared at her so hard that she dropped the curtain with a startled expression.

"Yazz, don't be like that. I didn't know you'd be so cross. Why can't we be friends again?" She seemed so genuinely penitent and at the same time so puzzled that for a moment I felt as though I should explain. I didn't.

"Please," she said, "Can't I at least come inside and talk to you? It's really important.........."

17

I lowered my voice. I could see the outline of my neighbour through her net curtain, hell-bent on her dose of free entertainment. "Lily, everything in your life is important to you and fuck the next person. I told Viv you'd be wanting something from me, but you know what? I want something from you too. I want you to go away and leave me alone." I started to close the door, but she had her foot blocking it. She moved her shoulder inside too. I stepped back, letting go of the door, not wanting her so close to me.

Surprisingly, she didn't follow me inside. She remained standing in the doorway. "OK, Yazz," she said quietly, all the playacting over. "I get that you don't want to see me. I don't know why, but I get that. But please," she reached into her handbag, took out a large brown envelope and held it out to me. "Please, Yazz. This is really important. You'll think so too. Just look at what's in here. Then you'll *want* to help me, I know."

How many times had I heard that? And how many times had falling for that line gotten me into deep shit? Maybe everyone was right. It was time I told Lily *why* I was glad she'd vanished from my life, *why* it was that I'd like her to disappear from it again. I took a deep breath. "And I needed your help, Lily. Remember? Ten years ago?"

She frowned. "Ten years? What…..oh," A look of consternation, then in a voice full of sympathy. "Yazz, you mean when you got pregnant?"

So she *did* remember.

She sighed, reaching out a hand as though she wanted to pat my arm or stroke my hair. She was so close, I could smell the lemon ingredient in her shampoo, the violet talcum powder she always shook over herself after a bath. I closed my eyes. Then she said, "I thought you'd got over it. That was so long ago."

"I got over it, as you put it," I said, snapping open my eyes. "What I can't get over is what you did."

"What I did?" Deep frown of puzzlement. "But I didn't do anything."

18

"Didn't ask. According to Viv, working for a Black Economic Empowerment organisation. Must pay well. You should've seen the clothes on her."

"Is she alright?"

My annoyance broke free. "Hey, this is the first time I've seen her since I found out about her treachery. I was thinking more along the lines of telling her what I thought of her, than exchanging air kisses and checking on her well-being."

"I only asked," he said, mildly. "Once upon a time if I didn't ask how your beloved Lily was, you'd be at my throat. So why are you fighting with me now?"

"I'm not." The protest was hollow. Seeing her had reminded me that Adam never shared my fury with Lily over her betrayal. I saw a disloyal friend, who should have stood by me. He saw a cadre who voted as she deemed politically appropriate, as was her right. "She's alright, OK?" I got up abruptly and started to clear the table.

"Really? She just wanted to say hello?"

"For god's sake, Adam" I snapped." If you'd said you were so worried about her I'd have given her your number and you could have sorted out her problems as usual."

"Maybe you should have," he said, following me to the kitchen.

"OK," I said coldly. "If that's what you want, I'll do it when she calls, which I am sure she will. You can take her to dinner, out for the evening. I'm sure you'd have a lot in common now, what with her working for a BEE company, exploiting the workers you're still trying to get international organisations to defend."

He sighed, ran water into the sink and started washing up, rinsing soap suds carefully from each item, stacking it all neatly on the draining board, plates in the slots, cups and glasses on the little points. Usually I would stand there laughing at his pernickety way of doing this chore, but now it merely grated on me. He washed plates the way he looked after comrades. "Adam, our conscience, our integrity," his best friend Simon, one of the CC members, used to call him. He'd never cared much for Lily when she was just a mate of mine. When she became a comrade, she was to be looked after at all costs, or so it seemed to me. It pissed me off. She wasn't a comrade any longer.

I took the pot I'd cooked in and scrapped the remains into the kitchen bin. "You know," I said, slamming the pot down on the surface next to the sink. "If she'd left the Party, if she'd left politics back then – fuck I'm sure even if she went over to the Stalinists or ratted us out to the SB – I'm sure you wouldn't care what's going on with her now." I shoved the bin back into place with my foot. "Oh, sorry, no, that's not right, is it? You're like the TRC – forgive and forget, kiss and make up. The Rainbow Nation can't afford to bear grudges, everyone's a comrade – or is that a citizen? - these days."

My good angel clapped her hands over my mouth. My bad angel opened my mouth wide and put both her size sevens in it. "But of course, this is different, isn't it? After all, it's just a personal betrayal. Only my so-called best friend making me kill my child. Not like it's happened to you either, is it? Just me. None of *your* business. You didn't have to go to that clinic on your own. You didn't have to take a bus back to a meeting feeling like your heart had been ripped out along with your insides and get on with the tasks of the day like nothing had happened. Did you even care that it was your child?"

He stared at me, his hazel eyes wide, his mouth tight-lipped as though he were biting back a response to this astonishing tirade. I felt sickened by it myself. "I'm sorry," I said, taking his hand, trying to pull him towards me. He took his hand away, stepped around me and left the room. I went after him. He was slumped on the sofa in the sitting room. "I didn't mean that. I really am sorry, Adam. I know I promised that we wouldn't do this again." I wondered when those threads of grey had crept into his dark hair, when those lines had formed around his eyes and his mouth, little white worms in the skin that was always tanned from running and biking in all weathers. He reached out an arm and I curled up beside him. "There really isn't anything else to tell, she is OK. Viv said it must be something pretty important that made Lily look me up now, but it wasn't."

24

"OK," he smiled, stroking my hair. "So the feisty woman is back. Did you really just tell her to go away and shut the door in her face?"

"More or less." I kept my face against his chest so he couldn't see it. I was sorry I'd said hurtful things to him.

"Which?"

"A bit more –I told her about the papers."

"What did she say about that?"

"Nothing."

"*Then* what happened?"

"Nothing!" Then I remembered. "Actually, she left something......
hang on a minute." I went downstairs.

Lily's plain white envelope lay in waiting for me, hidden amongst the rest of the stuff in the wire basket that caught everything coming through the flap. I lifted out the pile of junk mail, the afternoon post, the local rag delivered by the woman up the road who supplemented her lousy pay with menial odd jobs that kids used to do for pocket money. There was the explosion I'd been waiting for. Just one word on the outside of the envelope, in Lily's big bold, backward-slanting writing. "Heather". Oh God, I thought. Please, not this again. It was like kicking through a pile of beautiful autumn leaves, running across a pebbled beach, and suddenly having your foot hit a piece of broken glass. You could say, "Oh shit!" if it left just a little scratch and go on, maybe sticking a plaster on it. But if it's really something, you'd take a closer look, open it up just to check there's nothing in there which is going to do you damage in the long run. I was that careful, checking type. Lily knew that. My mouth dry, I tore the envelope open with shaking hands.

There was a photo inside. A young girl, perhaps seven or eight, in bright orange shorts and a white t-shirt, stood by a duck pond in a park, smiling at the birds. A typically London park on an atypically blue-skied London day? Or a park in ex-white South Africa, on a usual

25

summer's day? The child wore her long blonde hair in plaits tied with orange ribbons. She had a gap between her slightly crooked front teeth that her parents had declined to fix with braces. Wide, soft lips, a small mole on the side, slightly tilted nose, pale eyes that might have been green. I stared at the photo for a long time, telling myself over and over again that it could be of any child amongst the millions of blonde green-eyed little girls in London, in Cape Town, anywhere.

But there was the gap between those front teeth, between those soft lips, the mole, the smile I'd seen just that afternoon. And then there was the dolly she held in her sun-drenched, still baby-pudgy hand. A corn dolly it was, wearing a round hat encircled with a band to match the flowers in the basket it held and the band round its waist, the kind of dolly that you could buy on any market in any town in so many different countries. Prim-faced, with its dainty red-painted mouth and long flat-painted lashes, its eyebrows smooth thin arched lines - it resembled no-one as much as it did Lily before her Party days, when she'd switched from the hippy chick I'd first known, dressed in long dresses and floppy hats, to stern cadre in jeans and t-shirt. It looked like the Lily of the days when we were all just friends, debating politics hotly in the student union, partying wildly all over Cape Town. Heather had had such a dolly. Lily'd given it to her, over my and Viv's objections that it wasn't the kind of thing you gave a toddler. Lily, with no little brothers, sisters, cousins, had no idea that kids put such things into their mouths and choked on it. She wouldn't put it in her mouth, Lily had said. I'll tell her not to. And Heather never had. What she had done, was call the thing, "Mommy-dolly" because Lily'd given it to her, but of course it set us to winding Lily up about the doll looking like her and that being the reason she'd bought it for Heather.

"But Heather's dead," I said to myself out loud in the hallway "And her corn dolly was destroyed in the fire that killed her."

Still, I felt as though I'd been hit. We'd loved that child too, Viv and I. Co-mothers, Lily had called us, though nobody but Lily had ever been No.1 with Heather. Lily got all the kisses and cuddles, while Viv and I sorted out the finances and Sandy got all the shitty bits. I flipped the photo over. London and a date a few years ago written on the back in blue ink, in fat chain-link letters joined into words. Not Lily's handwriting. Not Lily's child. Heather had never grown to the age of

26

this child. Heather had never been to London, but Lily had written her name on that envelope. Lily believed she was Heather. I sat down on the bottom step, knowing now what Lily wanted from me.

"Yazz," Adam called from upstairs. "What's going on? Are you alright?" He started down the steps towards me.

I stumbled breathlessly to meet him halfway. "Here." I thrust the photo at him.

He looked at it. "Who's this?" He turned it over as I'd done, then looked at me with raised eyebrows.

"Doesn't that child remind you of someone?"

He raised his shoulders, turned down the corners of his mouth and shook his head.

"Lily left it for me."

"Why?" He looked at the photo again, then back at me.

"I guess she thinks that child's Heather." I pointed to the name on the envelope.

He ran a hand over his face. "So," he said quietly. "She's at it again. Poor Lily."

"You can see why this time, though," I said. "I mean, I know you never saw much of Heather, but doesn't that child look just like Lily?"

My voice rose with excitement. He took my hand and drew me up the stairs and back inside the flat. He shut the stair door softly, as though there were still student lodgers living below, instead of just his books and computer in one room, my stuff in the other. "Look," he said, pushing me down onto a chair. "Don't you start too. Lily's child is dead. This is someone else's child." He smiled. "Don't they say everyone in the world has a double somewhere?"

I looked at the photo again. The resemblance was uncanny.

27

"You were probably right to send her away before this gets out of hand. It's cruel to encourage this fantasy of hers. Remember the last time?"

"How could I forget?" I said. The last time Lily had let an accident of feature lend a stranger's face the familiar cast she'd loved, she'd nearly got us both arrested. I tried to put the photo back in the envelope and a slip of paper fell out. A mobile phone number and the words, "Call me, please" in Lily's writing. Adam picked it up, read it, crumpled it and threw it into the bin. He was about to throw the envelope and photo after them when I took them from him. I retrieved the paper and straightened it. "I have to call her," I said.

"Why?" he asked. "One minute you can't be bothered to even exchange a greeting with her. You get all upset with me for even wanting to know how she is. Now I tell you to leave her alone, that you did the right thing, and you want to call her? What's the point of your wanting my opinion, if you just ignore it? And you're the person who wanted me to make major decisions in your life? Bit of a waste of time, don't you think?"

I was taken aback at his sudden sharpness. I could count on the fingers of one hand the times when Adam had raised his voice to me. "I just want to find out where she is. She'll want the photo back."

"Why? So she can go round every park in London on the off-chance she'll see a little blonde girl she can – what? Kidnap?"

"She wasn't going to kidnap the girl that last time…but don't worry. I agree with you, OK? I'm not getting involved in this new madness of hers." I didn't sound too convincing, even to myself. Viv's words kept ringing in my ears. How had we come to this? From friends to comrades to wounded women, all of us grieving for something or other. Viv was right. Lily had suffered too. "I could almost feel sorry for her," I said. "If it wasn't for –"

Adam sighed. "Look, I feel sorry for her too. That's why I'm telling you. The kindest thing you can do for Lily is to ignore this. That way she'll get over this latest bout of obsession faster." He put his arms around me. "I didn't mean to snap at you. I know how close you and Lily used to be. But the past is past. Let it go." He kissed my forehead. "Here, let me put that in the bin."

I let him hold me a while then I pulled free. "No," I said. "She might want it back. I'll just call to find out where she is," I said. "I'll post it to her hotel."

"Yazz, why bother? It's not just Lily who can't let go of Heather – I know the whole thing upsets you too. Just leave it be." I didn't answer. He looked at me a while, then said, "Well, you must suit yourself. I'm going to watch the match at the pub," He went swiftly out to the small entryway. He took his jacket from one the hooks behind the door where he'd hung it. "See you later."

When he'd come in, he'd said he was too tired to join the blokes from work at the pub. He loathed crowded smoky pubs, preferring to ask some workmates over for a beer if it was a weekend, or go to see friends at home. But I let him go. I reached for the phone, but I didn't dial. I sat rehearsing what I'd say to her. I put the phone back down. No amount of rationalizing would get to Lily. She'd never let go of the dream that Heather was alive somewhere, no matter how many shrinks she saw.

Damn, I thought bitterly, if the Party was still around, I'd have written a party paper on how my personal experience had proven the correctness of the party position that angst-spilling to therapists and others was so much bourgeois crap. Which had essentially been its response to my attempts at treatment for the near nervous breakdown I went through after the abortion it had ordered me to have. I say "near" because comrades weren't allowed actual nervous breakdowns; breakdowns were security risks. You had your abortion, you got on a bus and went to your next meeting, remembering always how lucky you were. Working women in South Africa didn't even have the luxury of a good clean clinic and modern medicine. They couldn't indulge in the petty bourgeois self-indulgence of month-long crying jags. This was the gospel according to Comrade Zac, Lily's lover, Heather's father, who'd brought this wisdom, amongst much else, to our fledgling party from the Marxist prophets in the world outside apartheid South Africa. Part of the "else" was the rule that cadres could not have children.

I jumped as the phone rang. I let it go to answer phone. It wasn't Lily. Just my mother to ask whether we'd put up some kids travelling to the UK for a couple of days. I cut into her message by picking up the phone. "Hang up, Mum," I said. "I'll call you back." She was forever sending us this new brand of young South African. Not rich and white and backpacking round the world until the time came to settle down in the promised land, but black kids who were discovering that overseas travel wasn't marked "whites only". This generation had no ban on their passports. Their education was uninterrupted by boycotts and book burnings. Jobs were uninterrupted by strikes and protests - jobs where they earned the same as whites, many times what their parents had earned. There was no struggle to which they handed over their money, and the old way of handing it to parents had disappeared. After all those very parents had been the rebellious ones who'd made the townships ungovernable, who were they to stop the young gadding off, footloose and fancy free? So the young people packed up and came over, first to London where they irritated the shit out of me, they took it all so for granted.

I had little choice but to take them in. I knew my mother'd already said it would be OK. I might at well get kudos for being a dutiful daughter as well as a generous hostess. Anyway it was a treat for Adam. He liked the live feedback from home, even though it mostly ran to endless complaints about the new South Africa, crime and corruption being the main gripes. Adam liked that. He could get into debating mode, sit round the dinner table for hours, the way he used to in the students' union when he was their age, talk to them about the apartheid years, which they seemed to know nothing about or wanted to sweep aside as so much distant history. He'd remind them that apartheid had always made black life cheap, so that rape and mugging and murder could take place in the townships unpunished, as long as we kept it amongst ourselves. He'd talk about how the struggle years had made things worse, had created brutalised people who brutalised one another. Now it was spreading into the erstwhile white areas, into the areas newly inhabited by the blacks enriched by the changes, by these new elements of the ruling class. The white areas – which black women could at least run through before without being raped and mugged, because white police kept it safe for white women in the old days, because there were too few of us invading their space to matter – were no longer safe for anyone.

I was less patient, angry and resentful to see them so easygoing, so free, so unlike we'd been, taking for granted the things they'd never fought for and then still having the gall to complain instead of struggling to rectify the situation.

My mother nattered on for a while, catching me up on the births, deaths and marriages of my extended family and everyone I'd ever known, it seemed, in greater Cape Town and even beyond. We exchanged phone kisses.

I didn't call Lily. What would I say that hadn't been said already? Sandy, Heather's carer – foster mother really, considering that she'd had Heather full-time with all of us only visiting when we could – had identified the child's remains. There'd been an enquiry, an official report. Not much of either, because after all, it had just been another fire in another squatter camp, just some black kids burnt to death, not something the apartheid era police could be worried about. They had their hands full, as far as they were concerned, policing the political situation, far more important than the loss of several young lives, and anyway, they probably thought it good riddance. Maybe the fire had been caused by an adult carelessly leaving an oil lamp burning with kids around; maybe it had been sparked by barricades burning close by, in which case, it serves them right, black bastards, their own kids dying in the fire they started. Still, there were records.

The problem was, Lily didn't believe any of it. Not really. Sometimes she'd go for months, years even, believing it and then something like this would happen and she'd be off again. As Adam said, there was no point in even talking about it with her. It would only give her room for arguing. I went to the attic room and put the photo in a book, put the book in the suitcase which held all I'd brought with me when I'd fled South Africa and shoved it under the bed. Lily, I knew, could not be shut in some equivalence to that suitcase in the attic, but for now, I would have peace. I unplugged the phone, ran a bath and lay back in a mass of bubbles.

31

The thing about bubble baths is that they don't just unwind the knots in one's body, they loosen up all the screwed tight bits of one's mind too. And into my empty mind Lily had brought back our political past. We had started out as just a group of friends and like-minded acquaintances on campus. As a minority on an all-white campus which we attended under special permit – whereas in the rest of the country we were members of the vast majority – we were necessarily flung together in our own little campus ghetto. It was there that I learnt politics left of my father's, which I had once thought the height of revolutionary thinking. It was there with the members of that ghetto that I learnt to swear, drink and fuck. I owed my fag habit to Lily's lover, Zac.

Then had come the Soweto uprisings of '76 and the bus boycotts, murmurings of strikes and suddenly we were no longer just talking the talk in the student's union, we wanted to walk the walk in the townships. So it was that the Party was born and the parties ceased, to an extent, except for cover. A Trotskyist Party of young people trying to change the direction of the struggle from one for bourgeois democracy to one for socialist revolution. Those of us with day jobs paid dues to keep the illegals working at politics full time. By night we were all at it – canvassing tenants across the townships, forming housing associations, organizing youth movements, working in unions and sometimes forming them. It was wonderful. It was exhilarating fighting shoulder to shoulder with young people for better schools and facilities in the townships, with tenants for housing, with workers for unions and a living wage. Nobody talked about devoting their lives to the struggle or about working 24/7 for the Party. People just did it. It had to be done.

Until we got caught and forced into exile. Suddenly the struggle was all in the realm of theory. Endless hours of meetings in airless rooms in New Cross and Southwark and any one of half a dozen places I'd never heard of before. We borrowed basements and attics from friends of friends who'd moved to London long ago. People sympathetic to the struggle but who didn't really want an active part in it. We spent days on meaningless leftist nit-picking with the groups in the UK, mainly Zac's group, which was busy imploding. Unending debates on the minutiae of Marxist theory – what was real Marxism, what was revisionism, all manner of crap that went way over my head. I didn't recognise the struggle I was committed to. I hated Ben, our megalomaniac EC leader. I detested his neurotic wife. If there was ever a revolutionary's bimbo, she was it. And while we dallied, back home the left, our Party for whom we were meant to be building support, was losing the direction of the struggle to the wheeling and dealing of the mainstream organisations who would eventually take over the country. The only real part in those bitter years was work, like the 24 hour picket outside the embassy, the gathering of support for the struggle back home amongst working people.

I had buried that past. And now here was Lily, stirring it all up again, the time we'd both gone a little mad. Me walking the streets of London, crying for months post-abortion. Her seeing her dead kid everywhere. I pushed it away, got out of the bath fast and went to my computer to drown it all in work.

The tinny voice of AOL announced: "You've got mail!" I sat looking at the address for a while, ticked the selection box, moved the mouse towards "delete", but didn't click. Clever Lily, I thought. Even if you are mad, you know I find email irresistible. I am Pandora. I have to open boxes, even when I know better. I must know what's inside.

"I always told you I would have known if Heather was dead," Lily's email repeated the refrain I'd heard a thousand times before. "And that photo is proof!" She'd found the photo, she said, in a book Viv had returned. A book she'd long ago lent to "that woman". Several exclamation marks. "That woman" meant Sandy. Lily'd always known "she" was lying. Sandy knew where Heather was. More exclamation marks.

Poor Sandy, I thought. No wonder she'd sent the book via Viv. I wondered that she hadn't just burnt the book, knowing what Lily thought of her. I felt like a few exclamation marks myself, after some reminders of what Lily'd conveniently forgotten. All Lily remembered was that Heather had been in Sandy's care the night the child had died. Forgotten was the fact that Lily might never have had Heather without Sandy. Forgotten were the many times Lily'd been too busy, away for a few days, a week, a month, unable to visit Heather, just expecting Sandy to sacrifice her own activities, or go about her business with the child strapped to her back, African style. Never had Sandy pointed out that what she did - voluntary nursing in the squatter camps when the government shut down the clinic she'd worked in – was at least as important as Lily's work. She'd never pointed out that if Lily had been looking after her own child, instead of off being what Sandy called "a career woman" or "doing her political stuff", the child would not have been in the camp the night the fire broke out. Like Lily, Viv and I, who'd sworn to take it in turns to look after the child, never found enough time and increasingly we took Sandy for granted, as if clubbing for a full-time salary could pay for what she'd done. "No worries," was all she'd say. "Little darling's company for me, isn't she, Amos being gone half the year round." Amos, her partner, was away on field trips. All Sandy got for her trouble was Lily screaming abuse at her for being reckless, for not taking proper care of Heather, as if Sandy wasn't suffering too, wasn't suffering even more, beating herself up, without getting the care and sympathy which those of us who knew about Heather heaped on Lily.

"She won't see me," Lily's email went on, "because she's got something to hide. I know it. You have to go home and make her tell the truth!"

Was it, I wondered, because of how successfully – albeit unwillingly – Sandy had lied – or at least omitted to tell the truth – that Lily couldn't believe she'd tell the truth *to* her? And why should I be more successful in getting this "truth" when I'd helped convince Sandy to hide that other truth? Lily's answer was in the next lines: "She'll talk to you. After all, she was your friend. It was your idea to ask her to look after Heather."

Her memory was suffering a lapse in this regard too. I put it down to her Lutheran upbringing. No amount of Marxist teaching would get some of its concepts out of her psyche, like original sin. According to Lily, my original sin with regard to the entire Heather affair went a lot further back than my response to her plea for help when she'd had the baby. To wit, I'd brought her into the party, therefore I was to blame for her meeting Zac, sleeping with him, not using protection with him, getting pregnant by him. I remembered things differently. I remembered Lily begging and pleading with me to tell her where "everyone" - meaning our crowd of friends – disappeared to from time to time without telling her. I remembered that she got me drunk

34

enough to tell her about the Party. I remembered that I got disciplined for it and nearly expelled. I remembered that she was totally thrilled with being involved in real political work, and a lot else. I remember her reaction when she first saw Zac. Just one word: "Wow!" I hadn't been the one who'd argued for Lily to replace me as party liaison with Zac. I hadn't been the one to suggest that if she was seen with him they'd look like any white couple, unlike if he and I were seen together. Now it was all my fault.

And then there was the way she referred to Sandy. Lily really knew how to piss me off. I hit the reply button: "This child looks nothing like Heather. You're imagining things. Anyway, if Heather had lived, she'd be a lot older than this by now." And then, the final nail in the coffin of her dreams –I said that Adam agreed with me. I binned the lot of emails and was about to log off, when the line of a new email appeared in my inbox.

"I know she'll be older. You remember that time on the bus? You said it wasn't her. But I knew it was. Look at this photo. This is what she looked like on the date on the back. Think about that girl on the bus. It all fits, the ages and everything."

I remembered alright. All evening since Adam's reminder, I'd been pushing this event from my mind, but now it came right up, playing in my head like a film. We'd been on a London bus, coming home from a meeting shortly after Lily had joined us in the UK. The single-decker bus was full, so Lily and I stood at first, pressed up against each other and all the other standing passengers. When the bus began to empty we made our way to seats near the back. Soon it was just us on the bus, plus one other passenger. She was a teenager, maybe thirteen or so, fast asleep in the seat across the aisle from us. That child too, had a dolly like the one in the photo. At the time I remembered thinking the girl seemed far too old for dollies, but then remembering that teenagers often found such things "cute". It was probably the cool thing to carry around corn dollies. My mind was filled with what had happened at the anti-apartheid group meeting, hoping I'd written down everything I'd undertaken to do, that my report was fulsome enough for our cadre group meeting next day. Then Lily said, "Look Yazz," pointing at the girl."Heather's dolly."

I'd looked more closely. She was pretty, with thick smooth skin, the kind seldom affected by teenage acne or left unscarred by the odd pimple. The flush of sleep on her cheek reminded me of a Cape apricot on a tree in the early morning – it looked fresh, moist, as though it would be firm to the touch. Her eyelashes looked painted on, more brown than blonde, but the hair on the head leaning against the window of the bus was the colour of damp beach sand – exactly the colour of the corn dolly she was holding. Exactly the colour of Lily's. It seemed to me that if Lily had been sitting next to her, any stranger getting on that bus would have assumed she was Lily's. The top of the child's head pressed against the window, but her chin rested on her hand as she slept. I'd seen Lily sleep like that on countless bus journeys to and from meetings across South Africa. Had I not known it was impossible, I too would have been sure it was Lily's child, Heather grown from a plump toddler into a slender young adult like her mother.

Lily's eyes shifted back and forth between the doll and the girl's face. Then she breathed one word: "Heather," and stood jerkily, moving trancelike across the narrow aisle towards the empty seat next to the sleeping girl.

"Lily, no!" I hissed, snatching at her arm and yanking her down, more roughly than I intended: "For god's sake, are you mad? That's not Heather and you can't just hassle other people's kids!"

Lily slumped back down next to me. Tears rolled down her face. It hurt me, watching her force herself to look away from the sleeping girl as reason asserted itself, and then turning back, helplessly, to look again, when longing won out. The bus jerked to a stop. The girl woke and yawned loudly, in total contradiction to her delicate looks. "Hey, Mommy Dolly," she said, "why didn't you wake me? Nearly missed our stop." Snatching up her backpack, she ran lightly down the aisle and jumped from the bus just in time before the doors closed.

Lily stumbled down the aisle after the girl, but the bus was already moving off. She lurched to the back of the bus, gripping the tops of seats to steady herself. Kneeling on the last seat, she pressed her face up against the window. She knelt there long after darkness and distance must have made it impossible to see the girl any longer.

I went to her and sat down beside her, tugging at her arm. "Sit down, Lily. Come on. It's just coincidence. Forget it!"

"Coincidence!" She turned on me so fiercely that I shifted back uneasily against the side of the bus, the window cold and damp against my scalp, my ear. "Mommy Dolly!"

I said cautiously, "Lily, listen to me. You find dollies like that all over. Kids all call their dolls one name or the other from a limited range. They call their cat Smokey. They call their bears Teddy. They call their dollies Mommy or Daddy or Baby. That's how they are."

"And how would you know?" she snarled. Then she got up and went to sit down where the girl had sat, ignoring me.

At the last stop, I got up to go. I stopped in the aisle next to Lily. She sat with her face against the window, making no move to leave. I reached down and tapped her on the shoulder. "This is ours," I said.

"I'm not getting off," she said, "I'm going back on this bus to where she got off."

"Don't be crazy, Lily." I tried to lift her from her seat, as the driver called last stop.

She struggled. The driver came lumbering down the aisle. "Time to go, ladies."

Lily screamed obscenities at us, kicking out until her boot made contact with driver's leg. He rubbed his shin angrily.

"If you don't get off this bus right now," he said, "I'm gonna call the police. You can kick them around, and get arrested for assault."

I nearly laughed out loud. If he knew how many times the two of us had been arrested for assaulting cops in Cape Town, he wouldn't have looked as though he was making a serious threat. I was getting as deranged as Lily. "Please," I said. "She's just had a shock." I turned to

Lily. "Hey, look, the driver's tired. He's been working all day. Is it fair to keep him from going off shift?"

The fight went out of her. She stood up, hanging her head like a reprimanded child, and sweetly apologised to the driver. I smiled my own apology at him as I urged her ahead of me, helping her off the bus as if she was very young, very old or very drunk. I'd taken her home with me, where she'd lain for hours with her face turned to the wall, weeping hysterically, until Adam – Adam whom she trusted more than any of us – had come to comfort her, rubbing her back till she stopped crying, then talking to her gently, persuasively, until she saw sense.

Adam who now didn't want me to involve myself in anything like we'd gone through that night. Whose sanity did he fear for, I wondered, mine or Lily's?

AOL's announcement of yet another email broke into my reverie. This one was free of exclamation marks. "I thought you'd got over your abortion. Please believe me when I say that. And when I say that I voted for it because I really thought it was for your own good. The way things were going for us, you wouldn't have been able to look after your own child. You would have gone through the same problems that I went through, run the same risks, handing your child over to someone else's care. I wanted to spare you that. You *must* believe me. Don't punish me by not helping me to find Heather. Finding her will help you too, Yazz. We'll share, like the old days."

I felt like curling into a ball and howling, like throwing something, hitting, kicking, screaming with rage. Acting on that was more Lily than me. I typed: "Leave me alone, Lily. I've got a life." I clicked on "send" and pulled the plug on the machine. Then I sat smoking before giving up on Adam and turning in.

Adam came home from the pub beery, his clothes and hair reeking of smoke. He stripped and tumbled into bed beside me without showering. I wrapped my arms around him. "You stink," I said into his hair.

"So do you," he murmured. "Everything stinks." He fell asleep. I didn't think he meant the beer smells in the pub, or the heavy fug of smoke I'd created in the house, chain-smoking. I too fell asleep eventually, deep, exhausted sleep devoid of all bad dreams.

To my surprise, Lily left it at that. After a couple of days my life resumed its usual tenor. The guests my mother sent me came and went. Lily receded from my mind as the Summer wore on. I had other things to think about. Just after our young guests left, I realized that my period was late. I tried hard not to get too hopeful. It was no big deal. I'd been later than this before only to have nothing come of it. I didn't tell Adam. If it was nothing again, there'd be only one of us disappointed and I wouldn't have to face his sympathy. Only when we had our home to ourselves again, did I chance to look at the calendar. Yes. I was very late. Again I tried to suppress the hope, but my heart was singing when I put on shorts and t-shirt. I topped it with a hat and sunglasses, got on my trainers and headed out into the warmth for a big park some distance off. I would need to be fit, if what I thought was happening to my body was in fact happening. As I jogged along gently, I thought about whether I could take a chance on telling Adam. Perhaps I should see the nurse at our doctor's surgery first. Check before I told him. I made up my mind to do that and turned for home. Just then a woman ahead of me stepped onto a zebra crossing, mobile phone in one hand, toddler hanging onto the other, expecting cars to stop, too engaged in conversation to make eye contact with drivers. I looked up in time to see a convertible, driven by a man also on a mobile phone, speeding towards the crossing. It was coming too fast to stop. I flew at the woman, snatching up the toddler, shoving her into the gutter. The car sped on, unheeding.

"Amy," the woman whimpered, reaching for her screaming child. "Oh, Holy fuckin' Christ, is my baby alright?"

Wordlessly, I handed her the child. The mother sat on the kerb, rocking the girl. Then she got up to look for her phone. She retrieved it from the gutter and checked up on it. Then she remembered me. "Fuckin' arsehole never stopped at the crossing, did he? Near fuckin' killed me kid."

"Here darlin'," she said. "You better get home quick's you can," she pointed at my lower half. I'd not moved. It wasn't so much because I wanted to see whether they were alright, but because I didn't know

39

what to do about the blood, warm and sticky, running down the inside of my legs. The shock of the near accident had brought on my period.

"Here," she took off the top of her shell suit. "Don't want no-one seeing you've come on, do ya? Never mind getting it back. Saved me kid's life dintcha?" I thrust it away. She shrugged and put the phone to her ear, swung the child onto her hip and started telling the person still apparently on the other end what had happened as she stepped onto the crossing, still not checking for cars.

I wanted to run after her, snatch the child from her, keep it safe. "Stupid!" I shouted after her. My voice was lost in the traffic. "Bloody idiot!" I muttered, feeling the tears start to my eyes. "It's not fair!"

"Some people," said a woman, passing by with a dog. "They don't deserve children."

I rounded on her with a ferocity that startled both of us. "She loves her child!" I yelled.

Standing in a shower, I washed away the evidence that there was no child growing inside me. Once there had been and I'd been forced to destroy it. Ever since, the god I didn't believe in had deprived me of what I wanted, cruelly allowing me to think, like now, that I was pregnant, only to laugh in my face. At other times, allowing me to fall pregnant, only to tear the child from my womb before it could grow much beyond what could be seen in a grainy picture that the nurse insisted was waving a fist at me. Perhaps the woman with the dog was right. Those of us who couldn't look after children didn't deserve them. If I'd looked after that first pregnancy, fought harder for my baby, I'd have a half-grown child now. If Lily'd been looking after her own child, Heather would never have been with Sandy the night the child died. She'd never have been caught up in that fire.

I dried myself and sat on the side of the tub, thinking, no, that wasn't right. I'd wanted that first baby and I'd done all I could to keep it. Just as Lily had loved Heather above all else. Heather had to be fitted into the lacunae in Lily's life, but every one of those was filled with love. I could see her, swinging that child high into the air, the sunshine creating a golden aura around their blonde heads. "Remember, nobody

40

loves you like I do!" Bringing her down in a swoop into a smothering hug. "Nobody ever will." She'd repeat that to Heather a dozen times in every visit. She'd heard my mother say the words to me, even though I was grown up and had never forgotten. It became something Lily said to me, teasingly, when I was pissed off with her. She wasn't teasing with Heather.

There was no way of snatching Heather out of the past as easily as I'd snatched that child from the crossing. I couldn't do it, however hard Lily might wish it. As my mother loved to say, "If wishes were horses, beggars would ride." Lily would have to go begging.

CHAPTER THREE

I had no intention of seeing Lily when Adam and I made our annual visit to our folks in late December. I *did* intend to see Viv, but that didn't happen until a fortnight into our trip. She and Simon had been out of town when we arrived. So had a lot of people we were still in touch with, so was half of Cape Town, it seemed. Once they'd fled the arrival of the Northerners in the Mother City during the summer. Now word had gone round the world that Cape Town put the "festive" into "festive season", so it was tourists that Cape Townians left home to avoid.

In the absence of almost all our old friends, we spent most of our time with my extended family. Adam and I even saw in the year 2001 at a huge family *braai* on the beach. Overseas travel was a common occurrence these days. In my tribe, however, travellers or people who lived overseas were still accorded the status of celebrities. The usual hospitality battles between various aunts and uncles and cousins went into overdrive. I loved them all. I loved the fuss and appreciated the food, but a visit to Cape Town always threatened my waistline and left me feeling as though I needed another holiday. I could also have done without all the proud parading of new children in the family. I smiled. I kissed infant cheeks. I patted toddlers' head. I tried not to begrudge my cousins, most of whom had been parents when Adam and I left South Africa, their several children and even grandchildren. As always, there was lot of ribald speculation about the reasons for our childlessness and offers to give us lessons in human reproduction. Adam grinned. I bit my lip and didn't scream. Finally Viv called. She wanted to make up for neglecting us with an invitation to a "little get-together" as soon as she got back.

"So who else is coming?" I asked Viv. My question was addressed to her backside as the whole of the rest of her was inside the oven of the huge old-fashioned stove that she'd inherited from her folks, together with all the other ancient furnishings in this rambling old house in what was once the outskirts of Cape Town. "You look as though you're getting ready to feed the masses." I swept my hand across the large wooden table laden with food, trying not to look disappointed.

I'd been looking forward to a quiet evening of food and wine and music with just Viv and Simon. It looked to be anything but. I certainly wasn't going to get the time I wanted with her to talk through all the things we never dealt with properly by phone and email.

"Not exactly the masses," she said, backing out of the stove and slapping down a tray of foil-wrapped garlic bread next to the kitchen sink. The aroma filled the kitchen. I reached for one but she slapped my hand away with her cloth. "Hot!" she said severely. "I've invited a few friends."

"Oh, god, not that new lot again?" I rolled my eyes.

"No," she said, turning to face me with her hands on her ample hips like some small round grandma, "you were too rude to them last time."

"I can't help getting *the moeren* with all these gravy train passengers, more bucks than would feed, clothe and house a township full of people, while said township people sit unemployed and starving in shanty towns."

"Get down from that soapbox!" she said, starting to put salads together. "A lot of people are just trying to earn a living. If the only way they can do that is by working for the state, or for a multinational, or a BEE company, can you blame them? Who did we do our paid work for back in the day? Somebody had to work for company or state to fund the struggle. So no lectures, please."

"You make me sound like a real pain in the arse." I said, aggrieved.

She looked me sternly in the eye. "You were, last time. I almost didn't throw you a party."

I didn't say I wished she hadn't. "So who *is* coming?"

"The people you won't accuse of – and I quote – 'spurious justification for betraying and abandoning the struggle' before you throw my glasses around. All just old friends."

I sighed. Meetings with mutual old friends was almost worse than those with her new acquaintances. At least I could be rude to the latter. The former wrenched my conscience totally out of shape. Invariably, there'd be reminiscing about the old days. This or that campaign, what we'd done and whose arses we'd kicked. It was all great fun until inevitably we came to the present and the dissecting of where the Left – we - had gone wrong. Without meaning to, they made me feel as though I was personally responsible for our failure. Viv, Lily and I – our cadre group was called the Rovers –were responsible for recruitment. We'd dragged young people, workers, tenants, sportspeople, out on campaigns which took every waking hour and then some, with promises of working class victory. It didn't help for people like Simon and Adam to go on about how young we'd been, how small and new, compared to the established liberation organizations with their massive overseas support. My conscience had already taken a battering with the extended family, just ordinary bewildered poor township folk who'd expected to see the fruits of change, seeking an explanation. A former activist who'd lectured them on the need for struggle should be able to explain why so-and-so had been mugged/burgled/carjacked umpteen times, why so-and-so couldn't get a job, a house, a loan, why they'd not been white enough before and didn't feel black enough now. Political talk wore me out these days. But, I thought as I sipped the wine Viv handed me, it could be worse. Lily might be coming. I checked, "That include Lily?"

We hadn't really spoken about Lily since Lily's trip to London. In fact, we hadn't spoken about it at all. I'd left it to Viv to debrief Lily about our meeting. "I said old friends," she said firmly. "Lily's a friend of mine, just as you are. If she'd been here, of course I'd have invited her." She paused. "As it happens, she isn't."

There'd been a time when it was impossible to have a party without Lily and her guitar, jamming with Adam and Simon. They'd have been banging out the Beatles by now, switching to Sixties protest music later with everyone joining in loud drunken chorus, making up rude lyrics to popular songs to uproarious laughter, crooning love songs into the night when everyone was drunk and half-asleep. The times they are a changing, I thought with relief. "So where is she? Off with a new bloke?"

44

Viv shrugged. "I have no idea. I did want to see her, though. I'm a bit concerned about her."

"So what else is new? You're worse than Adam. I swear, the minute that woman arrives, he's like a broody hen, fussing over her. We only had a *moerse* dingdong when she was in London a few months ago. Never a cross word between us, as the saying about magic marriages goes, then Lily arrives and it's world war three."

She grinned. "With you doing the fighting on both sides, hey?"

"You don't know Saint Adam!" I said indignantly. "He fights a good battle. Albeit not very loud." We both laughed. "But why're you pissed with Lily? She's gone off somewhere without reporting to you first?"

She sobered up. "I'm not 'pissed', as you put it. Concerned was the word I used." She paused, then said slowly. "Look, have you heard about Sandy? No, I suppose you'd have said the minute you came in."

"Sandy? No, I haven't seen her. I thought she went back to her job in Dubai? Why, what's happened to her? Don't tell me. She got carjacked? Burgled?"

She looked at me with a serious expression. "Sandy's dead, Yazz. Before you shout at me, I know I should have said something earlier, but it's not the kind of thing you tell someone the moment they arrive. I didn't want to tell you on the phone, because I knew you'd be coming. I thought I'd tell you in person."

I stared at her in disbelief. "Sandy? How can Sandy be dead? Lily said she saw her a couple of months ago!"

"She died of AIDS, the week before we went away."

"AIDS? Sandy?"

"Why are you so shocked? One in nine members of this wonderful rainbow nation is HIV positive. People are dying of AIDS every day. Young people, kids even. Don't you read the papers? And don't tell me Sandy couldn't have it because she was a monogamous, heterosexual, non-drug injecting female. It doesn't work like that here. This is South Africa. Everyone knows someone. Someone who's positive, someone who's got AIDS, someone who's died."

Her recitation of the statistics rolled over me. From the yard, where Adam and Simon were preparing the barbecue, came the smell of wood smoke, sounds of chatter and laughter. More people must have arrived and stopped to talk to them, open a few cans of beer before coming in. Across Viv's head, through the kitchen window, I could see the big barn type structure at the far end of their property. It was left over from when this had still been a farming area, or at least somewhere people had kept animals. The barn's inside had long since been converted into human living quarters, first rented out by Viv's people, then taken over by her when she'd gone to university. We'd always had a place to party where we didn't have to turn the sound down in case the neighbours called the cops.

Viv had gone on living there when she'd started work. There wasn't that much choice for young black people back then. If you were poor, you lived at home until you got married, and some for a long time after. If you were lucky, your parents built a "granny flat" in the yard for you while you were on the council waiting list for a house. If you weren't, you could be raising your kids in a room in your parents' house. Even those of us who were young professionals lived at home until we got married. A mixture of tradition, family expectations, community mores, call it what you will, and economic necessity – and the lack of housing for blacks. Viv was lucky. We were all lucky. We still had a place to party. We still had our lives, our health. All of us, except Sandy.

"Sandy's dead and you're throwing a party?"

"People do," she said. "They celebrate the lives of those who die." She topped up my wine glass and poured one for herself. "We don't stop living because someone else dies. If we did, the world would come to a standstill. Anyway, that's not what the party's for. It's just a party." She raised her glass. "Here's to Sandy."

I raised mine in an echoing salute. "Why didn't you tell me she was ill? I didn't even know she was back in South Africa."

"I didn't know until a couple of months ago. I'd lost touch with them. You know that Sandy was in a terrible state after Heather died. Amos took her on some field trips with him. Then I heard that they'd bought a house in Obs. I saw them a couple of times, then Sandy got the job in Dubai. When they got back, they didn't seem that keen on getting together. I was never that close to them before Sandy started looking after Heather. As I've said, I lost touch with them. I only heard she was ill just before Lily came to see you."

"How was she when you saw her? How was Amos?"

"I didn't see her."

"What?" I slammed my glass down on the table. Wine spilled over my hand and onto the table. I ignored the mess. "You were afraid you'll get it from breathing near Sandy. I thought you knew better!"

"Thank you for that, Yazz," she said dryly, taking a tea towel and wiping both my hand and the table. "I know you're upset, so feel free to be more than your usual rude self. I didn't know she had AIDS. *Nobody* knew. I didn't see Sandy because Amos wouldn't let me."

"Why ever not?"

She grimaced. "You remember when Lily came to see you in London? Apparently just before she left South Africa, she turned up at Sandy and Amos's place. She made such a *skandaal* that she drove Amos frantic. He was going to call the police. I think it was Sandy who made him call me instead. He said, very politely, that he didn't like to burden me with his problems, but he couldn't think of anyone else who could deal with Lily in your absence. If I couldn't, he'd be forced to call the police next time or go to court to get an interdict to keep Lily away from Sandy."

I was still reeling from her news about Sandy's death. This was like a further tremor after an earthquake. If she'd told me that Sandy's gentle old tabby cat had turned rampaging lion, I might have been less shocked. "Amos threatened you with the cops?"

"You don't call it a threat when the person telling you this sounds as though he's crying. You can imagine how startled I was. I asked him what exactly Lily had done. He said it didn't matter. What mattered was that Sandy was ill and seeing Lily had upset her. He didn't want her upset because she was having a hard time as it was. So of course I went round there to see how she was and to see if I could help. He wouldn't let me in." She pulled a face "I think there are still people who labour under the illusion that you, Lily and I are joined at the hip. See one of us, see all of us."

"Lily must have known that Sandy was ill. That's why she was so frantic to see her. Imagine hassling a dying woman!"

"Hey, steady on. I said, *nobody* knew. That includes Lily."

"Even if you weren't aware Sandy was ill, you could have stopped Lily from abusing her. You know Lily as well as I do. You realized she'd go to Sandy the minute she saw that photo. In fact, she probably told you she was going."

"Yes. I could also have stopped a volcano from erupting."

"You expected me to."

She smiled. "You're so much stronger, Yazz."

"Don't start that again. Amos must be devastated." I glanced at my watch. "I'll go and see him tomorrow. I suppose it's too late to go now. It'll only scare the poor old boy. It's a pity Adam's leaving tomorrow. He'd have liked to see Amos. Bloody Lily. She could have told me Sandy was sick. And don't tell me she didn't know. Amos would have told her, if only to get her to back off."

"He didn't tell me that Sandy was dying of AIDS. He probably didn't tell Lily either."

"Oh, go and pick someone else's nits, Viv. She might not have known that Sandy was dying, but she knew she was sick, and she didn't say a word about it. Did Sandy have to be dying for her to show some sympathy, for her to think it important enough to tell me? She said a lot else about her – oh, too bloody right she did, but that the poor woman was sick? Not one bloody word. Fucking self-centred...."

Viv cut me off mid-invective. "Lily's in pain."

"So was Sandy. And she didn't cause her own."

Viv's deep-set little eyes burned into me. "That's a terrible, terrible thing to say."

"Yeah," I muttered. "But it's true, isn't it?"

The egg timer she used in place of an oven timer went off. Viv picked up a cloth and went over to the oven. She opened it, took out a pan and put it on the sink. Shutting the oven, she turned to me. "Do you know something? You and Lily have a lot more in common than you think. Each of you thinks you're the only one who suffered. Each of you thinks the other one could have stopped what happened to her. You need to talk."

"When hell freezes over," I said. I got up and went outside.

What effort I might have made to enjoy the party was scuppered. As soon as I could, I dragged Adam away. I lay awake all night in one of the twin beds in my childhood bedroom. My mind was a maelstrom with Sandy's death dominating, followed by Lily's behaviour and its cause. Then there was my conscience, reminding me that if I'd known Sandy was in Cape Town, I would have gone to see her as well, at least partly to clear up the mystery of Lily's photo. To be sure I'd have backed down on seeing she was sick, but if I was in Lily's position, I couldn't in all honesty say what I'd have done. The thing was, I wasn't in Lily's position.

Next morning I dropped Adam at the airport with assurances that I'd go and see Amos straight away and convey his sympathies as well as my own, plus his apologies for not delivering them in person. I had told him only about Sandy's death. There was no point in telling him about Lily's behaviour. Ranting at Viv had calmed me down a bit. Talking to him about it would only enrage me again. I didn't want us parting with him worrying about me. Driving to Amos's place from the airport, all I had in mind was comforting an old friend. I nearly gave up after hours of trying to find the place. Observatory was a warren of narrow half-cobbled, half-tarred streets bordered by narrower pavements, which twisted and turned every which way. Unlike the council built township my parents lived in, the streets weren't numbered and there was no logic to the names. I could find my way around most townships, even squatter camps, but this ex-white area where I'd never had to organize, baffled me. Finally I was there, in front of a house built nearly onto the narrow pavement of an only slightly wider street. I parked awkwardly and got out, looking around me in amazement.

This was the only part of Cape Town I knew of, except the sub-economic areas in Cape Flats townships, in which the houses were all joined together in a single storey version of what the English call a terrace. The houses all looked alike. The streets had no distinguishing features that I could see. The tiny frontage of these houses gave the impression that they were as small inside as a township house. That was an illusion. The similarity ended at the front doors. When I was young, this had been a white area, a bit seedy by the standards of the suburbs. Very seedy by the standards of the families from whom came a lot of its occupants. We'd sniggered and scoffed at the white students who lived here when we were at 'varsity. Pseudo-radicals, a step up from their liberal parents, slumming it until the degree was acquired, the grand job landed, or until Daddy bought tickets for a world tour. After that, the scions of the fine houses in Constantia would wander home from Obs and settle down in the mink and manure belt. In the eighties, black students had begun to slip into some of the houses, the cops turning a blind eye, as the area became "grey". It was, after all, only a ramshackle few streets occupied by "youngsters sowing their wild oats". There was more to occupy the cops in the townships.

That was a long time ago. The area was being transformed, the colourless dirty walls with only graffiti for decoration, the aging window frames and sagging or missing gates were largely gone, replaced by spruced-up houses with warnings of "armed response" on their front. The gate I pushed open was a smart wrought-iron one, set in a newly built wall around a tiny front patio filled with containers of flowers. The windows had the ubiquitous burglar bars of windows all over the city. There was a security gate outside the front door. I rang the bell, set into a pretty pastel wall which had well-maintained windows on either side, each with heavy curtains drawn across it. The bell echoed hollowly down the passage, a much longer one, I knew, than that of any township "train" house, because these houses were so much bigger inside.

I pushed the bell again. Still no response. Finally I sat down on the garden wall, reluctant to leave. He might not be long. Meantime, I looked around me. The township house Sandy and Amos had lived in when she'd looked after Heather was one built around a central tarmac. The entire township, like many others, consisted of such squares. They were meant to be play spaces for kids, with a few swings and a slide. By the time we started organizing in Sandy's area, most of the squares had long been taken over by gangs, for fights, smoking and trading dope, and just generally as a place to smash up things. Sandy's square was different. Mothers kept a strict eye on the kids in the playground. Fathers kept a strict eye on the gangs to make sure it stayed a play space. The gardens round the square were bright with flowers. The tenants maintained the swings and slides. It was a perfect place for open air meetings at night. It was a perfect place, by day, for Heather to play with other kids, though it provided a challenge to our principles. We socialists – Lily, Viv and I – would so much rather have equipped a private playground in Sandy's backyard to keep our communal chick safe – even though the happiness of all her little fellows proved there were no monsters around.

From the corner of my eye, I saw movement at one of the windows. I rapped on the window. "Amos? Amos, is that you? Won't you open up for me please?"

There was a shuffle of footsteps, a jangling of keys, a struggle with locks and then the wooden inner door opened. Except for the square-rimmed glasses, Amos used to resemble nothing as much as an oversized elf, with his large ears and round red cheeks. When he smiled, it only heightened this impression. He wasn't smiling now. He stood just inside the front door, peering at me through the security gate with red-rimmed, glassless eyes. His trademark thatch of wild hair, now greying, looked as if it hadn't been combed in ages. But then it had always looked like that. He had a nervous habit of running his hand through it, literally making it stand on end. "I heard you were in town," he muttered.

"Howzit going, Amos?" I said, inwardly cursing the township drums that beat so loudly in Cape Town. Now he'd think that neither Adam nor I had deemed it important enough to come and see him. Pity the bloody drums hadn't sent the news about Sandy overseas, together with all the trivia and moaning about the new state of things. "Sorry I didn't come before. I thought you were in Dubai."

"Sandy was ill. We had to come back."

"I know," I said gently. "I only heard last night. Can I come inside?"

He took his glasses from the pocket of his shirt, hooked them round his ears and peered out. "Are you alone?"

"If you're looking for Adam," I said. "He didn't come with me. Sorry. He ran out of leave. He had to go back to London first thing this morning."

"Oh, that's a pity." He ran his fingers through his hair. "I would have liked to see Adam." He pushed the glasses up his nose. They slid a bit on the shiny protuberance and he pushed them up again. Once more he looked around. Apparently satisfied, he took the glasses off, wiped them on the front of his shirt and put them back in the shirt pocket.

I took the proverbial bull by its equally proverbial horns. "Amos," I said. "Look, I heard Lily was here. I'm sorry. She's just *bedonerd.* I've nothing to do with her any longer. Really. I just wanted to have a cup of tea with you, see if you're alright. If you're not that way inclined, it's alright with me. I'll go. Just tell me you're OK."

"I'm fine," he stammered. He was still the shittiest liar I knew. "Sorry." He took the keys from the front door and came towards the gate, fumbled to find the right key, dropped the whole bunch.

I reached through the gate, sorted through the keys for a likely one and opened the gate. I stepped inside and planted a kiss on his cheek. It was damp and slightly salty. "Hello, Amos," I said gently. "It's good to see you again."

He put his hand up, as though holding the kiss, then turned and shuffled down the passage. I locked the gate. I'd been back home long enough to know to do that everywhere I went. Then I turned and followed him. All the doors off the passage, barring the kitchen at the end which spilled light into the far end, were shut. The house was a body missing its heart. In the kitchen, Amos tried to fill the kettle. The jet of water from the tap missed the kettle and wet everywhere. I took the kettle from him, filled it and set it on the electric stove. The yard wasn't as large as Viv's, but it was bordered with well-tended shrubs. The small paved area, like the front, was filled with containers overflowing with blooms. I made tea and set one in front of each of us. "I don't know how she got it," he said. "She thought perhaps it was when she was donating blood. Perhaps the needles weren't clean. Perhaps she got scratched or cut when she was working with someone who was infected. We never found out."

I wasn't really interested in how Sandy had acquired AIDS, more in how she and he had coped and how he was doing now, but I let him talk about what he wanted to. He stammered on for a while, the tea untouched. Finally I asked, "What will you do now?"

"I have work. A field trip," He waved his hand vaguely in the direction of a couple of travel bags which stood packed against the wall.

"Well, I'm sure you've got loads of preparing to do." I stood up to go.

I was already on the stoep, turning to kiss him good-bye, when he drew back and slapped his forehead in the classic gesture of remembrance. "Oh, she left something for you. Wait here." He hurried back down the passage and opened one of the doors off it. There was the sound of things being moved about. Then he came out of the room, carefully shutting the door behind him. "I was going to post it," he said. "But you might as well take it now." He shoved something into my hand.

53

I'd been expecting some small token of remembrance. Perhaps a book I'd liked, or an ornament I'd admired. Instead, I saw that he'd handed me a small brown envelope. It looked as though it held a letter or perhaps some documents. "What's this?" I asked.

He stared at his shoes, tugging at his hair like an embarrassed schoolboy. "I don't know." He blushed and started fiddling with the keys again, anxious to lock up after me.

I said, "I'll come back. If there's anything you need.........."

"No," he said, quickly. "There isn't anything, thanks, Yazz. Just that." He pointed at the package. "She wants you to do something for her."

I fingered the package, shivering, perhaps because he still spoke of her in the present tense. "And you? Will I see you again before you go?"

"No," he said, not looking at me. "I'm leaving this afternoon. You were just in time." I wondered why Amos didn't want to see me again. He was packed, but he didn't have the air of a man in a hurry to leave the country on a long trip. "I would have posted it," he repeated. "I promised her."

I shivered again, looking at the sky to see if clouds were gathering over the sun. The sky was clear. It was probably just some goose wandering across my grave. "Good-bye, Amos. Call if you need anything." I hugged him hard.

"She always trusted you," he said, for no reason I could fathom. He locked the security gate and retreated beyond the inner door.

In the car, I slammed my hand on the steering wheel. "This is so fucking unfair!" I said through teeth gritted against the threatening tears. Then I remembered one of the things Amos had said. "She knew you'd come once you heard. She said to tell you, it took a while, but she got her Bo Derek figure in the end." I didn't want to think about how she got there. I'd seen pictures of AIDS victims. But I'd laughed at the standing joke between me and Sandy. "She said to tell you she's sorry you only got middle-aged spread," he'd continued. And when I'd laughed at that, he'd said seriously," You haven't got any middle-aged spread." I'd laughed more loudly, slightly hysterically. Sandy always maintained that she'd long ago have lost her "melons" and "loaves" meaning her ample bosom and bum, if it hadn't been for Amos wanting something to hold onto. I'd never been able to think of Amos having sex, or even capable of sexual innuendo. I'd been wrong. Amos did notice women's bodies after all.

I drove on autopilot and found myself at the lighthouse at Mouille Point. The promenade ran from here, all along the seafront. Where it ended, there was a short walk up and then one could continue along the cliff tops to Lily's beloved Llandudno. I got out of the car and locked up, leaving the envelope on the passenger seat. I needed to shake out the dead feeling of Sandy's house, but I had no intention of walking to Llandudno. It was there that Viv and I had taken Lily when we'd had to break the news about Heather. The breathtaking view had meant to be comforting, to soften the terrible blow. How young we were. Talk about forever ruining someone's favourite beauty spot.

One of the ubiquitous "car-guards" who patrolled every parking area and curb side the length and breadth of the city, came limping over. He was a grown man, as were most of them, earning the price of a meal for themselves, maybe for a family, by spending an entire day obsequiously guiding drivers to empty parking spaces and out again, hoping for a handout. It was one of the worst "jobs" in the "informal sector", out there in all weathers. In summer, with tourism a booming industry and Cape Town now a prime feature of package holiday brochures, they could probably earn a bit, but in winter, the pickings were slim. I handed him a twenty rand note, which he took with some astonishment in both cupped hands. He expected this much of tourists, whom he probably thought of as too rich or stupid to know that a coin or two would do; he wasn't to know how little twenty rand meant in pounds, euros or dollars. Cape Townians were kind and polite and usually gave what coins they could, but there were many who had scant thanks in words or money for people like him, whom they treated at best like beggars to be sent on their way, at worst like thieves. These were usually those driving cars that cost more than my parent's house, to whom those cars were more important than this man's poverty. He wasn't to know that I'd probably have been as bad as the next driver, if I'd had anything but twenties in my pocket or could have been bothered to hunt for coins in the car. His profuse thanks shamed me. I felt like giving him all the money I had.

I looked back at the car seat. The envelope was in full view of anyone looking into the car. I walked away, hard and fast. "Hypocrite," I could hear Lily say. "You just gave that poor man money so he'd go and have a decent meal. You want your car broken into. You want the letter stolen by someone hoping it had money in it. That way you're off the hook." I lifted my face to the sun. In winter the Cape of Good Hope often earned its alternate name, the Cape of Storms. Then the ocean could easily turn into a boiling mass of grey water meeting grey skies, huge breakers smashing against the sea wall, sending foam onto the promenade and even as far as the palm-shaded lawns between it and the road. Today the sky was clear. There was no wind to lash the waves into mountains of water, but the spray still hit the sea wall hard enough to shower me as I walked along the rail. I walked hard, head up, revelling in the smell of the sea, the taste of salt in my mouth, the feel of the cold water pricking through my clothes.

The rainbow nation was out in force, walking or running along the promenade, enjoying picnics on the lawns beneath the palm trees or on the white-sanded beaches. Not too long ago, the only black faces under the trees or on the sand belonged to uniformed servants cum nannies watching their small white charges. The only black men were cleaners. I stopped at the Pavilion, a set of four pools –diving, toddler, laned, general – surrounded by paving and lawn. The place was packed. Bare-breasted women who had to be tourists, sunned themselves, apparently oblivious to the stares from small boys. I grinned when a mother who'd caught her boy staring snatched him away with a clip around the ear and a glare at the bare boobs. I couldn't hear what she said above the din, but I could guess. A few lane swimmers, largely white, tried to wend their way around the, largely black, bodies leaping in and splashing every which way. There were a few confrontations or disgusted departures from the water. I laughed out loud. It didn't take much to imagine what either side was thinking. I'd heard those thoughts spoken out loud often enough. The first varied from "these fucking people!" – this of course *sotto voce* – to the more frequently defensive, " I don't mind, but they could at least behave like…………". The latter varied from a "Fuck you. It belongs to us now too" to a totally uncaring shrug and a very rude gesture. No *sotto*

56

voce. The hues of the rainbow were still separate. My relaxing walk was fast turning into an exercise in cynical amusement. I turned and walked back.

My reliable car guard was gone. I picked up the letter, re-locked the car. The guard came hurrying up, breathless. "Sorry, Mem, I jus' go over dere ten seconds, Mem. Me, I watch de car alla time, Mem, cause you leave dat parcel on de seat, Mem," he said. "Somebody break de window, dey steal it, so I watch but I go quick to de toilet, Mem."

I took out the roll of twenties and gave him several. His eyes widened. "No, Mem, is too much Mem!" He glanced around fearfully, stepped closer to shield my hands. "Mem, you don' min' me saying, you don' let anyone see you walk 'roun' wit' so much money. Dere's bed people roun' here. Dey take your money, maybe hurt you. Put it away, please, Mem."

"*You* put it away," I said, peeling off one for myself and giving him the rest. "Here. Now I'm safe and you're the one has to take care." I laughed at his worried look. "Hey, it's OK. I've got this now. You go do your job."

I took the letter down the steps, across the narrow gold strip of shell-strewn sand to an outcropping of rock. I lit a cigarette, using the letter to shield the match. I studied my name and address on it for some time, listening to the goose which had caused me to shiver at Amos's house, have a right hard stomp on my grave. I held the cigarette's burning end to the corner of the letter.

"Trust," Lily used to say, "Is just blackmail. It's forcing suckers to do what you want. You know, bosses trust workers, so a worker doesn't steal to make up for his pathetic wages. The boss is free from worry about his profits."

"You're so full of crap, Lily, I'd laughed, secretly thinking how right she was.

Then she had to go and spoil it with one analogy too far. "Your parents say they trust you. That way when you go to a party, you don't want to get drunk, get high, fuck around. Your folks are free from worry. Trust just means making people put handcuffs on themselves."

That had cut too close to the bone. I'd responded viciously, "All parents aren't like that. You should have had someone to worry about you. Then you'd know."

She was right, my bad angel whispered in one ear. The Party trusted you to keep its secrets from the SB, you ended up on the run and in exile. It trusted you to obey the rules, you ended up having an abortion. Now Sandy trusts you with whatever's in here and God knows where you'll end up. A breeze blew the letter from my hand. I ran after it and stomped on it. The flap burst open. I picked it up. Inside were several sheets of thin, old-fashioned blue-lined writing paper of the kind my mother used to write to me when I'd first left home. They were wrapped round a photo. I straightened the pages and found myself looking yet again at the little girl whose picture Lily had left for me in London.

What made me feel as though I'd gone mad wasn't her pretty little face. It was the faces of the man and woman holding each of her hands, swinging her between them. I looked carefully from one to the other, trying to make sense of it. I knew that man. He was Lily's ex-lover Zac, Heather's father. I knew that woman. She was Mel, one of my few white friends from my undergrad days, my only friend who was avowedly apolitical. It wasn't politics that Zac was playing at with her, though. It looked like mommies and daddies. It was as though I was watching a photo taken in an alternate reality.

I'd met Mel the same day I'd first met Lily. In fact, I met her earlier. I'd been standing about to board the special bus I'd been told would take us up the steep drive to campus, when the driver turfed me off, with a "Students only" warning. "I am a student!" I said, embarrassed. I'd not been chucked off a bus since I was a small child, travelling into town with my illiterate grandmother who couldn't read the signs. He demanded my registration card. I remembered that I had my letter of acceptance in my bag. I started to fumble for it, awareness of the muttering people gathering behind me making me drop half my stuff. "Never mind, I'll walk." I gathered my papers and turned, expecting people behind me to give way.

"No you won't!" A girl thrust herself through the crowd, angry blue eyes flashing, a hand impatiently shoving aside a mass of tangled, streaky blonde curls as she readied herself for a fight. All five foot nothing of her. She said to the driver, "You didn't ask anyone else for their reg cards. Why are you hassling her? I haven't got a reg card." She gestured to people on the bus and those behind her. "They haven't. Nobody has until we get to campus to register. So we'll all walk and you'll drive an empty bus to campus, right?" Without waiting for him to answer, she pushed me ahead of her down the aisle and into a seat. She sat next to me. I knew her entire sexual history by the time we got to main campus.

That had been the first of many times Mel had stuck up for me on campus. I'd needed it, being a minority of one black person in our class. I never knew why she was so determined to befriend me. I just thanked God for it when the chips were down and we had to leave South Africa in a hurry. Lily had always scoffed at my friendship with this woman, Mel, but she'd come through for me.

By what fluke, of any of the billions of men on the planet, had she ended up playing happy families with Zac? It made no sense at all. Mel didn't even know Zac. Then it came to me that she did. It was no fluke. First Lily. Now Mel. How many friends had I handed over to this man? With shaking hands, I put the photo under a stone to secure it and started reading Sandy's letter.

Lily used to say, when I complained of a movie being totally over the top, that I should suspend disbelief and just enjoy. This was no celluloid fantasy, so perhaps it was *belief* I had to suspend. The contents were so incredible. I reminded myself that it was a dying woman's statement and read it again a bit at a time, responding to it as though Sandy was there, telling me. It was only on the third reading that the full horror of it struck me. I felt hot and queasy. I wanted to throw up. What Sandy *knew* Zac to have done was appalling. What she *suspected* him of having done in relation to Heather was, if true, unspeakable. If Sandy's recollection was true and her suspicions were right, there were no words for the actions he had taken in order to achieve his goal. Monstrous wasn't enough.

59

There was a tap on my shoulder.

"Please, Mem. I go now Mem. You go too. Not safe for lady now, Mem."

The sun was sitting low. The beach and promenade was emptying. I couldn't dredge up a smile for the solicitous car guard but I let him help me to my feet. The trembling in my hands and legs had long since ceased; my legs felt as stiff as though I'd sat there for days. My mind had cleared, though, by the time I headed in search of Viv. One of the conclusions I'd come to, was that she had some explaining to do. No-one else could have told Zac about Heather. Another was that we had a needle to find in a haystack, Lily and I. Sandy had left no clue other than a city whose size I didn't know. Sandy had entrusted me with helping Lily, but three searchers were better than two. I had to hope that when I found Lily she wouldn't draw my first conclusion, only my second. Otherwise she might just kill Viv.

I knew I just might, in her shoes.

By the time I reached Viv's house, another thought had crept into my mind. I had no doubt that we would find Heather. However long it took, once Lily knew her to be alive for sure, she'd scour every inch of the world for her. And when we found her? Would I again be the one telling a friend sad news about her child?

CHAPTER FOUR

Viv's place was deserted when I got there. Big gates that had been flung wide the last time I'd been were shut, chained and locked with a huge padlock. Nonetheless, I parked in the street and dialed Viv's mobile number. Her phone was switched off. Frustrated, I tossed mine into the seat beside me, and sat shivering, despite the warmth of the closing hours of the day. I lit a cigarette, letting the deep drags calm me down. Perhaps it was as well that Viv wasn't home. I was so livid when I'd arrived I'd have throttled her. I couldn't afford that. With Adam away, she was my only sounding board for talking through Sandy's letter. If I flew at her, she'd just send me packing, tell me to come back when I could hold a reasonable conversation. Besides, I knew that whatever role she must have played in Zac's discovery of Heather's existence would have been an inadvertent one. It was probably just some careless word, spoken in the wrong company. That didn't absolve her of responsibility, but it wasn't as bad as the alternative, which lingered at the back of my mind. My phone rang. I jumped, snatching at it and the cigarette fell onto my lap. "Shit!" I yelled, scrabbling for it with my free hand.

"That's no the way to answer the phone, Yasmin!"

My mother only used my full name as a disciplinary measure. I stumbled an apology and, slightly mollified, she asked where I was. I'd been gone all day without a word. Adam had called and they hadn't known what to say to him. I apologized again, like a recalcitrant teenager caught playing truant. She heard the agitation in my voice and mistook it for annoyance that I had to account for my whereabouts. "It's nearly magrieb," she said defensively. "This isn't London. You can't drive home alone in the dark."

"Don't worry. I'll get Simon to drive behind me when I come home," I promised. "I won't be too long. If Adam calls again tell him I'll call him later. He can talk to me at Viv's if he's desperate."

"Oh, you're at Viv's place." The relief in her voice was palpable. "Why didn't you say so, instead of worrying a person for nothing. I know you're alright when you're with her."

61

I was nearly forty, but still didn't qualify to look after myself as well as Viv could.

Twenty-odd years ago, that sort of comment irritated the shit out of me, perhaps because then, it had the ring of truth. Now it made me laugh. "Yes, Mum," I said, "I should have remembered that." I rang off just as Viv's old Citroen puttered past me and stopped in front of the gates. She got out, waved and went to unlock the gates. I drove in behind her, leapt from my car and yanked her door open as she was gathering her things. "She was right!" I shouted, ignoring her obvious alarm. The bit of composure that cigarettes and conversation with my mother had instilled was gone. For hours, I'd held back the shock and revulsion at Zac's behaviour, the guilt and remorse for never trusting Lily's instincts and believing her, the doubts about Viv. Now the floodtide of emotion which Sandy's letter had opened shoved that finger right out.

"All these years! She was right!" I paused for breath, gasping. "But how did he find her? That's what I want to know!"

"Steady on!" She pushed me away so that she could get out. "What are you so excited about? Who was right? About what?"

I waved the letter in her face. "Lily," I said. "Lily was right all along. Read this!"

At last my agitation got through to her. "OK!" She piled her stuff into my arms and took the letter from me. "But calm down, alright?" I followed her into the house and chucked her stuff on the table, causing a "tsk!" and a tight-lipped whisking away of things onto hooks and into drawers. There were times when Viv would try the patient of all the saints in the good place, and I wasn't even a member of that collective. "Did you not hear me?" My voice had risen even further, but I didn't really care. I could have shaken her. "Read the letter, dammit! Heather's alive!"

"I'll tell you what." She looked at me just as she did at Lily when Lily was in a state, and put down the letter on the table between us. "I'm parched and I'm useless to you without a cup of tea. You look as though you could use something hot and sweet. Why don't you tell me the whole story while I make tea? From the beginning."

"Sandy wrote it all down." I said, tapping the letter. "You have to read this. See for yourself, it's better than if I tell you. Heather's alive. Living in a place called London, Ontario, in Canada. That's where Sandy saw her. When she went with Amos for that stint he did at the university there."

She placed a plate of biscuits and two cups of hot milky tea on the table and sat down, gesturing at me to do the same. She opened the letter. Her face paled with shock and then reddened with anger. She looked as though she wanted to throw it down, but she read it through with grim determination. When she'd finished, she folded the letter carefully and set it aside, studied the photo, then put both back into the envelope. She sat very still for a while, staring into her tea, considering. I struggled to stay still through all this, but I knew she wouldn't be hurried. Finally she said, "So, let me get this straight. Sandy thinks –thought - that Heather is alive. She thought that Zac abducted her. And you –" She took a deep breath. "You want to show this to Lily?"

"That goes without saying."

"I don't know if it does." She sipped her tea. "You read this letter – what, a couple of hours ago?" I nodded. "Have you thought through it?" I nodded. "You're absolutely sure that Zac has Heather?" I nodded again and she studied the photo. "That's your friend Mel, isn't it? How does she come into it, I wonder?" She ran a thoughtful finger across Mel's face in the photo. "But, we'll get to that. Look, before we set Lily haring off halfway across the world, looking for these people, why don't we just examine things a bit more closely?"

"What's to examine?" I mimicked her word. "It's all there. We've got to tell Lily!" She raised an eyebrow at the "we", but said nothing. "Viv? How can you not see that? I need you to help me tell her!"

"Tell her what, Yazz?" she asked, gently. "That Sandy saw Zac and a blonde woman playing with a blonde child? That blonde child could be Zac and the woman's. She's blonde like her mother. If she

63

resembles Heather, it's because they're half-sisters. The child may be some other relative of Zac's, again with some family resemblance to Heather. The child could be the woman's and the resemblance may be totally coincidental. There could be any number of such explanations. I'm not saying Sandy's lying. But it may all be pure conjecture, based on what Sandy experienced and what she wanted to believe. Think about it. She's ill. She has this child's death and Lily's grief on her conscience. She sees this child. She remembers a man coming to see her about Lily's child. She puts two and two together and makes twenty two."

I picked up my cup with a shaking hand. "How can you......" I spluttered, returning my cup to its saucer without drinking. Tea spilled into the saucer. "I mean, aren't you even bothered? You're the one always telling me I don't care about Lily any more. Here I am, trying to help her. It isn't even anything to do with me, but I'm willing to try and........."

"Yazz!" The single word was like a pistol shot. "This is the situation," she said after a minute. "I'm not entirely dismissing this. All I am saying is that I am not prepared to show this to Lily unless I am one hundred percent sure that everything in it is true. You've told me several times how terrible it was in the UK when Lily thought she'd seen Heather. She took ages to recover. She seems better able to cope with the loss now. True, there are blips, such as this last time when she shouted at Sandy. But then she came to see you. You told her you weren't interested and for some reason, she accepted that. She dealt with it. What do you think will happen when she sees this?" She answered her own question. "Lily won't rest until she's tracked Zac down, even if takes the rest of her life. That's fine, if she gets her child in the end. If she doesn't, it will destroy her. I know that. " She paused, slid the photo from the envelope and laid it on the table between us again. "Besides, she's not the only person involved here, Yazz. There's Heather to consider. There's your friend Mel." She pointed to each of them in turn as she spoke their names. "All I am asking is that we make absolutely sure." She picked up her cup and drained it.

"OK," I said, getting up to put my cup of cold tea in the sink. "I know that. The point is, Lily's still got to be told about this. I think it would be wrong to keep it from her." I stood with my back to the sink and

64

looked at Viv. "As you well know, Lily's not my favourite person right now, but I don't think I could keep this from her. Even if I wanted to, even if I do, and she somehow finds out afterwards, there'll be hell to pay. The lord only knows what the fallout will be for Mel and Heather. So yes, they need to be considered. They need to be prepared for what happens when Lily gets this."

"Hey," she said. "You're jumping the gun. Let's take things one at a time -who, what, when, why, how." She ticked her fingers on each of the questions. "Alright?" I nodded and returned to my seat. This was Viv's usual way of reasoning. "We know when, and we've looked at one 'who'," she continued. "The child in the photo. She may or may not be Heather." She looked at me for agreement. I nodded again.

"The second 'who' then. Sandy says that a strange white man came to see her a few weeks before the fire, claiming to be Heather's father, demanding to see her. What makes you think that's Zac? We know that the security police used to play tricks on people. They threatened your parents to get at you. They arrested Adam's little brother to get at him. Do you think it impossible that they discovered Lily's visits to Sandy? They might have established that Heather was Lily's daughter. It's not inconceivable that they stored that bit of information to use against her later. Sandy's uninvited guest need not have been Zac. Agreed?"

This time I didn't nod.

"That's Zac in the photo. She says that's the man who visited her and asked for Heather." I took out the letter and ran my finger through the words. A man had come to see Sandy a few weeks before the fire, it said, at the old township house where she and Amos then lived. I skipped the bits where Sandy mentioned how shocked she'd been to see a white man in the township, when so many other townships were burning. White people didn't venture into the township under those conditions, even with troops and police patrolling. As well as getting stoned by protestors, they risked being shot by the cops on the assumption that they were anti-apartheid activists, in the townships for anti-government activity. Yet this man had gone into the townships with a state of emergency declared. Finally I found the passage I wanted and read out loud, "*So you can imagine my surprise when this white man shows up on my doorstep, asking about Heather."* I read. At first Sandy had thought he was a policeman, but then, the letter went on, *"He greeted us with the nicest smile…".* I looked up at Viv. She didn't say anything. We both knew what a sucker Sandy was for anyone with good manners and a smile. Zac could produce both, when he wanted to turn on the charm. The description of her mysterious visitor which Sandy went on to provide left no question in my mind that it was Zac: *"… shiny straight brown hair that was too long for a cop and the brown eyes that laughed even when he wasn't smiling."*

"That could be anyone," Viv murmured.

I went on reading. *"When I asked who he was and what he wanted, he tells me he's there to see Heather. He's Heather's father. He wants to see her and take her out."* Sandy hadn't taken his word for it. Despite the charm of her visitor, she'd demanded proof. "Here it is," I said, pointing at the place. *"I said to him, I'm sorry. No way can I just take his word for it. Every day children are stolen by bad men for all sorts of reason, especially kids who look like Heather and I'm not saying he's like that, but I've got no proof, he could be anybody. He was nice as pie, never got upset with me for saying all that. He just smiles and says he understands. He takes out his ID to show me his name. Then he takes out a birth certificate. It's Heather's."*

I put the letter down on the table. Viv put her elbows on the table and clasped her hands. She rested her forehead against them for a moment. Then she raised her head and looked at me, forearms on the table, hands spread towards the letter but not touching it. "Alright. Let's assume for the moment that these things can't be faked and it was Zac who visited Sandy. How did he find out about Heather?" I kept my head down, fiddling with my teaspoon. When the silence between us was almost tangible, she said, "Well, that's easy, I suppose. Zac used to have all cadres followed to see that we were taking the right security precautions. He probably caught Lily stopping at Sandy's en route to a meeting."

I snapped my fingers. Eureka! That was it. Relief washed over me. Then I felt my face flush with guilt and remorse. Why hadn't I thought of this simple explanation, instead of thinking my old friend guilty of being part of Zac's vile plot? She studied me for a while, the blood draining from my face. "Never mind that. Let's get to what he would have had to do to snatch Heather and make us believe she died in that fire. I know that you hate the man. I don't particularly like him myself. But mass murder? Think about it. He'd have had to deliberately set fire to people's homes, killed children, to get his own. Well, I know he wouldn't have got his own hands dirty, but he'd have had to find someone else to do it. Can you see him doing that?"

I'd seen the results of fires in squatter camps. The thought that anyone would do this deliberately made the bile rise up inside me. "No," I said. "Not even Zac." OK, he was a charlatan. He played at leftwing politics when it suited him and abandoned it when he was bored. I hoped there was a socialist hell where blasphemers like him would roast for eternity. Yes, he messed women around. I'm sure Lily would like to cut his balls off and stuff them down his throat for that. But murder I could not believe him capable of. I re-read the parts of the letter where Sandy described how a few nights after the strange man visited her, Sandy had gone to a squatter camp to help out as a volunteer at the clinic of a doctor friend of hers. She'd taken Heather along because there was nowhere to leave the child. She didn't say that the three women – Lily, Viv and I – who were meant to look after the child when she couldn't, were too busy. She'd thought it would be alright because the doctor had said that part of the camp was quiet.

"Zac must have been watching Sandy," I suggested. "He was waiting for an opportunity to see Heather. Then there was the fire and he just took the opportunity to snatch her for good."

"So now," she said, "Ask yourself this, why would he want Heather?"

I had no answer for this. Zac's party had forbidden cadres to have kids because it would interfere with their work. They'd said that in our case, children would also give the security police leverage against us – hostages to fortune. We knew now that Zac's obedience to his party's rules had been a sham. Even so, someone like Zac wasn't into ties, and, party or not, clearly hadn't wanted the burden of children. He'd paid Lily to have an abortion. Why would he want that very child, or any child at all? "I don't know," I said. "Only Zac can tell you that."

"Yes," she said. "And I can't really see him doing that, can you?"

"Maybe he did it to spite Lily," I said. "For disobeying him when he told her to have an abortion? To punish her for taking his money and pretending?"

"Perhaps," Viv said, "He went to see the child because he was curious – and then decided that he wanted his child. People often change their minds about an unwanted pregnancy, once the child is born."

"People," I said. "I don't think Lily would call Zac, 'people'."

Viv took up the letter up and read through it again. I went outside and stood looking at the stars hanging over the backyard. I breathed deeply, trying to clear my head. Viv's reservations troubled me. They raised doubts in me again, doubts which only she could resolve. I went back inside. As I resumed my seat, she got up and went into the pantry, emerging with a bottle of vodka, which she set down on the table, following it with one of lime and another of lemonade. She fetched ice and put glasses on the table. Her chair scraped as she pulled it back and sat down. "You thought I'd told him," she said, as she began to mix the drinks. It was a statement, not a question. I felt my face flush as I started to protest that the thought had never crossed my mind. It was useless. She knew me too well. "Yes you did!" Her voice would have frozen a volcano. "Well, thanks for casting me in the role of ogre's helper in this tale. Sorry I had to decline the role."

"I don't know what came over me." I sat looking at my hands spread on the table. "It's just hearing about Sandy's death last night. Then this letter and the photo. It gave me a shock. I tried to work out if I could have let anyone know accidentally and…well, I know I didn't. *Lily* wouldn't have. She was paranoid about keeping Heather a secret. You can't really blame me. What else was I to think?"

"Blame," she said coldly. "That's it for you, isn't it? You read this letter and the first thing you thought of was who's to blame. Not how Sandy must have felt. Not the effect this will have on Lily. Not the effect, God help us, that it will have on your friend Mel and on this child, if and when Lily tracks them down."

"I'm sorry, Viv," I said. "I didn't think there were any other options."

68

"So you chose the easiest one," she snapped. She tossed back half of her drink. "Fuck, but you can be pathetic sometimes!"

I recoiled as if she'd slapped me. I'd seldom seen Viv lose her temper, let alone hear her swear. She wasn't shouting or anything. Her voice was still at its usual pitch, but she was furious. "Just tell me this. What did I ever do to deserve such contempt from you? To make you think I'd enter into some sort of conspiracy with Zac to abduct Lily's child and then watch Lily suffer for all these years?"

My head whipped up. "I *never* thought that!" I remonstrated, making myself look her squarely in the eye. "Don't be absurd! Sure, I thought maybe you inadvertently let slip something to someone who repeated it to Zac and he worked it out. But I never, really – Viv, you must believe me, I never thought you actually told him! It never crossed my mind that you were party to his...my god, Viv!"

She finished her drink and mixed herself another. In more than twenty years of knowing her, I'd never seen her drink like this. "OK." The ice was melting in her voice, but it was clear she was still none too pleased with me. "You can stop squirming. I accept your apology. Goodness knows, there are so many others in this saga to feel sorry for. If I had my way...but then I don't. You need to establish whether this girl is Heather or not. I assume you'll need help with that. Much as I am inclined to run and hide from this, I don't think that I have any alternative but to provide whatever help you need." She paused. "All I ask is that you remember *that* is your priority. Getting to the truth. Once you've done that, I suppose we'll have to deal with what follows."

"We?" I raised my eyebrows in disbelief. "Who's 'we'? A minute ago you were saying-" I broke off at the sound of her phone ringing.

Viv let the answer phone pick it up. The caller rang off before Viv's recorded message ran its course. Viv made a dismissive gesture with her hand. "I was saying," she finished my sentence, "that we have to be one hundred percent sure of the facts, before we tell Lily anything. I didn't say that we simply shouldn't tell her." She paused at the sound of a car outside. "Besides, you owe it to Mel, don't you think – to prepare her before Lily descends upon her?" I opened my mouth to respond, but she held up a hand. Car doors slammed and footsteps approached the house. "Later," she said, as Simon banged open the kitchen door.

"Hey," he said, grinning. "Is this a private party or can anyone join?" Before Viv and I could answer, he continued, "Look who I've found." Oblivious to the atmosphere, he reached out a hand and swung Lily lightly into the kitchen, exclaiming, "The third musketeer!"

My fingers tightened round the glass I'd been holding. "Shit," I muttered under my breath to Viv. "Did we conjure her up?"

"Hello Viv," Lily said, laughing. "I heard you were looking for me." She hugged her and smacked a kiss on each of Viv's cheeks. Then Lily saw me. Her smile vanished. "Hey, Yazz," she said, peering at me out the corners of her eyes. "What's up?"

I exchanged a quick glance with Viv, then swallowed and finally I managed an uncomfortable, "Hey Lily."

"You look like you've seen a ghost." Lily slid into a chair and reached for a biscuit. "You been gossiping about me?" she demanded of Viv around a mouthful of biscuit.

"You're not the only topic of conversation in our lives, Lily," Viv said, without a trace of irony in her voice.

Lily grinned at her and turned to me. "You still pissed with me? Want me to leave? Or can we can we play nice in Viv's sandbox?" She spoke like it was just a minor spat we'd had. Children squabbling about destroying each other's sand castles. It was hard to find in myself the resentment I'd been nursing against her for so long. Sandy's letter, my discussion with Viv, had pushed it to the back of my mind.

Viv rescued me. "That sounds like an excellent idea, Lily," she said. "I was just about to cook something. Have you eaten?" Without waiting for an answer, she went into the pantry, tossing over her shoulder, "Simon, if you're going to be the thorn amongst us roses, make yourself useful. Open some wine and put on some music." Her recovery amazed me. It was as though none of the past hour had happened, yet I retained the feeling that a character from a movie I'd been engrossed in had suddenly stepped from the screen. The problem was, this character, Lily, wasn't aware of the chapter of her life we'd just been discussing.

Viv came back laden with eggs, mushrooms, onions. She cracked eggs into a bowl and started beating.

"I'll help," Lily offered, getting up.

"No, thank you," Viv said, dryly. "We're all familiar with your cooking. But *you* can do the salad, Yazz."

"Oh, come on," Lily persisted as I went to the fridge for salad vegetables. "I can help. Here," she reached out a hand. "Let me wash those for you." She took the lettuce from me, then turned as Simon came back into the room, playing an imaginary guitar. The sound of The Band playing "The Night They Drove Old Dixie Down" followed him. Simon stopped "playing" and clutched his chest in mock horror. "Viv! You're not letting Lily near the food, are you?" He ducked as Lily aimed the lettuce at him.

"I'm not," Viv said, taking the lettuce from Lily. "If you must do something, Lily, set the table. Simon, get the bread out and set the table." She set a pan on the stove and put a knob of butter into it.

Simon did as he was bid. "What the hell is that stuff you always cooked at Langebaan?" he asked Lily as he moved around her to get to the bread bin.

"Stew," Lily said tartly, swiping a hand him. Simon stepped smartly out of the way, still sniggering. Langebaan was one of the out of the way beauty spots where we'd camped when we needed to do major planning for our public political work. People came with papers, books, ideas. But they never remembered to bring enough food. By the last day, we were generally out of most things. That's when Lily would raid everyone's bag. She'd tip all of her booty - odd cans of baked beans, peas, corn, sausages, the odd tomato, onion and potato, plus whatever seasoning had been packed for a barbeque which we hadn't had because someone had forgotten the meat at home – into the big pot Viv always brought for such events. The result was a vicious stew which you had to be starving, drunk, or insane to eat. Everyone moaned, but everyone ate, including me. I grinned at the memory.

"You can laugh, Yazz." She came over to where I was washing vegetables. "If it was up to you we'd have lived on muesli and raw vegetables the whole time." Despite her complaints, she took a carrot and started munching. "So," she said as I started slicing tomatoes, "while you're temporarily not pissed at me, Yazz – what's new in your life?"

Viv was chopping onions so hard and fast it was unnerving to watch, considering the size of the knife she was wielding. I stopped, looking on in fascination and trepidation, before turning to answer Lily. "There's nothing new in my life, Lily," I said. "As I've always told you. Ninety percent of life is mundane."

"Yeah." She took another bite of the carrot. "And as I always told you, make sure that every second of the other ten percent is fun."

Viv tossed the onions and mushrooms into a simmering pan. "Careful children," she said as she added seasoning. "Casual sniping can lead to real fights. Why don't you tell us what *you've* been up to, Lily? I've been looking for you for weeks. Where've you been?" She shook the pan, returned it to the stove and poured the beaten eggs into the pan.

"Away," Lily said, vaguely. The Band had started playing "Georgia". "Oh, my favourite song!" she suddenly exclaimed. Lily went over to Simon, who was lying back in an armchair, legs spread out in front of him. She prodded his foot with hers. "Come and dance," she said. Simon groaned, but she pulled him to his feet. They did a slow shuffle round the room, which was the only dancing Simon knew how to do, but it suited the number. The whole scene felt surreal, Viv cooking, Simon and Lily dancing, music playing. I felt like yelling: "Stop!" and blurting out the contents of Sandy's letter, but the track ended. Lily let go of Simon. Viv called out that the food was ready. The moment had passed.

Simon sat down at the table and Lily slipped onto a chair next to him. Viv divided the huge omelette into quarters and slid a portion onto each plate, handing one to Simon, then one to me and finally one to Lily. We ate and made small talk until Simon got a call from a friend who needed help with his computer. There was nothing mechanical or technological that Simon couldn't fix. A short while later, a hooter blared outside and he went off, after I'd made him promise not to be too late so that he could drive behind me when I went home. When he'd gone, I sat back down at the table. Lily started to clear away.

"Oh leave it," Viv said. "Let's have some coffee first and catch up." She rose and put on water to boil. "So," She said as she measured ground coffee into a cafetiere. "You were going to tell us what you've been up to."

"Oh, nothing much," Lily said, walking over to the shelf on which Viv kept her cookbooks. She trailed a finger along the spines of the books, pulled one out and began to flick through it.

"Well." Viv poured water into the cafetiere and put the coffee on the table. "You said you've been away. Where's 'away'?" She took down mugs and put them on the table.

"Just gone." Lily leaned against a kitchen cupboard, arms crossed, scowling at Viv. "You got a problem with that?" Viv stared at her until Lily lowered her head and muttered, "What are you, my mother?" She scuffed the toe of her shoe exactly like a mutinous child lying to her mother.

"No." Viv wasn't rattled by Lily's annoyance. "Just someone who cares whether you live or die. You could be lying injured in a ditch or dying under your bed. Wouldn't you want someone to be looking for you then?" She poured coffee into a mug and held it out to Lily.

Lily took it and sat down at the table. She added milk and sugar to her coffee, stirred and drank before she answered. "I went to London, OK?"

I drew in my breath sharply and looked at Viv but she was still intent on cross-examining Lily. "You went to London?" Viv asked. "What on earth for? I thought you'd just been."

"Why not? I build up frequent flyer miles travelling on business. I have to use them up. So I did. I used them all. There'll be more next year."

I couldn't help myself. "London, UK?" I burst out.

Lily raised her eyebrows. "Is there any other? I know there's Paris, Texas and Athens, Georgia, but my dear," – she put on a mock posh accent –"there can only be one London."

"So what did you do?" asked Viv.

"Not see old friends, obviously." Lily looked at me. "If you must know, there were a couple of shows I wanted to see. I didn't get a chance last time. I had to work, remember? Besides, you get to see great shows really cheaply this time of year." Viv's disbelief was clear on her face. "Oh, come on." Lily switched from defiance to wheedling. "A girl's got to have some time out. Sorry I didn't tell you, right? You know you're all I have in the world since Ouma died, except…well anyway, I promise I won't fuck off anywhere without telling you again, OK?" She got up and dropped a kiss on the top of Viv's head. "Thanks for caring."

"And that's all you did?"

"What else?" Lily spread her hands wide. "Hey, don't knock it. Wait till you see what I've brought you!" She grabbed Simon's keys and rushed outside, returning moments later with several shopping bags. The Body Shop. Waterstones. Virgin Records. "Presents!" she announced. "Since we good atheists don't celebrate Christmas, these have nothing to do with Christmas or New Year, but –" She giggled. "Our being good socialists does not prevent us from taking advantage of the January sales!" She handed Viv a set of books from the Waterstones bag. "For you!" It was a complete set of Vonnegut, one of Viv's favourite authors. She took some plastic bottles from the Body Shop package. "And some sexy smelly stuff for those joint baths I know you luuurrvvee to take with Simon." She licked her lips lasciviously then returned to rooting in the bags to show us what she'd bought for this or that friend.

Viv smiled. "Thanks for this, Lily," she said, stroking the set of books. "It was really thoughtful of you. And I'm sure that Simon and I will enjoy the bath stuff." I reached out a hand for the books and Viv gave them to me to look at. Our eyes met briefly. Then she turned to Lily and asked, "Come on, Lily. You didn't really just go shopping, did you?" She paused for a beat. "Was it something to do with that photo again?"

Lily stopped fidgeting with the shopping bags. A shadow crossed her face. "The photo?" she asked without meeting Viv's eyes. "Oh, that! God, Viv. That was months ago." She resumed looking through her bags. "I've forgotten all about it. Isn't that what you told me to do?"

"And you always do as I say," Viv said, with gentle irony. Lily shrugged. Viv made a motion of brushing crumbs from her lap, gathered the things from the table and stood up. "Alright, I give up. You're right. You don't have to tell me. What you do and where you go is your business. All I ask is that you give me fair warning to get a decent umbrella before you blow up the next storm, OK?"

Lily left the bags and picked up her coffee cup. She drank her coffee and then sat gazing into her cup as though the grounds were tea-leaves which would offer some idea as to what to do next. Finally, as I had known she would if Viv pretended indifference , she cracked. "Alright yes, if you must know!" she burst out. "I went about the photo, OK?" She put her elbows on the table and buried her face in her hands. There were no tears or sobs, but Viv's words had seen off the light-hearted, mocking Lily of a few minutes earlier.

I had visions of her aimlessly hunting for Heather in London, UK and it made my head ache. I opened my mouth to speak, but Viv laid a hand on my arm and shook her head. I glared at her. No-one should suffer like this unnecessarily. At the very least, I could tell Lily that she was looking in the wrong city, in the wrong country, on the wrong continent altogether. I pulled my arm free. "It's wrong!" I hissed.

Lily raised her head. "Don't worry," she said bitterly, "I didn't kidnap any kids. You didn't want to help me, so I asked someone else." She paused, toying with her cup. "I went to some organizations which look for missing children, OK? If you must know - that's what I did."

Viv and I exchanged glances and Lily intercepted the look. "Yeah, right. Most of them looked at me exactly the way you do," Lily said. "Pity for the poor mad woman who can't accept her child's death. Oh, they take notes, they open files, they give me tea and sympathy and assurances. But when I leave, I know they'll be onto the SAP, find out that Heather's supposed to be dead and decide they can't waste time on me, when they can be finding other live children. So I went to the police." She laughed ruefully. "Can you imagine that? Me? Going to the cops for help? They told me that, a, I've got no real basis for believing Heather's alive and b, if she is, she's a grown woman now, so basically not their business to look for..." She waved a hand, shaking her head, "Talk about a waste of fucking time. I'll think of something…maybe I'll hire a private detective or something. I'll handle everything myself and fuck agencies and cops, OK? "

"I'd rather not if you don't mind, Lily," Viv said, straight-faced. "It's rather a lot to take on."

Lily didn't laugh. "What I mean is," she looked hard at me. "From now on, I depend on nobody." I looked away. Lily put all her unpresented gifts into their bags, then piled coffee cups in the sink. "Yeah," she muttered, turning her back on us and beginning to run water into the sink. "You can both rest easy."

Just then, there was the sound of a car outside. A moment later, Simon flung open the kitchen door. He stood in the pool of light just beyond the door. "So?" he asked me. "How's that for time, huh? Ready to go?"

"Drop me off after you take Yazz home, Simon?" Lily asked. She took her hands from the sink and dried it on a tea towel.

"No probs," Simon stuck his head through the doorway. "See you Viv. Thanks for the food. Come on then, you two." He gestured for us to go with him.

76

Instead of following him all the way to his car, Lily followed me to my dad's old jalopy. "I noticed you had a drink earlier," she said. "I'll drive if you like." I was tired. My night vision wasn't brilliant and I wasn't thinking that clearly, though the bit of booze I'd drunk had little to do with it. Gratefully I slid over into the passenger seat.

Viv came round to my side of the car as Lily started up. "Be careful," she said briefly. She wasn't talking about Lily's driving. I'd never been very good at keeping things from Lily. The moment Lily suspected I had a secret, she'd wheedle it out of me.

"Yes, mother!" said Lily as she pulled away.

I simply said, 'Bye'.

We'd barely left Viv's place when we were pulled over by traffic cops. Instead of staying in the car, Lily got out and stood waiting for them to come over to us. Whatever they'd been going to ticket us for was forgotten the moment they saw her. They ogled, she flirted, there was an exchange of sexual banter. They didn't even bother to check the car over for minor reasons – and South African cops were expert at finding minor reasons for fines, now as in the past. At last Lily got back into the car, laughing as they walked off with a wave and a wink.

"Well," I said. "I'm glad to see you've still got the touch."

"Never lost it," she sang out, pleased with herself. "Remember that time I got them to change the tyre?"

We'd been on our way back from a party meeting, out in the mountains at a campsite. Cars had left at intervals, so it wouldn't attract attention. When our turn came to leave, we'd crawled for a few kilometres along the ten or so of potholed dirt track which led to the main road, then the car started to list and sway.

"Lily," I said. "I've got to stop. I think I've got a flat."

"Don't be silly," she mumbled. "It's just the road," She'd fallen asleep as soon as we'd set off, as had the three blokes in the windowless back

77

of my Escort panel van. We'd been up most of the night. She curled away from me against the cushion she'd propped up against her door.

I yelled to the back, "Hey, guys. I'm stopping. You'll have to get out so I can change the tyre."

"Nothing wrong with the tyre," came one response from the back. "Just keep driving."

I swore, but went on driving.

I was just about to turn onto the tarred road when I saw the unmistakeable white car with the blue light on its roof, parked across the way. A cop with his trousers stuck in his boots was already leaning against its door, book in hand, probably envisaging making up a whole year's quota of arrests and fines with the line of jalopies coming towards him. He smiled and waved me over.

"I bloody told you so!" I said, shaking Lily roughly. I was resigned to paying about a thousand rand in fines. They might even take the car off the road. The problem was, I had three African guys in the back. I didn't exactly look like a farmer taking his labourers around. I wasn't even sure if the guys at the back had their passes. What anti-apartheid activists checked her friends' papers before letting them in her car? If the cops opened the back door of the van, there'd be a lot of questions to answer. At the very least, there'd be more than fines on the car to pay. And the guys would be arrested. The thought made me nearly crap my pants.

"Oh, shit," said Lily, straightening up with a yawn. "Let me handle it." She got out of the car, still in the halter top and shorts she'd worn practically all weekend in spite of the chilly Easter weather. Playing the camping part, she'd said. "In case the ranger drops by."

I knew what she had in mind. I hated it. I wasn't very good at it anyway. Still, if we were to stop the cops opening up the back, we'd better put on a show. I shrugged of my jacket, knowing my tight sweater would keep the focus on my boobs, and detract from the plain face above. I needn't have bothered. Lily literally stopped them in their tracks. They let their eyes linger over her, before one of them recovered sufficiently to cast a glance over the car.

"What's this then?" He was pointing at my back wheel.

I got out of the car. The wheel appeared to have a black puddle beneath it. It wasn't a puddle. It was most of the tyre, looking as though it'd melted, lying upon the road covered in red dust. Lily came over to look, as though she could do anything about it. "Oh, my God!" she wailed. "My dad's going to kill us, Bobbi." This was my code name. "I told you it was flat. That tyre's ruined. What'll we do now?"

I burst into tears. Two hysterical women were always better than one, especially if one looked like Lily and another had tits like mine. "My" cop put his arm around my shoulder soothingly, reassuring me there was no real damage done. Just put the spare on. Drive to the nearest garage and buy another. In fact, they'd change it for us. The thought of having to open up the back to take out the necessary equipment scared the hell out of me. I wailed more loudly, "Alex" – this was Lily's code name – "I told you not to let the guys borrow the jack. Now what will we do?"

"No problem, meisie." The cop let go of me and sauntered over to his car to fetch his own equipment. The other made to go and take out the spare from the back of my car, but Lily clung to him, making some inane conversation I was too panicky to hear. I opened the back. The blokes obligingly shoved out the spare they had ready. I quickly shut the door. There was still the small problem of weight. The minute the cop tried to jack up the car, he'd feel that there were people in the back. I needn't have worried. With a new-fangled jack, the cop lifted the car without any hassle. In two ticks the spare was on. Now to find out what the damage was. Fingers crossed they were too law abiding to demand payment in kind.

Lily had that covered too. "Oh," she squealed, looking at her watch. "Oh dear! I've just realized. I promised my parents I'd take granny to church this evening!" She batted her eyelashes as though it were an Olympic sport and she was after the gold medal "Officers, don't you want to tell us where we can contact you? So we can thank you properly?" The poor fool she'd been driving crazy scribbled down his details - no doubt he thought he'd get his payment in a more comfortable situation. He waited a long time. The much embellished story of two white cops changing our tyre while three Africans slept at the back, became part of Party mythology.

I watched Lily performing her act with the present-day cops. Lily wasn't a twenty something any longer, but she was right, she hadn't lost her touch. Most men were still fools led by their cocks and she could spot the suckers and play them. Thank God for that. For a while, laughing as she pulled the car back on the road, it was as though we were teenagers again. Lily started a run of "remember when" stories, from the time before firm friendship mutated into warm comradeship, and then declined into ill-will and bitterness.

"Hey, Yazz," Lily said, as she swept into my parents' driveway. "It was good to see you again. I mean that. I had such a gas. You must come round to my place before you go. Get Viv to bring you."

"I'll call you," I mumbled as I got out. Tonight I'd managed – with help from Viv and memories stirred by traffic cops – to keep from telling Lily. I didn't think I could do that again. I wouldn't see her, if I could help it, until I could come to her with the whole truth, one way or the other. "When I can," I said. "I will."

I slept like the dead. Both deeply and, amazingly, without dreams. It didn't last long though. My old rooms were on the side of my parents' house which caught the sun first, and it woke me at dawn. Despite my low intake of alcohol at Viv's, I had a headache. I rose, made coffee in the little kitchen which Dad had built alongside my old bedroom, and took my mug out to the table under the fig tree where I'd sat when I was growing up and had hard things to ponder. Last night Viv had been the one with reservations about giving the letter to Lily. Now I was the one with doubts about the wisdom of giving Lily the letter.

I lit a cigarette and blew smoke into the ripening figs above my head. As if in displeasure, a fig fell from the tree onto the ground beside me. Automatically, I stooped to pick it up and peeled it, but the thought of eating it made me feel ill, so I flung it away. Withholding the letter from Lily wasn't a real option. Even if my conscience would stand for it, secrets had a way of coming out. My response to Lily's betrayal

80

would be as nothing next to her response if I concealed Sandy's letter and Lily found out about it. Or was I just covering my own arse at the expense of Mel and her family? Wasn't the secret of Heather's existence one which was best kept?

Assuming Sandy was right, what would revelation do but cause but trouble for all concerned? I had no idea of what magic Mel had worked to change Zac from what he'd been into what he seemed in the photo – a happy family man. I did, however, know exactly what would happen to that happy family once Lily read the letter. She'd find them, if it took every penny she had and every moment of her entire life. I couldn't begin to imagine the vengeance she'd wreak on Zac. That was fine by me. He deserved whatever he had coming. The problem was that Lily's vengeance would punish Mel. Viv and I hadn't got round to really discussing Mel, but I was sure she felt as I did. Mel would have played no role in Heather's abduction. The girl who'd spontaneously and generously befriended me on campus, the woman who'd risked going to jail and probably worse, to smuggle Adam out of South Africa, couldn't possibly have connived with Zac in abducting Heather and faking her death. Whatever lie Zac had told her had deceived her thoroughly. Mel would be horrified if Lily were to appear on her doorstep, accusing Zac of being a kidnapper, of having deprived his daughter of her real mother, of perhaps having murdered in the process. Mel would be devastated if she'd raised Heather as her own and were then to be deprived of her. Heather wasn't a child any longer. She was seventeen, nearly eighteen. Lily couldn't physically take her from Mel and Zac. There were other ways, though. And what of Heather herself? Would Lily restrain her vengeance for the child's own sake? Would she shatter Heather's world to find a place for herself in the ruins?

I buried my face in my hands. Why did I have to be the one in the middle of this mess? Around me the morning had warmed up fast. Soon, even in the shade my arms started to prickle with sweat. I gulped cold coffee and spat it out, tossing the dregs under the tree. There was no point in sitting here driving myself crazy. Sandy had entrusted me with a task. If I found Lily's daughter, then nothing that had happened between Lily and me justified keeping Heather from her. As for Mel – I'd cross that bridge when I came to it. I stood and stretched. My legs folded abruptly and I sat again on the bench, lowering my head onto the table. How on earth did one find anyone in some strange city in another country? Did Viv expect me to go to Canada? Easy for her to say. It was time she came up with some of her own ideas. I went inside and called her.

"Go away, " Viv mumbled into the phone. "I'm sleeping."

Lily could snap awake and be totally on the ball in seconds, regardless of what kind of night she'd had, but Viv was a slow waker. I heard her fumble with the phone, then the dialling tone. She should have left it off the hook. I called back and this time, the fumble ended in a clatter followed by an exclamation of frustration. Now she'd feel obliged to find the phone, even if was only to hang up again. That should wake her up, I thought smugly.

"Who is this?" she barked. "It's the middle of the night."

"No, it's not," I answered. "It's morning. Wake up. I need you."

"For goodness sake! What's so important? Couldn't you call later?"

"Early bird catches the worm and all that," I said cheerily. "It is a worm we're after, isn't it? Zac? How am I supposed to find him? This London in Canada may not be as big as London, UK, but still, it isn't exactly a township, is it? I hardly think it will lend itself to a door to door search, certainly not by a single person. Even if it would, I can't afford a year off to do it. So – just how do you expect me to find these people? Hire a detective like in the movies? You know someone in Canada who can look one up for us?"

She was awake now but still grumpy. "Please do not rant at me at the crack of dawn, Yazz." She yawned. "I am fully aware of the likely size of a Canadian city. There is no need for either a single-handed door to door campaign, or for the services of a detective, assuming such persons exist outside of films."

"I'll put an ad in the papers then, shall I, asking Zac to come forward?"

"Don't be absurd. What do you think the internet is for? Everybody's on the net these days."

82

"Really?" I said, "The 'net' hey? Since when do you know so much about 'the net'? Been around Simon too long, huh? Anyway, I'm pretty sure I'm not on it. Not being so au fait with the net and all that."

"You may well be," she said. "If anyone's made mention of you on their website, or something you've written has been published, something like that - your name will come up. You won't know unless you've tried looking yourself up, and why would you do that?" She paused. "I should think that Zac's the easiest of the family to find. His father owned a big construction company, didn't he?" Her memory never ceased to amaze me. "Most companies have websites. Some have the names of directors. I doubt they'll have personal details such as telephone numbers and addresses, but at least you can find out where the company is. If they have more than one branch, you could call and ask which branch he's based at. If they won't tell you, call each branch and ask to speak to him."

"I don't want to speak to him!"

"I know that, Yazz," she said irritably. "You're only establishing *whether* he works and *where*. Then you can play at being a detective. You can go to his office and follow him home. Something like that."

I had to admit it was easier than my first idea. Still, the thought of going to Canada didn't appeal. "If it's that simple, how come Lily hasn't found him?"

Viv spoke with exaggerated patience. "Lily has a photo of a child. She has no idea that Heather may be with Zac and Mel. She doesn't have a name to search for. You do."

"And she wouldn't have looked him up, just to keep track of the love of her life?"

"For goodness sake, Yazz. Lily's had several relationships since then. She's been married. She's not interested in Zac any longer. She's moved on. Besides, she's a bit of a Luddite. She thinks of computers as glorified typewriters not as the means of finding people."

83

I let her go. In addition to building the kitchen, Dad had turned my sister's old bedroom into a study cum sitting room, when she'd married and emigrated to Australia. Mum thought they were being very progressive, giving me my own sitting room in which to entertain my friends, though she'd dropped many hints that she hoped this wouldn't include having "gentleman friends" over alone, especially at night, but Dad was more concerned about me having somewhere proper to work. Then I'd left home too. The little suite languished – a holiday home for my sister and her family when I was an exile. Now a holiday home for me. The big old desk my father had rescued from a second-hand shop when I was in high school held pride of place in the study. Its surface was no longer strewn with my books and papers. These days a cloth covered its polished surface. In the middle of this, sat a computer. Adam had presented it to my parents the last time we'd visited, and paid for internet access. It was meant to give them an additional way to contact us, but they'd forgotten how to use it as soon as we'd left. Now it was covered with yet another cloth to prevent it from getting dusty. I'd almost forgotten it was there. I whipped off the cloth and stared at the machine. The computer looked in perfect working order. I sat in my old chair and with trembling fingers, I switched the computer on, waited, then typed in Zac's name.

I don't know if I was relieved or annoyed to see hundreds of sites come up, mentioning "Zachariah Smith". It seemed that Zac's parents weren't the only ones who'd decided to distinguish plain "Smith" with a weighty first name. Zac couldn't have hidden his internet presence better if he'd deliberately chosen to do so. He was just another tree in a forest. No doubt Viv knew a shortcut to selecting the right references, but I'd have to go through one at a time. I had neither the courage nor the inclination for that. Besides, he wasn't my main interest, just a way of getting to Heather. There was another way.

If everyone was on the Net, as Viv claimed, then surely Mel would be too. I didn't want to hunt through a trillion Melissa Smiths. I hoped that Mel had kept her birth name. She had. There were several websites for her, but far fewer than for Zac. She was mentioned as a lecturer in history at the University of Western Ontario in London, Canada. She was also mentioned as a student at the University of London, doing a Ph.D. I wondered idly why a city of well under a million people would have two major universities as I gazed at the picture of Mel on her homepage. The pixie-face was quite a bit fuller than in the photo Sandy had taken. Perhaps it only seemed so because the long mop of tangled curls was drawn back. The mischievous grin was a demure smile, but there was no mistaking that this was my friend Mel. A number of random thoughts went through my head. Thank goodness I still had a couple of days of college vacation. Oh hell, after the trips to Greece and South Africa, we were probably too broke to afford a trip to Canada without digging into savings. Then I realized that I wouldn't need to use either my holidays or my savings. Closer inspection of the website revealed that the university at which Mel was doing her PhD was the very one at which I had done mine, in the London which had been my home since I'd last seen her. The one in the UK, not in Canada. The website contained references to her publications and all sorts of other things, but made no mention of a husband or a daughter. I didn't suppose people put such personal details on websites. I wondered if she'd come on her own, flying back and forth to see her family, or whether Zac and their daughter were with her. Whatever the facts , I had no excuse now. I'd have to go and see Mel. The information I wanted would surely come out in a simple catching-up conversation.

I jumped at a knock at the door. My dad, a light sleeper who'd probably been up since I'd been in the kitchen, came in with a fresh cup of coffee. "I heard you up ages ago," he said, dropping a kiss on my forehead. So much for being as quiet as I could so as not to disturb them. "Better not work too long on an empty stomach, cookie," he said. "Mummy made fresh scones for breakfast. Come and eat while it's hot."

I left the computer and followed him in to the main section of the house. It smelled of the freshly baked scones and the coffee my mother only brewed when I was home. The rest of the time they had instant. I didn't think she took the trouble to make fresh scones for breakfast either, when it was just the two of them. I tried to do justice to the special effort she'd made and to pay attention to the conversation, but after a while, Mum said gently, "You're not hearing a word we're saying, Yummy." It was the family's pet name for me. "Missing Adam already? He called you at Viv's place last night, didn't he?"

I tried to hide my confusion. I'd forgotten that he was meant to call. Surprisingly, he'd forgotten too. That was out of character. "We went out," I lied. "Viv and I and some others. Must have missed his call again."

"You can ring him from here, you know. It's not that expensive."

It was as good an excuse as any. "I'll ring him from my room," I said, getting up and clearing away my plate. "I was listening to you, Mum. I'll just ring Adam and then we can go and pick up his Mum and go shopping." I kissed the sceptical look from her face and turned to my dad. "Can we do the beach tomorrow, Daddy? It's just that I promised to see Viv after lunch. There's something she needs to show me on the computer."   As I reached the study, the phone rang.

"Are you still online?" Viv asked, without preamble. Her voice sounded uncharacteristically tense.

"Yes. I found Mel." Despite the situation, I couldn't contain my excitement at the prospect of having found an old friend. "She's in– "

"London, England. Yes, I know. She's a student up the road from your place. Have you tried looking for Heather?"

"Why would I? She's just a kid. She won't be on the Net. It's not like she's a businessman or an academic."

"It's the year 2001, Yazz. As I said, everyone's on the net. Heather is on the net." The strain in her voice was palpable, even over the telephone. "There's something new, especially in wealthy countries where people have a great deal of access to computers and the internet. They create personal websites these days. Young people do it for fun. Sometimes families create family websites as a means of keeping their friends abreast of what they're doing. If they're travelling, for example."

"Zac and Mel have a family website? How come I didn't see it?"

"Not a family website," she said heavily. "A personal one. I don't quite know why I did it. Simon calls it cyber-doodling. I was sitting

86

here, after I found Mel, and just typed in Heather's name without thinking. There it was. The website of Heather Yasmin Vivienne Smith."

"Hang on!" I tucked the phone between shoulder and ear and used both hands to type. "This I have to see." Viv said nothing while my fingers clicked. There might be a million Zachariah Smiths, but surely there couldn't be that many girls called Heather Yasmin Vivienne. I was right. There was only one. "Got it!" I said into the phone as Lycos found her website for me. Then the penny fell into the slot. Yes, there was only one. Not just on the Net, but in the world. How could it be otherwise? It was possible, but totally improbable that anyone else amongst the billions of mothers on this earth would name a daughter Heather Yasmin Vivienne. One baby's mother had named her thus, seventeen years ago. She'd been named for her two "co-mothers", in lieu of godmothers. Lily had been really happy with her choice. The child would be, she said, alive (Vivienne) sweet-smelling (Yasmin) and pretty (Heather). The chances that Zac and Mel had a blonde daughter named exactly the same were billions to one.

"He didn't even change her name," I said slowly into the phone. "The bastard didn't even change her name." Without thinking, I clicked on various "pages". Heather had inserted photos. The homepage had a posed family shot showing five people and was captioned: " Me with Mom and Dad and The Terrors." The last was a reference to twin boys of about eight, perhaps older. I was no judge of children's ages. They had their father's straight glossy brown hair and deep-set brown eyes, plus their mother's mischievous grin, spoilt by the straight white North American teeth. I wondered if they'd been an accident too, one that Mel had persuaded Zac to accept. At least he didn't have to steal them and pretend they were dead, I thought bitterly. "So what do we do now?" I asked Viv.

"You know the answer to that." Viv's voice was firmer now, as if she was readying to do battle with me. "Last night you wanted Lily told even before we had proof. We have proof now, more or less. I think the time has undoubtedly come to tell her, don't you?"

"No!" The explosion of sound shocked me. "No," I said more quietly. "You can't do that. You can't. What about Mel?"

"I don't know, Yazz," she said, sending panic coursing through me. "I honestly don't know. What would you like to do?"

"I need time," I said. "I've thought about what you said last night. The fallout from this is going to be terrible. I need to prepare Mel. I owe her that. I need to tell her to prepare Heather. That's only human. It won't hurt Lily…just a week or two……?" Images of Lily's reaction when we'd told her about Heather's supposed death flashed through my mind. I didn't know whether I had the strength to tell another friend she'd have to let go of her child.

CHAPTER FIVE

I spent a sleepless night on the plane to Heathrow. Added to the usual regrets about parting from my parents, friends, relations, sunny Cape Town, I had Mel on my mind. I kept flashing back to the last time we'd met, nearly a decade and a half ago.

Adam had called me at work. A colleague stopped him as he was about to enter his workplace to warn him that the security police were waiting for him. We'd always known the time would come, but usually the SB came knocking in the middle of the night. I told myself afterwards that this was why I went to pieces, because it was unexpected in the morning. Why else would I have collapsed onto my chair at my own workplace, feeling as though I'd wet myself? My insides felt like mush. Tears streamed down my face. Adam's voice seemed to be coming from far away, rather than from the receiver I was holding tightly to my ear. Before he ran out of money for the phone booth he was calling from, I managed to croak: "OK", though nothing was OK. Nothing would ever be OK again. The hard-nosed bitch in charge of the office where I worked took one look at me and decided I was in no fit state to see clients. I wasn't capable of feeling relief for the permission to leave. I would have left anyway. I stumbled around the streets for a while pulling myself together. Adam needed me. Not his panicky wife, but his clear-headed, organized comrade. I was a member of the Rover cadre group. It was my job, amongst other things, to put in place sympathizers, friends who weren't themselves activists but who would nonetheless do us favours without asking questions, like provide a place to lie low until contact could be made with the Party and instructions obtained.

I found a phone booth and called Mel. Mel was at the top of my mental list of sympathizers. Close enough to help, not close enough for the security police to trace. I hadn't seen her since we'd graduated but Mel asked no questions. She told me where to meet her in half an hour on a street corner. She couldn't have chosen better if she'd been trained by the Party's technical division on how to evade followers. Her red VW swung round the outer lane of the busy circle at the bottom of Adderley Street and she stopped briefly – and illegally – at the curb. I hopped in. She shot off. The Mount Nelson was an "international" hotel, the status accorded to certain places to avoid the embarrassment of black VIPs from overseas being barred from eating or drinking with whites. If anyone was looking for me , as a means of tracing Adam, they'd hardly think I'd be hiding in plain sight, on the balcony of one of Cape Town's foremost watering holes. I'd never been to such a place. We boycotted places where blacks were tolerated on sufferance and with special dispensation. I'd never been for a drink with Mel before. I'd never had gin and orange. This was Mel's response to the security police. Two stiff drinks for an activist. Two fingers up for them. I told her where to pick Adam up, gave her the fallback times and places. I never saw her again.

For nearly a year she took charge of Adam , moving him from place to place until, during the state of emergency, the security police had their hands too full to go after people long dormant. Like she'd met me, in plain sight, calmly sipping gin in the sunshine on an hotel balcony, she openly took Adam out of the country. He applied for a scholarship and a university place in the UK. When he left South Africa, he was seen off by Mel, nice white girl, apolitical daughter of a Methodist minister. If questioned, she'd know nothing about him, except what she'd learnt in her capacity as a worker for the internationally sponsored NGO who was providing Adam's scholarship.

In all that time I only spoke to her on the phone once. It wouldn't have been a good idea for her to be seen with me. I didn't think we'd be able to pull the international hotel trick again.

In any event, I had a lot of work to do. I was fighting for my political life inside the party. Comrades wanted me sidelined in case I got pulled in because of my relationship with Adam. They wanted me to appear to eschew politics until I too could leave the country but it was ridiculous to think the SB would fall for that. Besides, what would I tell all the youth members, all the community groups, all the workers I'd unionized? Nothing, the party replied. Simply drop out. Disappear. I argued that the Party couldn't spare an experienced activist and cadre leader like me, when it had just lost Adam. The Party argued that nobody was indispensable. This was what my friends, my warm-hearted comrades, had become under the influence of Zac's Party. Hard men and women. I could see Zac's hand behind my suspension and eventual exile. In the midst of all this, Lily lost Heather. Viv was out of the Party after a fight over some tactics or other. She made contact with Simon and told him that Lily was having a nervous breakdown. So there we were, the core of the Rovers Cadre Group, a bag of political cripples, looking after one another.

Now, on the plane back to London, I tried to rid myself of these memories, which belonged in the last millennium. All they did was cause more anxiety about what was to come. I made several trips to the lavatory. I went to the food area for water. I got up to stretch. I walked up and down looking at my fellow passengers. None of it helped clear my mind for sleep. The plane was filled to capacity. Mostly, I guessed, with others like me who had one foot in London, one foot in South Africa, returning from extended Christmas holidays "at home" to jobs in the UK. Many were young people, sprawled across one another or huddled in seats. Several families too - small children whining until bribed to sleep, babies wailing while harassed mothers tried to soothe with bottles and walks up and down the aisle while fathers read or slept. Finally there was the silence of the wee hours, with only snuffling and snores and the low murmur of the staff talking in the food area. I tried to settle down again, to work out some plan of action so that I could finally sleep. Exhaustion claimed me as the cabin lights went on. The breakfast routine and early morning scramble for the lavatories began. Revolted by the smell of the food, I waved the stewardess away. I'd tried eating the awful stuff the previous evening and ended up puking up the lot. Jovially the pilot announced the appallingly low temperature and grey skies awaiting us in London. In unison the planeload of people who had left behind the blue-skied warmth of a Cape Town January groaned. Glad that my UK passport allowed me to avoid the long queues of non-UK or EU citizens, I wearily cleared immigration, claimed my baggage and walked through customs, through the swing doors to where I knew Adam would be waiting.

He stood head and shoulders above the people leaning anxiously against the rope barrier. Some held up placards for tourists or unknown visitors. Others cried out welcome to relatives and friends. Adam just stood there. He didn't wave. He didn't call out. He just smiled his dopey smile. It felt as though a lifetime had passed since I'd last seen him. The tan he'd acquired in Cape Town, deepening his usually olive skin to the colour of coffee, reminded me that it had been a mere week.

Part of me dreaded telling him. He owed Mel a debt of gratitude. In the time Mel had looked after him, he'd come to like and respect her a great deal and the devastation which my news was going to wreak on Mel's life would sorely trouble him. But the rest of me needed the comfort he could offer. I also needed to talk it through with him, how to proceed with what had to be done.

"Hey kid," he said in his best fake American accent. "How's tricks?" His arms engulfed me in a huge hug.

I breathed in the scent of him. Warm skin, tea tree shampoo, freshly laundered clothes. "Not turning tricks no more, Mister," I countered, pushing aside firmly the thoughts which had troubled me for a week and kept me awake all night. "'Cept maybe for you."

He laughed. "I think," he said sternly, "you need to eat first, if you're going in for a long bout of exercise." He set off, dragging my trolley bag towards a coffee shop. After my disastrous attempt to eat the airline food, I still wasn't in the mood to eat, but I did need some decent coffee.

"Have this first." He put freshly squeezed juice in front of me. "You look shattered."

"Thanks for the compliment. Can't I have my fix first?"

He took a cup of mocha from the tray he was holding and put it in front of me. A plate with a fresh croissant, butter and jam followed. "That bad, huh?"

I stirred sugar into my coffee and sipped. "Yeah, the plane was full and you know it's like Piccadilly Circus, the stewards coming with this and that every two minutes."

"Anything exciting happen in Cape Town after I left?" He munched the almond pastry he'd chosen for himself, washing it down with a gulp of coffee.

The story almost spilled out but I snapped my mouth shut just in time. He looked at me enquiringly. I shook my head to clear it. . "Not

92

much," I lied, lamely. Costa's coffee in the arrivals lounge of the world's busiest airport was hardly the place to tell him my news.

"Sounded as though you were having a good time," he said. He spread jam on a bit of croissant and held it out to me. "Couldn't get hold of you day or night."

"Well, you know." I dutifully chewed and swallowed. "Viv wasn't around much when you were there. We did some catching up. How about you?"

"Not much. Work. Home. Running a bit. A week goes really quickly."

"You couldn't have missed me much," I pointed out. "Else it would have dragged by."

He waggled his eyebrows meaningfully. "Wait till I get you home, baby," he said. "I'll show you exactly how much!"

"I thought you had to be back at work at noon."

He glanced at his watch. "If you eat up," he said, "we'll get home with plenty of time to spare." He gave his version of a dirty laugh.

"Is it my imagination, or does your sex mania increase every time we're apart?"

"Says she, bolting her bread and gulping hot coffee in her anxiety to get me into her bed!" He got to his feet.

I unlocked my suitcase and took out the thick jacket I'd put there in readiness for the change of temperature from Cape Town, then swung the little backpack I'd used as hand luggage onto my shoulder. He took up the handle of my suitcase and gave me his free hand. We walked to the tube station, hand in hand like teenagers. I sat on the tube with my head on his shoulder, slipping in and out of sleep, unable to keep track of what conversation he made, until finally there was silence. Near our station, he patted me awake. I followed him home in a daze, the cold only waking me fully as he unlocked our front door. Next door's net curtain twitched. I couldn't be bothered to wave. "She's not yet broken her neck then?" I jerked a thumb in the direction of the curtain twitcher. "From all the craning this way and that?"

He grinned as he shoved in the suitcase. "Lack of sleep does give an edge to your tongue, my dear." He started upstairs, the suitcase hefted onto his shoulder.

I followed, deposited my bag on the sofa and settled into a corner. Adam eyed me with thinly disguised disappointment. "Looks like you won't have the strength to dig your clutches into me after all."

"You got time?" I yawned. "Get me another cup of coffee and we'll see what we can do to put you out of your misery, you poor wretch!"

In the end, it was closer to 1 pm than noon when he finally left for work. I sat for a long time in the bath we'd shared after making love. I listened to him dress. He came into the bathroom and dropped a final kiss on my head. "See you tonight," he said. "Probably have to stay late to make up for this morning. You'll be sleeping the afternoon away, in any case, won't you? If you ever get out of the bath?"

I got up and reached for a towel. "I actually don't feel like sleeping now. I'll unpack."

"Oh, leave it. Lie down for while. Sleep will come."

It was only when I heard the door downstairs close that thoughts of Lily, Mel and Heather re-entered my mind. I finished drying off and went to dress. In the sitting room I lay on the sofa, counting the ticks of the clock on the mantel. Sleep would not come. I got up and looked at my case. I didn't feel like unpacking. I decided to go for a walk instead. Outside, the cold stung my face as I walked under a dreary grey sky, past drab houses and streets and cheerless people whose dull clothes reflected their faces. It was all so unlike the bright warm friendliness of home. I dug my gloved hands into my pockets and strode towards the river. On Waterloo bridge I stopped and lit a cigarette. I smoked, watching the murky water flow below, feeling people flow past me. I could go to the university now and try to find Mel. I could put into action at once the plan I'd formulated and rehearsed endlessly in the previous week. I'd bump into her by accident. I'd start a conversation. One thing would lead to another and she'd tell me about her life, her marriage, her daughter. Somewhere in the conversation, the issue of the child's birth would come up. I would know for certain then. I'd be prepared for what I had to do the next time I saw her. I flung the cigarette into the water, getting a dirty look from a passerby and set off briskly towards the embankment, heading north to the university. Halfway there, I stopped again. This was silly. I had no idea how I'd find her. The university would be semi-deserted until classes started. She might not even be there. She might have gone home for the break. No, I remembered. Ph.D. students didn't have set schedules. They worked in libraries in the first year, reviewing the literature. Later, there'd be the primary research and later still writing it all up. There was a good chance she'd be in the library. I set off again.

The university was as unpopulated as I'd anticipated. A few students huddled over cigarettes outside the library. A few more hurried this way and that. The cold wasn't conducive to lingering. The library doorman who'd let me in on the many times I'd forgotten my student card at home was nowhere to be seen. I stood aside as one or two students slipped their cards into the slot which let them through the turnstile. I could ask the next one to let me in with her card or I could go home. A voice behind me said sharply, "Forgotten your card again?"

I turned. One of the librarians stood behind me. With her square black-rimmed glasses, grey hair drawn back into a tight bun, and frumpy frock made of some thick cloth, Brenda was still the perfect parody of her profession I remembered from my years spent in the place. I bowed my head and said humbly, "It's much worse, I'm afraid, Brenda. I don't have a card any longer." I gave her my biggest smile. "Any chance a visitor can get in?"

She tutted, letting me grovel a while longer before she relented. "I never expected to see you back here," she grumbled, slipping her own card into the turnstile, before handing it to me so I could repeat her actions. "Where are you teaching?"

"Local college," I said. "Only part-time. Doing a bit of this and that the rest of the time."

More tongue clicking." And you don't have your own library?"

"I'm looking for someone. An old friend. I heard she's started a PhD here."

"Old friend and you don't have her phone number or address?"

"You're so suspicious, Brenda! We were undergrads together in Cape Town. We both moved around the world and lost touch. As one does."

She hmphed some more, then finally gave in. "Well, help yourself," she said, waving a hand over her domain, and walked over to the door beside the main desk. She keyed in the code, went in and re-appeared on the other side of the desk.

The library. It had been massively refurbished in the few years since I'd finished my last degree. The main change of course, was the omnipresence of computers. I'd done my research without the benefit of the internet. JANET - the joint academic network - was in its infancy then, the internet's existence barely on the periphery of my consciousness. The library, as far as I knew, hadn't had more than a handful of computers, and those had been used mainly to examine the catalogue. I'd typed the drafts of my thesis on an old Atari without a hard drive, lent to me by someone in the anti-apartheid movement. I'd paid someone else – whose name I picked off the library notice board - to type the final copy for submission.

"God," I said to Brenda. "How am I going to find my way around your new kingdom?"

"If you tell me your friend's name or what she looks like," she sniffed, "I might be able to help."

Brenda was the library equivalent of my nosy neighbour. Nothing and nobody passed her by. Many PhD students were creatures of habit. They tended to work in the same areas of the library every day, sometimes the same desk. If Mel was like that, Brenda could direct me straight to her. "Her name," I said, reaching into my bag, "is Mel. This is what she looks like." I showed her the picture of Mel which Viv had printed from Mel's website.

"Already left," Brenda said. "She's like you used to be. Comes in first thing and stays quite late, in a rush to get it over with. She's taking a break today, though. I saw her leaving at lunch-time. I said, 'See you later' and she said, 'Not today, Brenda honey. I've had enough.' So," Brenda finished briskly. "Come back tomorrow. She's always here."

"Thanks, Brenda.' I turned to leave. 'See you, OK?"

I must have looked really crestfallen, because sympathy broke through the frosty exterior at last. She called me back. "If I see her before you do," she said, "I'll tell her you were looking for her. Leave me your number so she can call you. That way you won't miss her again."

I shook my head. "I want to surprise her. I'll take my chances tomorrow."

"Hang on," she called again as I was going through the door. "I've just thought of something." I came back to her desk. "She always has lunch at Pedro's. If you miss her here, you could always try there. She takes coffee breaks there too. It would –" She sniffed. " –save all our ears from the noise of your happy reunion."

"It would indeed." I grinned. "Thanks, Brenda."

Outside, I shivered after the warmth of library. I walked briskly over to Pedro's. The place seemed completely unchanged. There were still too many small round wooden tables and stools, in too small a space. The curtains seemed to be the same shabby ones I remembered from my time as a student. In the middle of the afternoon, there were few people in the tiny coffee shop. Most of its regular clientele were away on end of term holidays.

"Can I help you?" The Australian girl whose name I now failed to remember had been replaced by an Eastern European boy who looked barely sixteen. The name tag on his apron declared him to be Janek. I ordered a latte.

"Takeaway?"

I looked around the room. A couple engrossed in each other were half hidden in the shadows of the furthest corner. Two girls were bemoaning the time they'd been obliged to spend with their families over the holidays. A boy was playing some sort of computer game on a hand held device. A girl sat at a table by the window with her head bent over a book, blonde hair obscuring her face. "No," I decided. "I think I'll have it here, if you don't mind." I felt an urge to use the loo. "Hold it for a minute, won't you? I just have to use the women's room."

Toileting done, I emerged through the archway separating the dim passage leading to the lavatories from the coffee shop. I stopped as the door of the shop flew open and a woman stepped inside, swept in on a blast of cold air that made all heads turned in her direction. Oblivious of the glares of irritation, she dropped the shopping bags she'd been carrying and stood for a moment inside the door, a vision in red. Calf length red woollen coat, red beret jauntily perched on the blonde curls which framed her face. She stamped her black-booted feet as though she'd been out in mud or snow, clapping her black-gloved hands together and then rubbing her face with them. "Bloody hell!" she piped in a breathless, little girl voice. "When will global warming heat up this benighted place?" The last time I'd heard that voice it was on the other end of a phone, telling me that my parcel had been safely delivered. Adam had arrived in the UK.

A youthful habit of twenty filterless Texans per day had done nothing to coarsen the middle class, white South African accent that the English called "posh". The harsh exclamation of dismay at the weather was softened by a girlish giggle. I started forward unconsciously, hand half-raised. The greeting froze on my lips. "Oh, Honey! You're here already!" she chirped. She gathered up her bags and began to weave her way through the unoccupied tables towards the single girl sitting with her book at the window table.

As Mel approached, the girl put the book down on the table, tossing her head to shake back the long blonde bob revealing her face. Mel dumped her bags on a stool and bent to kiss the girl's upturned face. I gasped at the sight of it. Involuntarily, I took a step back into the shadows of the passage. Dismay coursed through my mind as I watched Mel drop her beret on the table, slip off her gloves and struggle out of her coat. This would have been the perfect opportunity to break the ice with Mel, but not with the girl here! Not with Heather present. My heart sank further. What if Zac showed up? My plan had been to tell Mel, and let her work things out with her family in the way she thought best. Now this plan lay in tatters. I hovered in the dim passage, waiting for an opportunity to slip out unnoticed.

"Sorry I'm late, Hon." Mel piled her coat on top of her shopping and followed it with a bulky black knitted jumper. She swept her gloves and beret from the table onto the rest of her outdoor things. The top items fell to the floor. Her companion bent to retrieve them and put them on the unoccupied adjacent table before sliding back onto her own stool.

"Where were you?' she complained in a strong North American accent. 'I've only been waiting, like, forever!"

"Don't whine, honey. I had a couple of errands to run. They took longer than I thought they would." Mel caressed the girl's hair. "Good thing you had your book, hey?"

The girl ducked away from Mel's hand. "Mo-om! Don't do that!" She ran a hand over her head to smooth the place Mel had touched. "It's pathetic," she said. "The way you little people always have to pat us normal sized human beings on the head."

"Size-ist!" Mel shot back as she slid onto the stool facing the girl. "Get your old mom an espresso, please Hon? And a Danish. And get yourself another of whatever you've had."

The girl looked around, then lifted an arm to summon the youth behind the counter with a careless wave. I'd never known Pedro's to do table service, but Janek stepped swiftly over to their table. He took their orders of hot chocolate with extra cream and banana muffin for the girl, double espresso and Danish for Mel, then came back to the counter. "Ah, Miss!" he exclaimed as he passed the doorway where I lingered. "You are still there! I think you go long ago, maybe not want coffee. Something is wrong?"

Startled out of spying on the mother-daughter banter, I muttered, "No, er, uhm. I just…." but he was already past me. From behind the counter, he called out to me, "I make your coffee now. Latte? One moment."

I cast a furtive glance at the two women. Neither of them was taking any notice of the waiter, or whoever he was talking to. Mel was showing the girl her purchases, explaining what was for whom, seeking the girl's opinion on each. This was the perfect accidental encounter I'd been hoping to engineer but I wasn't ready for it. I needed to go home and catch my breath first. I sidled over to the counter, keeping my back to the seating area of the coffee shop. "Make it a takeaway," I said to the boy.

Janek stuck the huge paper cup which passed for "medium" in the requisite space on the coffee machine, letting it run my coffee while he fetched down mugs for Mel and the girl's drinks. He placed them on the work surface behind him and took my coffee from the machine, put a lid on it and set it on the counter while I took a note from my purse to pay him. Reaching for the money, his hand knocked the cup straight at me. The lid which he'd not quite succeeded in fitting onto the paper cup flew off as the cup hit my front."Shit!" I yelped, leaping back. I hadn't yet zipped up my parka and my shirt took the brunt of the accident. "Shit," I said, looking at the mess. "Shit, shit, shit!" Janek stared at me in horror, then dashed to the counter where the milk, sugar, cutlery and paper napkins were kept. He snatched a handful of napkins and returned to dab at my front with them, apologizing in English and another language.

"Stop!" I said, grabbing at the boy's hands to restrain him. "It's OK. It will wash out." I wanted to get out of there unnoticed. It was too late. "Oh my God!" The little-girl voice behind me had become a shriek. "I don't believe it!" I heard the clatter of tables and chairs and turned to see Mel shoving them out of her way as she rushed towards me.

She stood in front of me for a minute, looking searchingly at my face. "Yazz! It is you!" she said, flinging her arms around me. She was tiny and hadn't picked up that much weight since I'd last seen her, but the movement was unexpected enough to nearly knock me into the waiter, who was still apologizing. "I knew it! I just knew it!" She chortled. "Still the only person I know whose sole synonym for catastrophe is 'shit'! It just had to be Yasmin Patel!" Barely lowering her voice, she pretended to shield her mouth with her hand, "And still the only person I know who'd stop a pretty boy touching her wobbly bits I see."

I winced, knowing that her voice had been audible enough to reach Janek. "Mel," I faltered, leaning down to kiss both her cheeks "How are you?"

She stepped back, holding both my hands in hers. "I'm fine. How are you? My goodness, fancy meeting you here! Haven't you had enough of this dreary place? Why aren't you catching a tan on Fourth Beach?"

"You haven't changed a bit," I said, returning her scrutiny. Without her layers, in tight-fitting black jeans and black and red top, Mel's figure was, if not as dainty as when I'd last seen her, still pretty good. Her face had acquired laughter wrinkles around eyes and mouth, but, like the added curviness, they suited her. She had grown from a pretty girl into a lovely woman.

"You mean I'm still so beautiful?" She patted her hair with one hand in a phony gesture of vanity and placed the other on one hip to strike a pose. "Art imitates nature well, hey?" She smirked.

"I meant," I said, "you're still the same dizzy blonde!"

She hooted with laughter. "You're not rushing off somewhere, are you?" she asked. "Come on. I'm not letting you go now I've found you. Besides, you must meet my girl." Without waiting for an answer, she took my hand and started leading me to her table, calling over her shoulder to Janek who had retreated behind his counter and was busying himself making coffee. "Sweetie, bring whatever my friend was having to our table, please!" She tugged at my sleeve. "Come on. Please. Even if it's only for a little while." With that we were at the table, where her companion had taken advantage of Mel's absence to once again bury herself in her book. She studiously ignored our approach until Mel patted her shoulder. "This is Heather," she said proudly. "My daughter. Honey, meet my old friend Yasmin Patel. We were at 'varsity together. We haven't seen each other in ages!"

101

"I got that, Mom." Heather rolled her eyes. "So did the entire world!"

"Hi!" I said, trying not to stare. Up close, her face wasn't as identical to Lily's as it had seemed from across the room. Her mouth was slightly wider. Her face rounder and there was something about her eyes that was not quite like Lily's. Nonetheless, the resemblance was uncanny. She muttered, "Hi there" to me and bent her head to her book again.

"Don't be so rude, Heather," Mel admonished, wagging a finger at her. "Put the book down and say hello properly." Mel bundled her clothes from the spare chair onto the next table where Heather had put her beret and gloves, to make room for me to sit.

The girl put her finger in her book to mark her page and drawled, "Hello properly, Mizz Patel," in exactly the tone of voice either one of her mothers would have used at around her age. Despite my discomfort, I had to smile at her sauce.

"It's *Doctor* Patel, you disrespectful minx! Behave!" Mel chided playfully slapping Heather's hand.

"Call me Yazz," I said to the girl. "Or Yasmin if you prefer. That's really my name, but everyone calls me Yazz."

Janek appeared with our tray. When he'd finished distributing the drinks and cakes, he said, looking shamefaced at my blouse, "No need for payment. This on the house. I pay for the shirt."

"Nonsense!" Mel extracted a note from her purse and tucked it into his hand. "If it wasn't for you, we'd have missed each other."

"She's right," I added my reassurances. "It was a lucky spill. Besides, I told you it will wash out." I looked at the stain on my front. The central heating had already dried it. There was no way it could be rescued. There was also no way this kid could afford to replace it. I slipped a note onto his empty tray.

The boy looked from one to the other of us in confusion. "It's OK, sweetie. Keep the change." Mel smiled and patted his hand consolingly. "So," she demanded when he'd gone. "What do you think of my girl? Isn't she gorgeous?" She reached out to stroke Heather's cheek.

Heather flushed. "Mo-om!" I noticed she didn't move away from the caressing hand.

I nodded. "She is."

"This is the part where you're supposed to say she looks just like her mother!"

"It's called fishing for compliments, Mom," Heather reproved. "You are shameless."

Barring the blonde hair and fair skins, there was no resemblance between Mel and Heather, but I could answer truthfully: "She does. She looks exactly like her mother."

At this, Mel let out peals of merry laughter. Heather grinned sheepishly. "Sorry," Mel gasped. "Private joke. Tell you later." She sipped at her coffee and quickly put it back. "Oh, god, all this laughing makes me want to pee!"

Heather held up her book to shield her face. "Motherrrrr!. Can you please not make announcements like that to the whole world?"

Mel chortled and kissed the top of her head. "Alright, darling," she said sweetly. "I'm just off to tinkle. Will that do?" She grabbed her handbag. "Be right back."

The girl looked after her mother in despair and I ventured, "In case you're wondering, the answer is yes."

She looked at me in surprise. "To what?"

"The question you were going to ask. 'Was she always so embarrassing'. Yes she was. But she's a gas and she's got a heart of

103

gold, so everyone loves her. But you know that. She's your mom, after all. Even if does make you want to crawl under the table sometimes."

Heather grinned sheepishly. "I guess everyone's mom is like that. And mine's not too bad."

"You mean she doesn't borrow your clothes and try to go clubbing with you?"

She looked so horrified at the image I'd conjured up, that it was my turn to grin.

Silence fell. Mel was taking an inordinately long time to "tinkle". Heather fiddled with the corner of the book but wasn't bold enough to resume reading. I considered going for another "tinkle" myself. Finally I reached into my pockets and produced cigarettes and lighter. I held them up to her questioningly, "Do you mind?"

She shook her head. "Mom does too. Only she does it in the garage? When she thinks we're busy doing other things or when we're out? She thinks we can't get the smell. It's so childish. Like everyone doesn't do it?" She had that young person's way of ending every sentence as though it were a question.

"Smoke?" I said. "Or do it on the quiet?"

The face might be Lily's I thought, but that giggle was pure Mel. Nature and nurture. I lit up, located an ashtray on one of the other tables and put it in front of me. "So," I said. "You're on holiday here?"

"Me? Yes. Kinda. Actually? I'm visiting my Mom. She's a student? Over at the college up the road?"

"She is? I thought she'd done with all of that. What's she studying this time?"

A note of pride crept into her voice. "Well, she actually teaches college back home, but she's off for a while, doing a doctorate." She spoke the last word with awe, even though she'd not taken much notice of my title.

I blew smoke carefully away from her face. "And what do *you* do?" I asked her. "When you're not visiting your mom?" I looked at the book. "Or reading Pride and Prejudice?"

"I'm at college. Back home in Canada."

"But you've transferred here for a while? While you're mom's studying here?"

"I wish," she sighed. "Dad wouldn't let me come." She pulled a face. "I have to stay home with him and my brothers."

"So it's your school holidays? How long will you be here for?"

"Oh, it's not our vacation. That's what we call them in Canada: 'vacations'?" she digressed kindly. "I just kinda missed my mom. Dad and the boys are great but they can be a pain. You know? Especially without Mom. Besides, they're doing some work to our school building," she said. "So we got kinda a long weekend?" The giggle again. "So I made Dad let me come see Mom."

"You really love your Mom," I said.

She grinned. "Yeah, but don't tell her I said that."

"I promise. So.... you go back in a day or two?"

"Yeah. Right. Wednesday."

Mel slid into her seat. "Still got the fag habit, I see."

Heather said airily, "You can have one if you want, Mom. You know you do. I won't tell." She made a zipping motion with two fingers across her lips.

Mel gave her a "Who me?" look and tucked her hands primly under the table. "What have you been telling each other behind my back?"

105

"Heather was telling me that you're studying here," I said. "A PhD? What in?"

"History, what else? But never mind that. Tell me what you're up to these days? How come you're back here? And where's that lovely man of yours? You've not gone and lost him, I hope?"

I held up my hand to stop the deluge of words. "No, I've not lost him, Mel. How could I, after all you did to save him for me? He's fine. And I'm not back here. I'm still here. We both are. We never went back, except for visits. In fact, we've both just been to SA. I got into Heathrow this morning."

She looked at me quizzically. "Bloody hell!" she said, then clapped a hand over her mouth and glanced at Heather. "Oh, Hon, you didn't hear that, did you?"

"Mom," Heather sighed. "I hear a lot worse at school every day. How many more times?" She shook her head despairingly and popped a piece of muffin into her mouth, following it with a gulp of hot chocolate.

"I thought you'd be back there like a shot," Mel said to me. "Once things changed, you know?"

I shrugged. "I guess it didn't change enough," I said. "Or maybe not fast enough. Don't get me wrong, I'm not like all those new emigrants slagging off the place now it's majority ruled. Democracy in itself is a great step forward. It's just…..well, we kind of knew things wouldn't turn out exactly how we wanted it to, you know, a workers' state, but I think personally I hoped for a bit more change on the ground, for the masses, before all the grabbing by the top brass started……"

She made a tsk-ing sound, reaching out to squeeze my hand. I smiled in acknowledgement of the sympathy. "To be honest," I said. "It's not just the political side of things. I guess we sort of settled down, got a house, got jobs, this and that. It's hard to uproot and move again – people back home have changed, things aren't what we thought. It's always next year. I can't explain it myself." A phone rang behind me. The woman who owned it launched into a loud conversation, without

106

drawing breath for the other party to join in. Mel rolled her eyes and I laughed. "Enough about me. How about you? Been back?"

She shook her head. "No need. My folks died. What family I have is in Canada. That's where I live now. Canada. You know me. I'm not hung up on SA. Nice beaches and mountains and all that – but Canada's got all of that and more."

"Mom," Heather interrupted. "Is it alright if I go to that bookshop over there while you chat to your friend?" Without waiting for an answer, she shoved her book into her small back-pack and rose.

Disconcerted, Mel reached out a hand to stop Heather as she started to button up the short thick coat she'd been sitting on. "But, Heather honey, we were going to…" she stopped, looking from Heather to me and back again.

"Hey, don't let me keep you!" I said, rising from my chair. "Go do what you were going to with Heather, Mel. She said she's only got a couple of days with you. You and I will have plenty of time to catch up. I live here, remember?" I scrambled in my bag for pen and paper. "I'll give you my phone number. Call me and we'll set something up when you've got more time."

"But we've hardly spoken a word!" she protested, taking the paper on which I'd written my details. "No, it's OK. Let her go. You be careful, Hon, won't you? Be back in ten, yes?"

"Gosh, Mom. I'm not a kid any longer," Heather said. "I'll be fine. Promise."

"Just don't wander away from the bookshop. Remember, you don't know this city. So be careful, it's getting dark…."

Heather made a face and kissed Mel's cheek. We watched the slender figure as she sauntered off, waving. "See you later," she said to the besotted waiter and went out the door, letting in a blast of cold air that made me shiver.

"So," I said. "You've got Heather and twin boys?"

107

"She told you about the boys?" She watched through the window as Heather crossed the road, then, satisfied, hunted in her bag for her wallet. She extracted a couple of photos. "Here they are. My lovely boys."

I took the photos. "Sweet," I said, with a pang of envy. "How old are they?"

"Nine soon." She gave a mock groan, slapping her forehead. "Going on a hundred and nine." She paused. "How about you?" she asked. "Any kids?"

"It's just-" I swallowed hard to rid myself of the lump in my throat. "Well, just me and Adam." My eyes stung. I handed her photos back to her without meeting her eyes.

"I'm sorry." She took her photos and slipped them back into her wallet. "Here's me bragging. I didn't mean to rub your face in it."

I shrugged. "Don't be silly. You weren't to know." I forced a smile. "What's the use of having kids if you can't show them off? Heather's lovely. So are your boys."

She looked relieved. "Take heart," she said. "Look at Cherie Blair. You've got, what, five years on her? Plenty of time. Plus," she added with a wink and a knowing grin, "There's all that fun in trying!"

I waited for her to finish chortling before I asked, "So are you going to tell me about bloke that the twins take after? Did you meet him in Canada? Is he the real reason you've not gone back to SA?"

Amusement tugged at the corners of her mouth, "Aha! At last! I thought you'd never ask." She cast a last look through the window. This time it was a furtive one. "Hey, do you mind?" She pointed at my cigarette packet.

I shook my head. "Don't be silly."

She lit up and blew out a stream of smoke. "Lovely." She breathed. "He's actually South African. At least, he was born there. Then moved to the UK and only came back to South Africa for a year or so to do a Masters at UCT."

"So you met him there? I thought you were with Hans then!"

"I was with Hans," she confirmed. "But I also met my man there. The first time anyway. We didn't get together until the second time I met him. In Canada." She tapped ash from her cigarette and leaned forward conspiratorially. "Want to hear a joke? You actually introduced us that first time."

"I did? Since when was I ever in a position to introduce you to men? "

"Well, in this case you did." The blonde head bobbed up and down in vigorous emphasis. "Only, it wasn't my glorious body he was into at the time." She paused for another long drag. "It was yours. Even though you insisted at the time that he respected your pure body and soul and was only after your political mind."

"There's but one person on this earth, I do assure you, Mel, who'd express a preference for me over you. And I've got him firmly pinned down. Reckon I'd have noticed if Adam was jogging back and forth across the ocean, don't you? So, much as I'd like to take credit for your marital bliss, Mel my dear, I haven't the foggiest notion of who you're talking about." I made a "give" gesture with my hand. "Come on. Show me a picture of this weirdo who made an honest woman out of you."

She handed over the picture she'd been holding back. A man with one of the twins on either side, all three posing with fishing rods, displaying their catches. "Here."

"Zac?" I said. "You're married to Zac Smith?"

"Aha! You do remember!" She chortled, bouncing in her seat with delight. "And I'm right, aren't I? You did have a scene with him. Come on. Confess. It's not like there's anyone around here who cares!"

"Mel, once and for all. I did not have "a scene" as you put it, with Zac Smith. He really was interested in my politics, not my body."

She dimpled mischievously. "I didn't believe you then and I don't believe you now." She wagged two fingers at me, the cigarette held between them. "You're so cagey, it's no fun pumping you." She stubbed the fag end out in the ashtray. "I don't suppose you even remember the day you introduced me and Zac?"

"I might," I said. There was no might about it. It was one of the memories that had tormented me on the plane back from SA. She was talking about an afternoon in our final year, when Mel and I had been sitting in the students' union. The union was almost deserted, since more conscientious students had long since gone to afternoon lectures, seminars, tutorials, or to the library where I'd promised myself I'd put the final touches to an essay I was working on before being waylaid by Mel and tempted into another round of coffee and endless filterless Texans. Mel was recounting to me, in graphic detail, her weekend sexual exploits.

Suddenly, she stopped in mid-sentence. "Will you look at that!" she exclaimed, spacing her words to add weight to them.

I followed the direction of her pointing finger. It appeared to be pointed at the back of a man walking towards the sandwich counter.

"What?" I asked.

"That, my girl," she said admiringly, "is the greatest butt I've seen on a bloke in a long time. And you know my motto. Great butt, great in bed. Wow!"

I couldn't see what she was on about. Bums, as far as I was concerned, were just bits of anatomy to sit upon. The subject of her admiration turned. In the instant before I ducked my head, I recognized him. I'd seen him at a seminar the previous night. Seminar was a euphemism for the Sunday evening gatherings at which the left in Cape Town came to debate the finer points of Marxism. I'd made a substantial contribution at the last meeting, which Mel's admiree had vociferously contested. That made me remember him.

And the fact that he was one of only a handful of whites present.

"He's waving," she said.

"Well, there's your chance," I muttered, my head almost down on the table. "I'll be on my way, shall I? While you explore your butt theory?"

"It's not me he's waving at," she said. "It's you. You *are* a dark horse."

"I don't even know the man's name. I certainly don't want to....." I broke off, seeing her disbelieving smirk. "You're terrible, you are."

She giggled. "Oh dear. You really should lose the chastity belt, Yazz. Sex can be so pleasurable."

"What your friend is trying to say," said a voice behind me. "Is that sex should be as easy as drinking water from a glass, in the words of Kollontai."

Annoyed that he'd eavesdropped on our conversation, I shot back, "I tend to agree with Lenin - who wants to drink from a soiled glass?" I clapped my hand over my mouth, feeling my ears burn at what I'd just implied about Mel. I started to stammer that I hadn't meant it like that, but she roared with laughter.

"I'm Zac," he said, looking immeasurably pleased at my discomfiture. "And you're Yasmin, I believe."

He didn't even look at Mel, until I said stiffly, "This is my friend Mel. Sorry to seem rude, but we've got a lecture."

"Oh." He seemed genuinely disappointed. "I was rather hoping we could pick up where we left off last night."

111

"Actually," Mel contradicted me, "we don't have anything this afternoon." She yawned delicately. "I'm going for a nap in the library." Then she bent and whispered a somewhat less delicate suggestion in my ear. That was how it had begun, my political involvement with Zac. Within weeks I'd introduced him to members of our fledgling party – the worst thing I'd done in my life. I'd also lost my virginity to him. The few minutes *that* took gave the lie to Mel's theory about men with great butts.

Still, I could truthfully assert when she asked me then, as now, that I'd never "had a scene" with Zac Smith. I didn't think a few minutes of extreme discomfort counted as "having a scene."

What I could tell her, was that my friend Lily was the one who'd had a "scene" with Zac and that she, Mel, was raising the product of that liaison. The thought brought me back to the present with a bump. Mel was chatting away merrily, still teasing me about the incident she'd recalled too vividly to my mind, when the door of the coffee shop slammed open once more. Again there was a blast of fresh air. Heather stood in the doorway, waving at us.

"Oops!" Mel dimpled at me. "We'll have to continue this another time, else my baby will have kittens." She scrambled around for her things, calling out, "Coming Hon!" Mel opened her bag and took a printed business card and a pen from an inside pocket. She scribbled a number on the blank side of the card and handed it to me. "Hey," she said, laying a hand on my arm and standing on tiptoe to kiss my cheek. "It was so good to see you again. Stay in touch, OK?" She kept her voice low. "But don't call in the next couple of weeks. I haven't told Heather yet. I've booked myself a seat on her plane. I'll be going back to Canada with her for a couple of weeks." She grinned ruefully. "I miss my boys so much. I haven't seen them in two months!"

"Now would be a good time!" Heather called out.

"You haven't given me your number," Mel said. "Quick. Enter it in that." She reached into her coat pocket and handed me a mobile phone.

"I'll walk part of the way with you," I said. "Let's move while I give you the numbers."

Heather heaved a dramatic sigh of relief when we reached her. Mel told her to wait while I entered my phone numbers in Mel's mobile. Then we stepped out into the icy dark, one of Mel's gloved hand in the crook of my arm, the other in Heather's. As we turned into Oxford Street, Heather spotted an accessories shop and, with an exclamation of delight, broke free from us and dashed into it.

"How old is she?" I asked casually, watching through the shop window as she held up earrings, looking at necklaces and bracelets.

"Seventeen," Mel said. There was a moment's quiet as we both continued to look at Heather. Mel turned to me. "You all done doing the sums?"

I said, "You had a kid of three or four back then? Where'd you hide her?"

"I didn't," she said. "I didn't have her. I mean, I didn't actually give birth to her." She looked at Heather through the window again. "She knows. That was why we laughed when you said she looks like me. Everyone says that, because she's blonde and fair like me." Amusement crinkled the corners of her eyes as she turned to face me once more. She paused, then said quietly, "She's not my daughter by birth…but she is mine." She spaced the last three words for emphasis, as though each were a separate sentence. "Actually," she said, "Heather looks like Zac. Didn't you notice that? I mean, she doesn't have his colouring, just his looks? He's her real father. She was about four when I bumped into him and her in Canada." She paused reflectively. "I think I fell in love with her before I even registered I'd met her father with you."

"You mean he used his kid to pull you?"

"No," she protested. "It was how good he was with her. You should have seen…"

"Only teasing," I cut in. "What about her birth mother?"

Her voice softened. "Long sad story. I'll tell you when we have more time. In a nutshell, she's dead. I'm all the mother Heather has. I'm all the mother she can remember."

I'd heard enough. I neither needed nor wanted to hear any more. I was suddenly deathly tired. "Listen," I said. "I must go before I fall down. I feel as though I've been hit by a truck. Delayed jetlag, I suppose. I'll call you soon. Promise." I leaned down to hug her.

"Are you sure you'll be OK?" she said, looking at me with concern. "Can I call you a cab?"

"No," I said, pointing in the direction of Tottenham Court Road. "My bus is just round the corner. Drops me practically in front of my house."

"Right then. See you soon." She bounded into the shop with a last wave at me.

For a minute I watched her and Heather through the window, then I turned for home. The bus was packed with commuters. I stood there with that last image of Mel and Heather in my mind, Mel on tiptoe behind Heather, trying to hold up a necklace round the girl's neck, the two of them laughing. I could end that sweet thing they had between them tomorrow. Or I could leave Mel a blissfully unaware couple of weeks with her family before I shattered her world. What a choice.

The smell of garlic hit me as I unlocked the front door. Adam was singing "The Boxer" along with Simon and Garfunkel. I looked at my watch guiltily, realizing how late it must be for Adam to be cooking already. He was bent over the oven, checking on my favourite dish, and the one he cooked best - vegetables roasted in garlic and olive oil. Having decided it needed more time, he shoved the roasting tin back into the oven, shut the door.

"Where on earth did you get to?" He offered a cheek for my kiss. "I thought you'd be knocked out by the trip!"

"Couldn't sleep," I said. "Had things on my mind. Let me help you get supper." I started to wash lettuce for a salad. "We can talk while we eat."

"Sounds serious." He peeked into a pot, forked a few grains of brown rice into his mouth and chewed. "Do I need a drink to brace myself?"

"I rather think so, but you'd better eat before you drink. You fit people are so light on petrol. I don't want you drunk while I tell you."

He didn't push it. While I made salad, he talked about this and that at work, set the table and put food into serving bowls. We carried various dishes into the dining room and sat down to eat. Usually the smell of this dish would set my stomach rumbling. Tonight I had no appetite, despite having eaten nothing since breakfast. I pushed food around on my plate watching Adam eat, until he said. "I think the waiting is worse for you than for me. Best get on with telling me. Maybe then you can actually eat that food."

"I saw Mel today."

The fork stopped halfway to his mouth. "Mel? You mean Mel from Cape Town?"

"You know any other Mel?"

He raised his eyebrows in surprise at my tone. "I suppose not." The fork resumed its path to his mouth. He chewed slowly. "So, how is Mel?"

"Sorry," I said. "Didn't mean to snap. Guess I'm more stressed than I thought."

"I'm sorry too," he said mournfully. "I thought I'd given you the total de-stressing treatment this afternoon. Sex, soak, sleep. You missed out the sleep bit, that's the problem. Jokes aside though, why's seeing Mel upset you? There's not something wrong with her? She's not ill? Injured?"

115

"No," I said. "She's fine. Really, fine. She's studying here. We had coffee."

He looked at me quizzically while I tried to find the words to explain why seeing Mel had upset me. "She…well, I went to Pedro's for a coffee and she was there. She asked how you were, you know, the usual…she's married now. She's got kids."

The news appeared to amuse him. "Really? Good Lord, I can hardly imagine Mel with a husband, let alone kids. So where are they, this family of hers? Here in London? Did you invite them over?"

I folded my hands in my lap, gripping them tightly together. "No, I didn't. I couldn't."

Puzzled, he prompted, "Why not? She rushing off back to SA? Or wherever she lives now?"

"Canada," I said slowly. "Her family's in Canada. She's based there. It was just...her daughter. She was with her daughter." I stopped again. "I couldn't…"

He poured water and handed me the glass. I sipped it slowly and tried again.

"Adam, her daughter…" I broke off, put the glass down and buried my face in my hands. "Oh God, what a mess! Adam, do you know who she's married to? Mel? She's married to Zac! And don't ask me which Zac! Yes, that Zac!"

Adam dropped his fork. It clattered on his plate and fell off the edge of the table. After bending down and taking a long time to retrieve it, he wiped it carefully on his napkin and put it on his plate parallel to his knife. He folded the napkin and put that beside his plate. "How did that happen?" he finally asked.

"Through me. It's all my bloody fault, Mel even made a joke of it, how she was with me when she first saw him…" I told him what Mel had reminded me of.

116

He was silent for a while. Then he said, "I know it makes you sick, a nice girl like Mel with that miserable sod. But come on. You can hardly blame yourself for her marrying him. Nice girls marry shits all the time. I mean," he tried a grin which didn't quite come off, "Look at us." When I didn't respond, he went on. "But what's to stop us seeing Mel? And even the daughter? Can't blame the kid for what her father is. Besides," he said triumphantly, "Didn't you say he's in Canada?" I nodded. "There you go. We don't ever have to see him. We simply won't see her when he's around – you know, pretend to be busy or out of town or something. It probably won't even come to that. I'm pretty sure he won't want to see us either, the way we left things!"

"I don't care two fucks whether we ever see that shit again or not!" I burst out. "In fact, I'd like to see him, so I can cut his balls off! Oh God, you haven't heard the worst of it, Adam. So much has happened…I don't know where to start…"

He looked at me in consternation, then came round the table and drew me to my feet. "At the beginning," he said. "Come on. It looks like a long story." He led me through the connecting doorway into the living room. "Let's sit on the sofa and you tell me all about it, hey?"

"You haven't finished your food."

"It'll warm up later." He pushed me down onto the sofa. "Now tell me. Or wait." He held up a finger to stop me. "It looks like you could use a drink."

He went over to the small cabinet where we kept our seldom used supply of alcoholic drinks and without asking what I wanted, poured brandy into two glasses. He went to the kitchen, returning with a can of coke which he added to each glass. Brandy and coke - the drink of choice in the townships when we were young. He handed me one. "Have a sip. Then tell me."

I took a deep gulp and started on a blow by blow account from the time I'd read Sandy's letter to the time I'd left Mel. He didn't interrupt. It would have been hard anyway, the way the story poured out me once I'd begun. When I'd finished, he sat swirling his drink around in his glass, mulling over what I'd said.

"Well?" I demanded. "Aren't you going to say anything?"

"I don't *know* what to say." He ran a hand through his hair, ending with a slight tug. It was like watching someone pinch themselves. "It's so absolutely incredible." He repeated, "Absolutely incredible!"

"You can see the letter, if you like." I rose and took the letter from my handbag. "Here." I dropped it on his lap. "See for yourself if you don't believe me." I'd fetched cigarettes too and lit up.

He didn't raise his usual objections, or even wave his hand in front of his face or open a window. "No, of course, I believe you…" He contemplated the letter, then picked it up, weighing it in his hands before opening it. I sat smoking and drinking as he read, his face impassive. "She's alive then?" he asked rhetorically. He repeated softly: "She's alive!" He laid the letter on the low table by his side, downed the balance of his drink and got up to pour another. He walked the length of the room, stopped at the bookshelves, turned and came to stand in front of me. "She's living with Mel?"

"That's what I said. Lily's daughter Heather is alive and well and living with our saviour Mel and Lily's bastard ex, Zac. You heard me correctly, you understood the letter correctly." I reached out my glass. He took it and refilled it without the usual raising of an eyebrow when I went onto a second drink. "The problem is," I said. "How am I going to do this?"

"Do what?"

"Adam," I said, patiently. "Viv's taking on the job of telling Lily. Thank God for small – or in this case not so small - mercies. But Mel's also got to be told and it seems I'm the only one who can do that."

"Why?" He swirled his drink round in his glass, drank some of it, swirled again, seemed to be pondering the issue, his face expressionless.

"Are you offering?" I asked. "I mean, you don't have to do it for me. We could do it together …?" My voice trailed off hopefully.

He mulled the question over for a moment before clarifying. "No. What I meant was, why does *anyone* have to do anything about this? Why can't you leave it alone?"

"You're not serious, are you?" I blew out smoke. "Can you imagine the size of the explosion when Viv tells Lily what Zac's done? Do you think for one moment that Lily will stop to consider the collateral damage to innocent bystanders like Mel?" I stubbed out my cigarette in soil of the delicious monster plant by my side that I'd been using as an ashtray. "Can't say I blame her either. I mean, listen to me. I was only Heather's pseudo-godmother. I was only Lily's friend. And *I* want to murder Zac. I have reason to have regard for Mel's feelings, but ask yourself, does Lily?"

"No," he said slowly. "I suppose not."

"The best we can do for Mel," I went on, "is to tell her ourselves instead of letting Lily land on her out of the blue. Mel wouldn't want all these lies and deception either. She's not that kind of person. We owe her the truth."

He leaned forward, elbows on thighs, hands tightly entwined, head hanging down, silent. He finally turned sideways to look at me. His face was deeply troubled. "What about the child?" he asked. "Viv is worried about Lily. You're worried about Mel. And rightly so. But they're both grown women. They can take care of themselves. But can that child? Have you and Viv stopped to consider that poor child?" He gestured helplessly with one big hand. "It's like she's not there. Or just an object in the middle of some dispute that you and Viv are mediating, rather than a real person with real feelings that have to be considered too. I haven't heard you say a word about how this will affect her."

"That's not fair!" I felt my face heat up. "The whole idea of telling Mel is so that she can prepare Heather. I mean, she's raised the child. She'll know how best to handle it…"

"But you and Viv never actually discussed Heather, did you?" It was an accusation rather than a question.

119

"No," I blustered. "We assumed...look why are you stressing? I'm the one in the hot seat here. You're not exactly helping." He said nothing. He looked at me. I lit another cigarette and inhaled a calming lungful. "As I was saying, it wasn't so much that we weren't thinking about Heather. It was more that we assumed that she'd want to know the truth about herself. I mean, if it was me, I'd want to know."

"That's you thinking as an adult! You've no idea how fragile young people are at that age."

"As a matter of fact, I do engage with young people quite regularly in the course of my work," I said, stiffly. "And if you ask me they don't like being lied to. They'd rather know the truth about themselves. They want adults to show them respect by being honest with them."

"Oh please!" He brushed this aside with an angry wave of his hand. "Which manual did you get that from?" He thumped a fist into his palm. "You can't tell me there's a single one of them who'd welcome someone conjuring up a mother she thought was dead because her beloved father lied to her. Show me the child Heather's age who would welcome proof that her father is a liar, a cheat, a fraud, a kidnapper, maybe a murderer! Tell me that you honestly believe a young person of that age would like to be told that she's at the heart of all her miscreant father's crimes."

"And there I was," I said bitterly, "hoping you were going to help me out with this. Ask our benefactress over for a drink or for supper, and break the news to her gently, together."

He picked up the glass I'd rescued, drained it and slammed the glass back down on the table. Both the wooden table and the thick-bottomed glass were sturdy enough to take it, but I jumped at the unexpected and uncharacteristic violence. "Well, count me out. I want no part of this. That poor bloody kid." He stood up.

I reached for his hand. "Adam, listen. You're right, OK. I can't honestly say that I know what that child would want or how she'd feel, but you can't either. The point is, it's out of my hands. I can't stop this explosion. All that I can do, is to contain the fallout, or cushion the impact so a friend doesn't get hurt. Viv is going to tell Lily. Lily's going to go to Canada and confront Zac and God knows what else. She might even stop off here to have it out with Mel first. I don't know. The only thing I know is that I have to tell Mel before Lily gets to her."

He pulled his hand away. "You could tell Viv to leave things be."

I snorted. "Tell? Tell Viv? I can ask, but I really don't think I can tell her. Have you ever tried giving Viv orders she doesn't agree with? Remember what happened when the Party tried? She called the Party's bluff. She was expelled and a couple of months later, there she was, back again without recanting a word or denying an action."

"I have to go out," he said. "I have to think. This is...this is all so crazy."

From the sofa I heard him opening drawers in the bedroom across the passage. Moments later, the door of the flat opened and shut. His steps sounded on the stairs and then the street door slammed down below. The music he'd been playing had long since stopped and the house suddenly seemed inordinately quiet. By contrast, all the sounds outside, London traffic, people talking and laughing on the pavement below, distant sirens, a train rumbling, were magnified. I sat, trying to work out what had just happened. I'd foreseen that he'd be upset about this issue on some level, but somehow I'd expected his concern to be about the impact of my involvement on me. I'd also thought he'd be worried about Mel. That was why I hadn't told him straightaway when I'd arrived. It had never crossed my mind that he'd be so concerned about Heather. It wasn't as if Adam even knew the girl. I sighed at my own stupidity. When had Adam ever needed to know someone to be concerned about their pain? I gave him the length of time it took me to smoke two cigarettes before I called his mobile. It was switched off. Forgetting that South Africa was two hours ahead of the UK, I called Viv. She was getting ready for bed.

"I saw Mel today," I said without preamble.

"We agreed it would take you a week or two to sort things out with Mel," she said. "I didn't expect you to see her the minute you landed!"

"It wasn't quite like that. I didn't expect to see her. I don't know what I intended – maybe follow her around, see what she does these days, how she is, I don't know. It was all very accidental." I related the afternoon and evening's events.

"Don't worry about Adam," Viv said reassuringly. "He'll come round. He'll see that we don't have much choice in the matter."

I sighed. "We're only the messengers. We haven't even delivered the message yet and already we're getting shot at."

"Sorry about that," she said gently. "I could say that you should have done it without telling him, but you'd be the first to tell me that you and Adam don't have that kind of relationship. It affects him too, in a way, Mel being what she was to him. I know none of this is easy for you..."

"I've made up my mind," I said. "I'll tell her when she gets back from Canada, OK? I want to leave her that at least - some time with her family before it all falls apart. Or rather," I added bitterly, "before I blow it all up in her face."

She didn't object to that. She said goodnight and hung up. I went to clear the dining room of our mostly uneaten supper. I'd already washed and dried the dishes and was putting the containers of leftovers in the fridge, when Adam got back.

"Where've you been?" I complained. "You didn't answer your phone."

"Just had to clear my head." He put a box of chocolate chip ice cream on the counter beside me. "Peace offering," he said and pulled me into his arms, nuzzling my hair. "I know none of this is your fault."

"No, it isn't," I murmured, enjoying the warmth of his hug. "But you're forgiven for being a horrible brute on my first night home. I don't know how much of a peace offering this is," I said, freeing myself to reach for the ice cream. "In case you haven't noticed, I've put on quite a bit of weight in Cape Town, courtesy mainly of your aunties." I pinched the beginnings of a spare tyre round my waist, but nonetheless opened the cutlery drawer and took out a spoon. "Still, waste not, want not."

He made to grab the spoon and ice-cream from me. "I'll put it away then, shall I?"

I hit at him with the spoon. We both knew that I could eat ice cream, especially chocolate chip, any place, any time, under any weather conditions, especially when I was anxious. He stood watching me as I put a dollop of ice-cream on my tongue and let it slide coldly down my throat, repeating the action several times in rapid succession. In times of stress, my love of ice-cream turned into total pig-outs. This time my body revolted. Halfway through, I flung the carton and spoon down and spewed all that I'd consumed into the kitchen sink. I washed my face. Silently, Adam handed me some squares of kitchen paper. I dried my face and drank the cup of water he'd poured from the filtering jug. "Don't even think about giving me a lecture on greed," I said, weakly. "This is the cumulative result of all the food forced on me in Cape Town last week. I've been puking my guts out every night. That is, after every time some bloody relative has force fed me." I looked into the sink with disgust. "One would have thought my body would be discerning enough not to include ice-cream in its anti-rich food strike!" I hunted under the sink for disinfectant.

Adam took the bottle of Dettol from me and pushed me down on a kitchen stool. "Dry bread and water for a week then, is it?" He set about cleaning up. I watched him, feeling overwhelmingly tired. When he'd finished, I let him lead me to bed. I fell asleep instantly, only to wake a while later. The red lights of the clock radio said 2:15. I'd only been asleep for a couple of hours. I lay in the dark, going through all the chores which usually awaited me on my return to London, trying to remember all my commitments, to think about work, anything to prevent another night of wakefulness over Lily's daughter. My wakefulness was contagious. Adam stirred beside me. I could tell he was awake from his breathing, though he said nothing. "It'll be alright," I said into the darkness. He sighed and pulled me into his arms. Finally sleep came.

CHAPTER SIX

The absence of a warm body in bed beside me woke me next morning. The smell of toast and coffee still lingered in the air but the silence that hung over the house told me that Adam had already left for work. I stumbled to the kitchen for my first caffeine fix of the day. A note was stuck to the coffee pot: "You were sleeping like a log. Don't work today. Rest. Love, Adam X." I poured coffee and popped the mug into the microwave, resting my arms on the counter and letting my head drop between them while I waited for the ping. Work was the furthest thing from my mind. When the phone rang, I left it to the answer-phone. My friend Maria chirped the kind of bright hello that could only be delivered by someone who'd just slept 10 sound hours. Maria always managed that, despite 3 kids and a menagerie of animals. She had a helpful husband. I picked up the phone and muttered a greeting. She burbled enquiries about my trip and my family. I made appropriate responses as I took my mug from the microwave, added milk and sugar and stood sipping. Maria sailed into the tale of her life since I'd been away. "Don't forget," she said, having come to the end of the tale of Christmas with her folks and New Year's with her in-laws, "staff meeting on Friday."

"Oh god," I groaned. "Already? When am I supposed to do the prep? I'm so jet-lagged I can barely move."

"That's no excuse," she laughed. "Not when you've just spent weeks in sunny South Africa!"

I'd just hung up on Maria when the coffee I'd been sipping throughout the conversation rose to the surface. I threw it up in the kitchen sink. I cleaned up the mess, took the phone off the hook and switched off my mobile, then went back to bed. I was asleep in an instant. I woke to find it was nearly noon. My stomach rumbled. I got up, boiled an egg and made some toast, then sat staring at the food with distaste. Thinking that some fresh air would do me good, I showered and dressed, put the toast in a bag and went over to the park. The morning had been bright for January, sunlight streaming into the kitchen and living room, but the light was already failing. The park was deserted.

Most of the parents and small children who were its main users had left. At the pond I tossed my toast to the ducks before starting my usual walk around the perimeter of the park. One side was all I managed before I was again overcome by the need to lie down. I went home and back to bed. I was still sleeping when Adam got in.

"I'm in here!" I mumbled in answer to his greeting.

"What's this?" He kissed me. "Delayed jetlag?"

"Must be," I yawned. "Unless I ran an ultra-marathon in my sleep last night. I'm shattered. And that's after sleeping the day away."

He brought me tea. I was too tired to eat at table. Adam reheated leftovers and brought a plateful to the sofa for each of us. I got several forkfuls down before stumbling to the bathroom and letting it all out. Adam followed me. He wiped my face when I'd finished. "Hadn't you better go and see the doctor?"

"It's just a bug," I said. "Probably picked it up on the plane. You know how germs circulate on planes. I'll be alright by tomorrow." I patted my stomach and pinched my waist. "I could do with losing this, anyway."

"I'll call Alan and cancel squash," he said, with a worried frown. "I don't like leaving you alone like this."

We spent the evening with Adam reading the paper while I listened to music. Neither of us mentioned the elephant I'd deposited in the middle of the room the previous night. I was loathe to initiate the debate. There was nothing in Sandy's letter that wouldn't keep for a day or two while I recovered from my bug and let my husband fuss over me. There was plenty of time to talk about it before Mel returned to London. As for Adam, either my illness had thrust the previous night's conversation from his mind, or he'd resolved not to resurrect the issue. Nonetheless, every so often, he'd look up from his paper and eye me speculatively. Whether that had to do with my illness or Sandy's letter, I had no idea, but dealing with the fallout from Sandy's letter was wiped from my mind when we discovered the source of my malady.

On Friday, feeling no better than I had all week, I dragged myself onto a bus and in to work. Halfway through the meeting, I excused myself, went to the loo and threw up. Afterwards, I sat on the toilet seat of the cubicle, resting my head against the wall. I didn't realize how long I'd been there until I heard the clatter of high heels in the corridor, followed by the main toilet door slamming open. "Are you alright?" Maria asked as I emerged from the cubicle.

"Fine," I muttered. "That room is just so stuffy." I turned on the cold water tap and washed my face. Maria handed me a paper towel. "Thanks. I don't know why they have to turn the heating on full blast."

"Are you sure that's all it is?" she asked.

"Stop fussing, Maria. I haven't brought back some dread disease from darkest Africa." I pushed open the toilet door. "Come on. Best get back." I trudged towards the staff-room.

Maria put a hand under my elbow. "You look terrible," she said. "Don't go back inside. I'll just pop in to tell them I'm taking you home. We've nearly finished anyway."

I stood leaning against the wall outside the staffroom as she made our excuses, then let her drive me home and tuck me up on the sofa with a cup of chamomile tea. She left as I started drifting off to sleep. I woke to the sound of someone thundering up the stairs. There was a jangle of keys, followed by a string of muttered curses as they were dropped. I sat up and swung my legs off the sofa just as the lounge door opened. "Yazz! My god, are you OK?" Adam flung his things on the floor and came over to scoop me up in his arms.

"I'm fine, Adam!" I exclaimed, wriggling free so I could talk. "What are you doing here?"

"Guy from work brought me," he said. "Maria called to say you were sick at college and then you passed out when she d put you to bed." His face was grey with worry.

"Oh, you know what Maria's like." I patted his hand. "I told her not to fuss. I'll be alright in a couple of days."

"It's *been* a couple of days," he said. "Come on. I'm calling a cab. I'm taking you to the doctor."

"Don't be ridiculous," I protested. "He'll probably tell you the same thing I just did. A few days' rest, that's all I need. It's the weekend. I'll be OK by Monday." Adam paid no attention. He picked up the phone and called the surgery for an emergency appointment. He was about to dial a cab when I stopped him. "There's no need for that. I can walk up the road, for God's sake."

It wasn't until the doctor asked the question, that the possible nature of my illness dawned on me. It would have occurred to me earlier, if I hadn't deliberately refrained from keeping a diary or noting my period on the calendar since the last time I'd got my hopes up in vain. The last period I could recall was way back in November. I had no idea what the poor doctor made of our reaction to his confirmation of his suspicion. I burst into tears. Adam sat dumbstruck. It was a while before we could assure him that we were actually delighted by the news. Everything else he said – making appointments with the midwife attached to his surgery, tests, antenatal care, noises about my age – went by in a blur. Adam and I walked home, our arms wrapped around each other. My legs had felt heavy coming to the surgery. I went home floating on air. I finally came to my senses when we got home. Adam insisted that I lie down on the sofa in my study instead of going upstairs to our living quarters.

"I am not," I said firmly, "going to live down here for the next few months. I'm pregnant, not sick. There's loads to be done before this baby comes and I'm damned if I'm going to lie here and watch you have all the fun. Besides, somebody has to work, unless we want this baby living on benefit. So make me a cup of ginger tea and shoo, go to work."

He brought me the phone with the tea. "I thought you'd want to ring your mum and dad."

"No." I thrust the phone away. "Please, Adam. Let's just keep it to ourselves for a while?"

He put the phone on the table and handed me the tea. "Alright, if that's what you want." I bit my lip and nodded. He sat down next to me and stroked my cheek "It will be OK, you know love. Just think positive." I said nothing. "We don't have to do anything unless and until you want to."

"Thanks, Adam. I'll tell them at the end of February," I said. "I know it's a bit of guesswork, with me not knowing my dates, but the magic 12 weeks will be over for sure by then. I... well, I just don't want to get them all excited for nothing."

"Hey, what did I just say about positive thinking?" He ran one hand over my abdomen. "I love you," he said, bending to kiss my belly.

"Which of us do you mean?" I asked.

His response was a mischievous grin. When he'd left, I rested my hand on the slight bump which I'd thought was the beginning of middle-aged spread, trying to recall what pregnancy had felt like the first time, the last time. I couldn't remember being this sick, or this tired, on any of the previous occasions. Perhaps all my nausea and fatigue this time was a good omen. I wished I believed in some deity, something which I could implore to just this once let things go right. I bent my head towards my belly, "You just hang in there, baby," I said. "Do you hear me? You stay there until it's time for you to come out. You do that for your mum and I'll be the best mum you could ever wish for."

The ringing of the phone interrupted my first conversation with my baby. I let it go to answer-phone. There was a click. No message. I turned on my side, patted the cushions and prepared to sleep. The phone shrieked again. I reached for it with a sigh of resignation. Maria knew I was home. If I didn't answer she'd come around. "Maria," I said before she could let loose. "There's such a thing as worrying a person into her grave. I'm meant to be resting. Call you when I'm better."

"Oh, I am sorry, Yazzie," A long-forgotten voice drawled in my ear. "Are you ill?"

With a clatter, I dropped the receiver. A rush of revulsion made me shiver. I could hear his voice calling my name. I fumbled for the phone, clamping my jaw and covering my mouth against the return of the nausea. I swallowed before uttering one syllable into the phone: "Zac?"

"Sweetheart! You still remember my voice. You don't know what good it does my heart." Canada hadn't robbed him of the upper class English South African accent his comrades had liked to imitate.

"How – how did you get my number?" Stupid question, I thought even as the words left my mouth. Stupid not to have known Mel would blurt out to him that she'd seen me. She'd been excited. Under normal circumstances, I'd have been excited to see her. Excited enough to tell my husband the first chance I got, just as she'd done.

"Mel mentioned she'd met you in London." He confirmed my unspoken thoughts. "She imagined you'd be delighted if I gave you a call. To talk about old times and all that. How's my old friend Adam? Not ill too, is he?"

I took a deep breath. "I'm not delighted at all, Zac. And Adam's fine, thank you very much. But that's not the reason you called."

"Dear girl, of course it is! Why wouldn't I want to enquire about the health of old friends? Especially ones with such special relationships with me and Mel."

"Bullshit, Zac," I burst out. "You don't care two fucks for either of us."

"My dear girl," he said, unaffected by my outburst. "So angry!"

"Let's not piss about, Zac," I said. "You called to find out whether I know what you did. You want to know whether I'm going to tell Lily and Mel what an abominable excuse for a human being you are." Before he could interrupt, I plunged on. "It's yes to all of the above.

129

Now I think we're done here, unless you're about to tell me that you'll come clean with Mel and save me the trouble. But then coming clean isn't a term you understand, is it?"

"Darling, I haven't the foggiest notion what you're talking about. Not been using Mel's special herb cake recipe, have you?" There was nothing warm or amused about his chuckle.

My stomach twisted with rage. "I'm not the one who's been at the herb cakes, Zac," I said. "You must have been, though, fifteen years ago, to think Lily would never catch up with you."

"Lily?" he questioned. "Oh, I have it!" I imagined him snapping his fingers as if he'd only just seen the light. "You mean your friend Lily?" He gave a little self- deprecating laugh. "The one who had a bit of a crush on me?" His tone became one of mock horror. "Oh please say she's not still after the old bod? And please, please, don't tell her where to find me. I don't know whether I could cope with the woman's demands again."

"You're unbelievable!" I said through clenched teeth. "As if you could ever forget, when you've got the spitting image of her with you every day!"

"My dear, truly, I carry no image of the woman engraved on my heart. It is a long forgotten, and even longer regretted, indiscretion, I do assure you."

"I think not, Zac," I snapped. "Not when the result of that indiscretion is called Heather. A child you stole from Lily. You think Lily's given you cause for regret in the past? Wait till she hears you stole her child, you bastard." I slammed the phone down breathing heavily.

It rang again at once. I didn't pick it up. The voice which left the message was far removed from the suave one with which I'd just had an exchange of words. It was hard and cold.

"Yazz, dearest. A word to the wise. Stay away from my family. More importantly, keep your crazy friend away from my daughter. Note that I do not use the word "crazy" lightly. You have no idea." He laughed and repeated for emphasis, "You have no idea of what I'm capable." Another laugh. "Or perhaps you have."

My hands shook as I searched in my bag for the bit of paper on which Lily had scribbled her number. I was determined to put an end to this. Her phone rang endlessly. No answer-phone message came on. I depressed the button and dialled Viv's number. Viv's answer phone came on, the standard business-like message that she was busy, leave a message and she'd ring back. "Viv," I said. "Call me as soon as you get this." Then I realized that she might not call back for hours. Cape Town's long Summer party, which went on from Christmas till the schools and factories re-opened, had finally come to an end. Viv was self-employed, but no doubt she had started back at work when everyone else did. I felt hot and faint, as though the walls were closing in on me. Taking my jacket and keys, I left the house, heading for my favourite walk by the river. I walked for more than an hour, out and back, until the cold air had cleared my head.

Back at my desk, I took the card which Mel had given me from the corner of my desk blotter. It had her email address and her Canadian phone numbers printed on it, her London one scrawled beneath them. I chewed my thumbnail. I couldn't possibly call her at home and risk him picking up. I emailed her. "I have to see you. Please call me as soon as you get to London." I hesitated, then plunged on: "It's really, really urgent." I inserted my mobile and landline numbers, just in case Zac hadn't given her back my card.

The grey day was already darkening, when Viv finally called. "I only just got your message. What's wrong?"

I told her about Zac's call. "I should have known she'd tell him," I said. "I just didn't think…I mean, the cheek, calling me here, threatening me!" Then, to my horror, I burst into tears.

"Hey!" Viv's voice in my ear was gentle. "Steady on, Yazz. He can't hurt you. You don't live in a township in the old days when people could get away with assault and murder because the police couldn't be bothered. Besides, you've got Adam."

"I know." I sniffed, reaching for the box of tissues. "I'm not scared of him. I'm pissed off. It's just…Oh, Viv," I wailed. "The best thing's happened and he…he just bloody went and ruined it all."

There was a brief silence before she said, "Nothing and nobody can ruin this for you, Yazz. Congratulations! When are you due?"

Too late, I tried to recover. "What are you talking about?"

"Yazz," she laughed. "What else would you describe as 'the best thing'? Unless it's having the actual baby, of course. How's Adam taking it?"

I gave my nose a final blow. "With a stupid grin plastered on his face, looking like the village idiot." I felt the smile on my own face. "He wants to start work this weekend on turning the spare bedroom into a nursery. I never thought he would be so boringly predictable."

"Normal and dependable," she returned.

"It's supposed to be a secret, at least until we know everything is going OK. Once I tell my folks it will be like taking out an advert on telly. And in all the tabloids back home."

"Oh good," she said. "Not a secret forever then. For a moment I got an awful feeling of déjà vu."

Talking to her about the baby had sent my heart soaring again. Her last words made me fall to earth with a jolt. "You mean Lily and Heather."

"I do," she said carefully. I heard the sounds of tea-making in the background and of Viv's famous biscuit tin being opened and shut. "Listen, Yazz, I know you're determined to carry out Sandy's wishes. I know that you also want to cause Mel as little pain as possible. I think, however, that you have new priorities now."

"You mean with my history I can't afford the stress."

She didn't answer directly. "None of us is getting any younger, Yazz. You're fit and healthy, but you're not an 18 year old." A biscuit crunched. Some tea was sipped. "And yes, I do mean that with your history this may be too stressful for you."

"And what do you propose, pray? That I put off telling Mel until I have the baby? Will you wait until then to tell Lily? You can't, you know. Zac will do something. He could have his family installed in Timbuktu by the time I have my baby."

"I doubt that," she said. I heard the smile in her voice. "It's not that easy to maintain the lifestyle to which he is accustomed in Mali. Even if it was, don't you think there'd be protests and questions from his family?"

"You know what I mean. I've just made things worse, seeing Mel and not telling her. Lily will blame me. She'll think I tipped them off on purpose."

"Leave it with me, Yazz," she said. "I'll sort things out."

"What? You'll go and see Mel? You'll fly over to Canada?"

"It's a thought. I've never been to North America. But no. I was thinking she'd have to be back in London soon. For her PhD? It's only a few weeks to Easter. I meant to come and visit you then."

"You're a stranger to her! She wouldn't even give you the time of day."

"We met on the odd occasion, on campus, back in the day," Viv reminded me. "I got the impression that she's a fair and reasonable woman. She would at least look at the letter, and consider the evidence, surely."

"She would. But I don't know, Viv. It's me Sandy asked to tell her."

"You're delegating."

"I've already delegated telling Lily to you. That's the hardest part."

"No it isn't," she said. "It's the best part, restoring her daughter to her. Yours is the worst, depriving a friend of her daughter."

I closed my eyes, trying to envisage how I'd go about it, what Mel's reaction would be, how I'd deal with it. It was beyond me. "I'll have to think about this. Give me time to work out how to do it. You won't tell Lily until then?"

"I won't tell Lily until then. Meantime, just enjoy your pregnancy. Join in the fun with Adam – once everyone knows or you deem it appropriate, of course," she added in a wry aside.

"I emailed Mel after he called," I remembered. "I was just so bloody livid. ...... What do I do if she emails me back? If she agrees to meet up?"

"Perhaps Adam could go with you? Or he could meet with her?"

"There's no way…he'd go spare. If *you're* worried about me, imagine the state he would be in!"

"Let me think this through, Yazz. Meantime, don't do anything. Or contact me before you do."

We left it at that. She hung up after asking if there was anything special she could bring over for me at Easter. I told her that I planned on telling my parents before then. She'd have to get a spare suitcase so that she could bring over all the gifts from my family and Adam's.

Mel didn't respond to my email. Zac never called again. I saw little point in bursting Adam's bubble by telling him about Zac's phone call. With nothing to galvanize me into thinking about the issue of Heather again, it slipped towards the back of my mind. In the next few days, talk of my pregnancy and plans for the baby dominated everything. Shamefully, it even trumped the floods in Mozambique, the war in the Congo and the earthquake in India as topics of conversation between us. I took Adam's odd speculative pauses, the starting to say something and changing his mind, as baby-related, or about a myriad other things in his life that he didn't want to discuss with me for fear of burdening me. My consciously adopted "wait and see" approach to the Lily saga became an unconscious "let sleeping dogs lie." Weeks slipped by. I was standing in front of Mothercare, wondering whether it would be tempting fate to go in, when my mobile phone buzzed to announce the arrival of a text message. My eyes still on the crib in the window, I fumbled in my jacket pocket for it the phone. No recognized name came up with the number. I peered at the message. It read: "When and where?" and was signed just M. Too cryptic for Maria, even if she had a new phone number she'd not given me. Mystified, I stuffed the phone back into my pocket and went on looking at the shop window. The phone buzzed again in my pocket. It was the same message. Intrigued, I looked up and down the street for somewhere to sit down so I could respond to my caller. Texting wasn't one of my strong points. It would take ages. There was a patisserie nearby. It didn't serve herbal teas, so I guiltily ordered coffee, telling myself I had to order something to justify taking up space in the shop. I sipped while I considered the text. Then it came to me. I knew only one person who signed off messages only with that initial, confident that the recipient would recognize her identity. Years ago, it had been notes, not text messages, ending in a slanting M, spiky at the top and flicking away gracefully at the bottom.

I slipped my hand into my pocket fingering the packet of cigarettes I kept there. My mother and all my aunts, most of my cousins, had drunk litres of coffee and smoked cartons of cigarettes when they were pregnant. Their kids turned out fine. My poor baby had already smoked lots, not to mention imbibed alcohol, before I knew she existed. One more could hardly harm her. It would be better than the stress I was feeling. I took the packet from my pocket, looked at it and put it back, keeping my fingers on it like a security blanket. I took my phone out and sent a text to Viv. "Mel wants to meet. Should I go?" Relief flooded me when my phone rang. I responded without checking who it was from. It wasn't Viv.

"I'm in the bar of the RFH." I could just about make out it was Mel over the hubbub around me. "Do you know it?"

"Mel?" I asked. "Is that you? Yes, yes of course I know the RFH."

"Are you free to meet now? Or perhaps later? I don't mind waiting."

I had been ready for her weeks ago. Now I wasn't. It reminded me of the exams she and I had swotted for. We could write them on the scheduled day. A month, a week, even a day later, we hadn't remembered a thing about the subject. At least it had seemed that way, especially if other things intervened. Momentous events had wiped out my preparation for Mel. She could hardly expect me to be available at the drop of a hat, I thought, wracking my brain for excuses. My mouth wasn't in sync with my mind. I heard myself saying, "I could be there in half an hour."

"Good," she said and hung up.

Puzzled by her abruptness, I sat nursing my coffee. It had started to rain outside. People crowded into the shop. A waitress came and removed my long empty cup. "You want anything else?" she asked. I declined with a shake of my head. She looked pointedly at me, then at the people waiting in the doorway. I got up, slowly pulling on my parka, then the woolly hat, scarf and glove set my mother had knitted for me. Outside the filthy grey skies, which had threatened rain whilst I was window shopping, had well and truly opened up. I lingered under the awning of the patisserie. People hurried past, splashing through puddles, huddling under umbrellas. Some took shelter alongside me, jostling for space. It would be warm and dry at home. I could call Mel and arrange another time. A bus headed for near my home pulled up at a stop just metres away. I dashed to it, soaking my feet in a puddle. The bus was packed, despite it being only early afternoon. I stood, hating the discomfort of my soggy shoes, hating being crammed amongst so many strange bodies, all their smells exacerbated by damp, hating being jostled. The bus stopped at the top of Waterloo Bridge, just by the Southbank Centre. A woman called out to be let off. I stepped off the bus to give way for her. The rain had let up. I didn't get back on the bus. I looked at my watch and was surprised to find that I was barely late for Mel. I went carefully down the wet steps, lingering at the Hayward to look at the posters advertising its current exhibition, before going on to the South Bank Centre. I pushed open the side door and stepped inside, savouring the warmth.

The huge foyer was almost empty. In the café area nearest me, a man appeared to be having an animated discussion with himself. A woman sat reading a novel at one of the tables alongside the sunken ballroom which doubled up as an exhibition area. Today a couple of toddlers were racing round, slipping and sliding on the polished wooden floor of the bare ballroom, turning it into an impromptu rain day playground. Their mothers leaned over the rail, chatting with an eye on the kids. Waiters and cashiers lingered languidly behind the counter of the café areas. There were one or two people at the bar. At one of the tables in the smoking area in front of the bar sat Mel. Her back was to me, smoke rising above her head as she drew on her cigarette, tilted her head back and blew a stream upwards. She glanced at her watch and looked around. A trail of smoke followed her hand as she saw me and waved, the cigarette between her fingers. Heather, I thought, remembering our last meeting, would have a giggle. I trudged towards her, my sodden trainers squeaking on the floor.

"Hello Mel," I said. "Howzit going?"

She looked up at me with expressionless eyes, dragged hard on her cigarette and stubbed it out in the overflowing ashtray. "Hi," she replied. "You alright?"

"Cold. Wet." I made a gesture of my hand down my front. "I need something hot. Get you another of those?" I nodded towards the empty glass in front of her.

"Best not." She looked at the glass regretfully. "I've been loitering here a while. Espresso. No sugar. Please."

I slung my outdoor things on a chair and went to the café. My stomach churned as I waited for our drinks. The terseness in her voice and manner made it clear something had happened in Canada. I had no doubt that Zac had said something to her. I just wished I knew what. I went back to her, deposited our drinks on the table and took the chair opposite her.

"Thanks." She pulled her drink closer, raised the small cup with one hand and sipped. The other hand held a freshly lit cigarette. She put her cup down. "Adam OK?"

"He's fine, thanks." I didn't ask how her family was. The words would have choked me.

She pushed her cigarettes and lighter towards me. "Help yourself."

I looked at the packet longingly before pushing it back. "Nope. Given up."

"Anti-smoking fascists got to you?" she mocked, offering me the packet again. "Go on, have one. You can go back on the wagon later. Everyone falls off and gets back on. Tried it once myself. Can you believe that?" A smile briefly touched her lips. It died before it reached her red-rimmed eyes.

"I can't," I said.

"Can't smoke? Or can't believe it of me?"

"Both of the above," I quipped, matching her flippant tone. "Remember what you used to say? Try everything once." I was glad my bulky pullover hid my growing bump. "So," I said brightly, "What's up?"

She tapped ash from her cigarette. "You wanted to see me urgently." She flung her arms wide. "Here I am."

I fiddled with the handle of my cup. "You didn't respond to my email."

"You know how it is," she said lightly. "Some people only check email now and then. Some take longer to respond to email than snail mail."

"I thought you didn't want to see me."

"Why wouldn't I want to see you?" She didn't sound as surprised as the question implied. "We're friends aren't we? But you didn't expect me to drop everything and fly over at once to rescue you, did you? Or is it Adam? No, you said he was fine."

A warm rush flooded my body at the reminder of that time she'd dropped everything to rescue Adam. "No," I said. "I mean yes, he is. Fine, that is….Of course I didn't expect you to drop everything…" My voice tailed off. My worst childhood nightmares used to end in this warm feeling. It was dread, not comfort. It ended by my waking in cold sodden sheets. I crossed my legs so I wouldn't pee my pants.

"Well, I'm here now," she prompted. "So spit it out." She waited, blowing out smoke, looking at me through the haze. "Has it all gone away?"

"No," I said. "It hasn't." My tongue felt thick and heavy. "It's just…I've been thinking about this for so long. You didn't answer my email. Then you wanted to see me straight away. It sounded like you had some urgent reason of your own, that you wanted to see me about." I studied my hands, looking at each finger carefully, at the wrinkles around my knuckles, at the solid gold band on the third finger of my left hand. I breathed deeply and plunged in. "Is there?"

She stubbed out the cigarette and stood up, catching her chair just before it fell. She took her bag from the back of her chair, but she didn't reach for her coat. "Don't worry." She addressed my startled look. "I'm only going to the bar. Think I'll have that drink after all."

I watched Mel wend her way through the scattering of small round tables. The rain had driven more people indoors. Several tables were now occupied. A number of people huddled over drinks at the bar, office workers in suits. Either they'd left work early to network over power cocktails, or they were out for late liquid lunches. Mel ordered the drinks. She tossed back half of the first one the barman placed in front of her, before he returned with a second. The other half disappeared when he returned with the third. She paid, picked up the remaining drinks and walked back to me without as much as a wobble. Admiring glances followed her from the bar. She placed one of the glasses of orange-coloured liquid in front of me. "Here," she said. "Drink up. Don't think I'll get anything out of you without oiling the wheels."

I sniffed at my glass. It wasn't orange juice. "I can't," I said, putting it back down. "You have it."

She raised her eyebrows. "What? No booze either? Have you found Jesus or are you detoxing? Have a sip." She led by example. "It will help you stop the verbal dance."

"I'm not dancing," I said. "I just don't know where to start."

"The beginning's usually a good place." She shook a cigarette from her packet and lit up.

"Right," I said. "But listen, Mel. Whatever I tell you now…I want you to remember that I'm telling you because I'm your friend. Please believe that. It's the only reason I'm telling you. I'm your friend and you need to know the truth."

Mel studied the tip of her cigarette. "Sounds like a soap opera where someone reminds you she's your friend, then says your husband is fucking someone else." She put the cigarette to her lips, drew deeply and blew a long stream of smoke at me. "You didn't come out in this wonderful British weather to tell me *that,* did you? Sweetie, my husband fucks around all the time. I never imagined he gave up his bad habits. I still have mine. It's called an open relationship. We just have to be discreet because of the kids."

I resisted the impulse to scream at her to drop the act. "After you left here, I had a phone call from Zac," I said. "You told him to call me?"

"I did," she agreed. "I was totally excited about bumping into you. Gave his leg a right old pull. You know, the one who says she got away, that kind of thing."

"He didn't think it was funny, did he?" I guessed.

"No." She stretched her lips into that humourless smile again. "I must say, I was just the teensiest bit pissed off. I mean, casual flings yes, but carrying a torch for you after so many years? I hadn't realized you had such an impact on him. He demanded to know every word you'd said."

"It wasn't about me," I said. "You told him Heather was with you when you met me?" It was another guess.

140

She nodded. "That was why he demanded chapter and verse."

The murmur of quiet conversations, the sounds of people coming and going, had grown round us. Above it a sudden screaming of children arose. We both turned towards the source. The women whose children had been playing on the ballroom floor were scooping up their kids. Reluctant to leave, one wailed and struggled in his mother's arms. The other joined in. The women staggered up the steps to where they'd left their prams, one with her child held round his waist under her arm, the other with both arms wrapped around hers. The children were deposited in their prams and strapped in, still yelling. The mothers wheeled their prams past the bookshop, towards the main door, out of our sight. We turned to each other again. Mel said quietly. "So tell me why."

I told her all of it, from the birth of Heather to Lily's loss. I told her about Sandy's letter and my fears of what would happen when Viv told Lily that Heather was alive. I related what Zac had recently said to me on the phone. Mel listened without interruption, completely unmoving save for the cigarette going back and forth between her mouth and the ashtray. Her eyes never left my face. When her cigarette burned down, she let it fall. She didn't light another. Around us people came and went. Their chatter made the air hum, drowning out the sound of the rain which had begun to lash the windows and glass doors around us again. I talked through it all, for what felt like aeons. When I'd finished, my throat was parched. My head ached. I felt sick on my stomach. It wasn't the nausea of pregnancy, which had mysteriously cleared up a few days ago. It was a general wretchedness pervading my body from telling the revolting story like this, all in one go. It seemed that hours more passed after I'd finished. When at last Mel spoke, her voice was rusty, as though from long disuse.

"It wasn't what I meant when I asked you to tell me why." She fumbled with her cigarettes. I reached over and took one from the pack, offered it to her. She stuck it between her lips with shaking hands. I held the lighter to the end. "He's already told me, you see," she said, blowing out smoke.

I watched her for a while, waiting for the nicotine to do its job before I asked, "If you knew it all, why'd you let me sweat? Tell it again?"

"He said you'd tell a different story from his. That it would be better if he told me the truth than if I heard your lies and distortions."

"So you think I'm lying, Mel? Why would I lie to you? I haven't seen you in years and the first thing I do is tell you a pack of lies that are guaranteed to hurt you? You're my friend. I owe you more than I can ever repay – what possible reason could I have to lie to you?"

She made a sound that wasn't quite a laugh. "You know, that's exactly what I said to him. Yazz is my friend. Why would she lie to me? And what's to lie about? I started laughing. Don't tell me, I said. You slept together after all? How's that dramatic news? How does it even matter?" She looked at me now, for a fleeting moment an echo in her eyes of her own remembered glee. "He said that wasn't what he wanted to tell me about, but it did prove his point. Kind of, if you could lie about that, you could lie about anything. You see?"

I did. A good liar laces lies with truths and half-truths. Zac was a good liar. "I didn't really lie about it," I said contemptuously. "I just don't count the five minute fuck I had with him twenty years ago as having a scene with him. It's hardly a lie on a par with everything I've just told you!"

"No." Then she said, "Will you get me a drink?"

I took my purse from my jacket pocket, went to the bar and got gin and orange for her, fizzy water for myself. She took hers and sipped before she said, "His version is that he knocked up a woman. Just a one night stand, but he did the responsible thing. He offered to pay for an abortion."

"Yes," I agreed, though I would have used the word "demanded" not "offered."

"He found out afterwards," she said, as though she hadn't heard me. "That this woman had decided to have the child. He was horrified, because she was high and pissed half the time, like she'd been the

142

night conception occurred. So, again he did the responsible thing. He offered to take the child off her hands. She refused. He offered her money. She took it. He took the child. He was afraid when she sobered up she'd want the child back, so he took Heather to Canada."

"You believe him?"

"Why not? He's my husband after all. He has no reason to lie to me about his past – or his present." Her mouth twisted in a grim parody of a smile. "The benefits of an open relationship. No lies." Ash fell unheeded onto her lap.

"You agree that it was right to take a small child from her mother?"

She glared at me defiantly. "Of course I do. In his place I'd have done the same thing. I'd kill for my kids. Sure I was pissed off that he'd not told me about it long ago, so we could have gradually prepared Heather for the possibility of this woman re-entering her life. But mad at him for taking his daughter from an abusive and negligent mother? Absolutely not."

I'd heard enough. I snatched up my still damp clothes. "I don't know why you came," I said bitterly. "If you believed him, why in hell call me?"

She reached out small strong fingers to encircle my wrist. "Don't go. Let's finish this."

I sat, my things bundled in my lap, ready to leave.

"A good liar," she said. "Knows when to quit. He didn't. He had to go on about you."

"Me?"

"I knew, you see, that it couldn't be you he was talking about – not unless you were some sort of Jekyll and Hyde, drunk and high by night, principled politico by day, having a kid on the quiet and abusing it…so no, I knew he wasn't talking about you. What beat me was, what did all this have to do with you?"

143

"And he said?"

"He told me Heather's mother was a good friend of yours. Lily." She mulled the name over for a while. "I remember her. Your crazy friend who doesn't like white people."

I opened my mouth to defend Lily. Then I remembered all the times Lily had found me chatting with Mel and dragged me off for some spurious reason, letting rip about my white friends when we were still well within earshot of Mel. I felt my face heat up.

"Not white *women,* perhaps." Mel read my thoughts. "Anyway, he had some idea that you'd make this woman out to be a saint and him out to be Satan himself.... I might be persuaded to hand Heather back to her. If that failed, he even had visions of the two of you, you and this Lily, trying to snatch Heather back."

"Christ!" I exclaimed. "What planet does the man live on?"

"I know." She gestured helplessly with her hand. "But he loves the kids. I had to point out to him that our daughter's grown up. She's hardly going to stand being handed over like a parcel. The entire notion was bizarre. As was his idea that we should take the kids out of school, up sticks and go and bury ourselves somewhere you and your friend would never find us."

I had to laugh. Bizarre wasn't the word for it. "So you put paid to his wilder notions. That doesn't explain why you're here."

"I offered to put Zac's side of the story to you. I was sure that you had no idea what a monster your friend was. You'd see how traumatizing it would be for Heather to be confronted with her abusive birth mother out of the blue. I'd convince you to let us tell Heather about her birth mother when it's best for Heather. To let us leave it to her to decide if and when she wants to meet the woman. He said he'd already spoken to you and you weren't budging. *I* said *he* wasn't *me.* You'd listen to *me.*"

"Because I owed you?" I put a hand to my mouth. "Sorry," I mumbled. "You didn't deserve that."

She shrugged. "He said you wouldn't give me the time of day if I defended him. You think he was a spy for the security police back then, perhaps even that he betrayed Adam. You were bitter because he got bored with leftie life and wanted to get his share of his old man's millions before the old man kicked the bucket. You're just looking for someone to blame for your failings. You don't care about who you hurt in the process, we're just collateral damage – me, my daughter, my sons."

"You didn't believe him." I reached over and put my hand over hers. "Thank you, Mel."

She drew her hand away. "There are two sides to every story. I came to hear yours."

"And now that you have?"

"Nobody could invent the story you just told me," she said. "You couldn't, anyway." She smiled bleakly. "You're just not a good enough liar. Besides, you said it yourself - he has reason to lie. Three reasons, actually – Heather and our boys. You don't. Vengeance isn't a reason."

"Some might say it is."

"Is it? For you?"

"If it were, what you did for Adam would have settled the score." I started at a clash of cymbals behind me. It was followed by a drum roll. Unnoticed by us, the band providing that evening's free foyer entertainment had set up and was getting ready to roll. "It's going to get noisier," I said as the other players started tuning their instruments.

"Do you want to go somewhere quieter?" asked Mel.

I looked at my watch. I couldn't believe the time, but if the band was about to start and the bar was full, it was way after knock off time for most people. "I should call Adam," I said. "He'll worry if I'm not home."

"I didn't take him for the type to watch his woman."

"He's not. There are reasons," I said. She didn't ask what they were. I called Adam. His phone was unavailable. I left a message. "So what happens now?" I asked her. "I assume he knows you've come to see me after all?"

"No," she surprised me by saying. "I couldn't reason with Zac. I had to let him take the kids out of school and off to New York. His father left him an apartment there."

I tried and failed to conjure up a picture of Zac in a flap. "And you're meant to be where, exactly?"

"Blitzing into London to pick up a few things, consult with my supervisor on working long distance, that sort of thing."

"What will you do?"

"I need time to think." She got up and slipped into a slick black raincoat. "I'll go to the digs I have here." She pulled on leather gloves and slung her bag over her shoulder. "Get a load of fags. Get some booze. Let the little grey cells sizzle."

The suddenness of her departure took me unawares. I watched her leave as I wrestled with my own damp parka. She was wobbling slightly as she walked, even in flat rain boots. I'd known her walk perfectly in stiletto heels with half a bottle of gin inside her. "Mel," I called after her, hastily hanging my scarf round my neck and shoving gloves and woolly hat into my pockets. "Mel, wait up." I dashed after her. "I don't like leaving you like this," I said as she pushed open the doors of the centre. "Come home with me."

"I'll be fine," she said. "I'll call you. I promise." She stepped outside. Three paces on, she stopped. "Is my children's father a mass murderer?" she asked.

"No," I said. "No, Mel, there is nothing to show that he is." A man is innocent until proven guilty. Even Zac had the benefit of the doubt. She walked off into the wet dark.

Adam was on the phone when I got in. "Oh, she's just got in, Maria," he said. "Hang on a minute."

I struggled out of my boots, dumped my wet things on a radiator and took the receiver. I'd forgotten that I'd arranged to go to the cinema with Maria. "Sorry, love," I said wearily into the phone. "Had a hard day. Can we do it next week? My treat. I'll even throw in dinner." I cut short her concerned questions. I was too worn out to feel guilty about taking advantage of her easygoing nature.

"You look shattered," Adam remarked, kissing me. "And you're absolutely frozen. Where've you been?"

"I left you a message," I said.

"It didn't say much. Why were you out in the cold and rain?"

"Mel called," she said. "She wanted to see me right away. Please don't ask me about it now. I'll tell you later. I just want to catch some kip, OK?" I ignored his look of concern and went into our bedroom to lie down. Too over-wrought to sleep, after a while I got up. Adam was sitting at the kitchen table, his head in his hands. He looked up as I came in.

"So," he said. "You told her then."

"I did." I poured water from the filtering jug into the kettle and switched it on.

"How did she take it?"

"How do you expect? He'd spun her some fairytale. Told her some weird things about me, trying to put her off seeing me again. Let me make myself some tea and I'll tell you all about it."

He went into the sitting room. I could hear him pacing while I made my drink. "So?" he asked impatiently when I came in carrying my mug.

"For god's sake, Adam," I said. "Sit down. You're making me nervous." He frowned, but did as I asked. "Look, I'm fine. I'm a bit tired, but the stress is over now." I told him the gist of what had happened between me and Mel.

"That was all he told her?" he asked.

"Well, what do you expect? It wasn't as if he was going to tell her the truth, was it?" He didn't answer. I sipped my tea.

"So what happens now?" he asked.

"I've no idea. I'll call Viv," I said. "Then it's up to them." I went over and sat on the arm of his chair, stroked his arm reassuringly. "I've done my bit, Adam. I'm out of it now. It's what you wanted, isn't it?"

"I suppose so," he said, uneasily.

I waited for the "but". It didn't come. Instead he said, "I'm going out for a run. I'll order in Chinese when I get back."

"I'll do it," I offered. "Tell them to deliver in about an hour or so?"

He nodded. When he'd gone, I ran a bath, threw in some lavender oil, stripped and sank into the sweet-smelling warmth. My belly was already round enough for the bump to be visible above the surface. I ran my hand over it. "Third time lucky," I said to it.

"The nice thing about being pregnant," Lily had told me when she was expecting Heather, "is that you have a living person to talk to all the time." She'd been lying in the bath like this, talking to her bump when Viv and I had come in. Lily loved to hold court in her bathroom, with me and Viv sitting on the laundry basket or the toilet, just keeping company with her. I liked my peace and quiet when I was in the bath, but suddenly, I wished they were here, she and Viv, talking for once about nothing in particular. Just keeping company. The tears slid down

148

my cheeks, down my chin, joining the bathwater at my neck. I got out and called Viv.

"Well," I said after I'd related what had happened that afternoon. "I've done what I set out to do. It's your turn now."

"Yes," she said slowly. "It is, isn't it?"

"When will you tell Lily?"

"As soon as I find the most appropriate time."

"Will you let me know?"

"I wish I could tell you to just forget about it now. You should focus on yourself and your baby and not worry about this."

"Easier said than done."

"That's what I thought." She paused. "Have you told your parents about the baby yet?"

"No," I said. "I was waiting to ensure nothing can go wrong."

"Is that fair on your mother and aunties?" she asked. She tutted several times. "When are they supposed to get knitting and sewing?"

"I'll tell them this weekend. When I've got all this out of my head. It's been like some dark shadow hanging over me." The doorbell rang once, and then again. "Got to go, Viv. Someone at the door. Call me when you've told her."

I put the phone down and hastily flung open the window. "Hey! Don't break the bell!" I shouted down.

The man on my doorstep looked up and raised a hand holding a brown paper carrier bag. "Your order," he called out.

I fetched the food, paid him, put the cartons in the oven to keep warm and set the table. Adam hadn't returned by the time I'd finished watching an entire episode of some courtroom drama on TV. The phone rang as I was about to call him. He'd bumped into a running mate and they'd worked up a thirst which went beyond what was in their water bottles. They were downing a pint of bitter at the pub. "You eat if you're hungry," he said. I wasn't interested in eating alone. I sat down in front of the telly again to let fictional drama erase for a while the real life one in which I'd been caught up. By the time Adam got in, I'd drifted off. He sneaked past the sofa, making straight for the bathroom.

"Sorry," he said guiltily, when he saw me arrive in the doorway. "I tried not to wake you."

"I wasn't sleeping," I said grumpily. "I was waiting up for you." The reek of beer and stale smoke hit me as he pulled me towards him and gave me a kiss. I pushed him away. "Phew, you stink! I thought you and Andy only had money for one beer each."

"Sorry." He slumped on the edge of the bath. "Andy met up with a couple of other guys he knew in the pub. You know how it is."

"You might have told them your wife's got dinner waiting!"

He raised his eyebrows. "I didn't know my wife got worked up about things like that!" He started to strip. "Come on. It gave you a chance for a nice rest."

"I would have been able to rest in my own bed," I snapped, "if I hadn't been worrying about you, walking home in the cold in only your running gear. If I'd known you had all that beer to keep you warm, I would have saved myself the worry." I stomped off to bed. I was still awake an hour later when he crept in beside me. "I'm really pissed off with you," I said, sitting up and flicking on my bedside lamp. "You know it's not about dinner waiting. I've had a helluva time with Mel and then you go and leave me on my ace."

"You said you were alright," he muttered, plumping up his pillow and burying his face in it. "How was I to know you'd still be stressing yourself about it?"

150

"You know," I said, getting out of bed and grabbing my pillow. "You've been clucking over me like a hen with a single chick ever since we found out I'm pregnant. If I asked you for the moon on toast, you'd grin and try to get it for me. Tonight when all I wanted was some company and comfort from you, that's too much to ask. You'd rather sit in a pub drinking, when you don't even like pubs."

He rolled over to my side of the bed and slid an arm round my thighs, pulling me towards him before I could stalk off. "Hey," he said. "I'm sorry, OK?" He pushed himself further up and nuzzled my belly. "Sorry I went out, sorry I had too much beer, sorry I came home stinky." He lifted a penitent face. "Forgive me?"

I sniffed, not ready to be appeased yet.

Adam stood up. "Hot milk and honey?"

"OK," I said, but I was asleep when he brought the drink. Sometime during the night, I reached out and found him gone. The hollow which his body had made in the bed was cold. Driven by my full bladder, I ambled yawning towards the toilet. I washed my hands and walked from room to room. Adam wasn't anywhere upstairs. I looked at my watch. It was five a.m. I opened the front door. Light spilled from the doorway of his study. He was on the phone. I looked at my watch again. It really was 5am. "Adam?" I called. "What're you doing?"

He came out of his study, putting off the light and pulling the door shut on the latch behind him. "I had to make a call," he said softly, as though there were people around to wake up.

"At this time of the morning? Are you mad?" I retreated into our living room as he came upstairs and shut the door.

"It's 7 am in Cape Town," he said, as if that explained anything. "I was trying to get Simon before he left for work."

"What's so urgent you couldn't call tonight? Or email him?"

"He told us he was coming over here soon," he said, following me into the bedroom. "I wanted to tell him it's not possible for us to put him

151

up any longer." He sat down on his side of the bed as I got into my side. "But you know Simon. He's never home and he answers email and phone messages when he feels like it."

"God, I nearly forgot he was coming." I snuggled under the covers. "Why can't we put him up?"

He made no move to join me. "The baby, Yazz."

"Oh, don't worry about him finding out," I yawned. "I'm planning on spreading the good news – starting with my parents this weekend." When he didn't reply, I said into the darkness. "Simon doesn't have to use your lovely nursery in waiting. There are two perfectly good rooms downstairs. If you won't give up your study for your oldest friend, he can have mine. Now can we please get some sleep?"

"It's not the space. It's the hassle for you."

"Oh, rubbish. Simon's never any trouble. Cleans up and tidies after himself. Come on. Get in. I'll call Viv later and tell her to tell Simon it's still OK. You want to get a message to Simon, you tell Viv. Sleep!"

Despite my injunction, Adam lay restless next to me for ages. I fell asleep amused by the change which the coming child had already wrought in my usually overly-generous husband. In the morning, when Adam had left for work, I called Viv. As I'd expected, I got her answer phone. I left a message then went down to my study and looked at the calendar. Simon was due in about a fortnight. I didn't want Simon booking an hotel. He couldn't afford it. He was one of the few comrades from the old days who still worked for an NGO. When the ANC came to power in 1994, most overseas organizations withdrew funding from NGOs, arguing that there was no longer a need for them and that they were giving whatever they had directly to government sponsored projects. This had left organizations like Simon's having to beg for continued funding every year. To save money, Simon stayed with friends wherever he went, rather than spend the organization's money in travelling around raising more.

For a while we heard nothing from Simon, directly or via Viv. Assuming he'd just rock up around the time he'd said, we carried on with our lives. It was a busy couple of days before he arrived. My part-time teaching was taking up a lot more time than I got paid for. I often wondered if it was worth it. Cuts in education funding meant that there was little administrative support, especially for part-timers. At the same time, the paperwork seemed ever increasing. There was also the necessary notification to the college of my pregnancy, and helping to find a substitute for my maternity leave. Once I'd told the college, I felt I had to tell Maria. That opened the floodgates. Friends dropped by all the time with this or that precious item they'd saved from their own babies – or advice for us on which way to hold a baby. Though I had ages to go, all the hardware – pram, crib plus linen, baby bath and stand - was piling up, courtesy of our friends. It was tiring but great fun. It also made the baby more real. She could hardly fail to turn up now, I thought, with so many presents already waiting for her. Adam barely had time to pump air into the futon in my study before Simon was there.

Without as much as a call from the airport, he arrived. At the ring of the doorbell one night, I looked out the window to find him grinning at me, the light from the street lamp glinting on his glasses. He had his laptop dangling from one shoulder, his suitcase at his feet. I opened the front door to be enveloped in a hug. He stepped back, inspecting me at arm's length. "Something's different," he said. "What is it?"

"Come inside, you fool," I said, "before we both freeze to death standing here."

He humped his case over the doorstep into the hallway. I shook my head, knowing it contained only toiletry essentials and a couple of changes of clothing. The rest would be books and papers. "Jesus, Simon," I said. "Have you been buying up the contents of every bookshop you passed?"

He looked at me, then doubtfully up the stairs. "Where's the man? Any chance of a hand from him?"

"He's getting your dinner," I said, then relented. "Don't worry. We've put you down here." I unlocked the door to my study. "Just put all your stuff in there and come up to eat." I handed him the spare keys for the front door and the study. He was only staying a couple of days, but I didn't want my movements restricted by his comings and goings.

After stowing his luggage, he trailed up the stairs after me. "Hey, howzitt?" Simon greeted Adam with a backslap. Adam put the spoon he was using to taste the curry in a saucer and turned to shake Simon's hand. I left them chatting and went to set the table. We were seated at dinner before I asked, "So what's happened to Viv? I haven't heard from her in ages."

Simon swallowed some roti he'd wrapped around a mound of curry before he answered. "I thought you knew. She's gone to Canada with Lily."

CHAPTER SEVEN

I felt free. Viv had lifted a burden from my shoulders. Whatever happened in Canada, it was out of my hands. Adam and I could get on with our own lives. I looked at Adam, expecting to see my relief mirrored on his face. He was staring fixedly at his plate.

"Beats me why they just had to bugger off without saying anything," Simon went on, looking aggrieved.

As I opened my mouth to answer, Adam stood up abruptly. His chair clattered against the sideboard behind it. Simon and I looked at him in surprise. "I think I left a tap running in the kitchen," he muttered. I could hear no tap running.

"I thought they left you a message," I said to Simon. Viv clearly hadn't told Simon why she and Lily were going to Canada. She was still operating on the need to know principle, even with Simon, who'd had several spells in the post of lover. I'd told Adam about Heather after the decision had been taken that both he and I should leave South Africa. Feeling guilty afterwards, I'd confessed to Viv. All she'd said was, "That hardly counts, does it? It's like telling it to a rock in a deep dark forest." She was right. Adam was the keeper of Party records, the only person who knew the movements of all cadres, the only person who knew what everyone was doing, when why where and how. He must have known that Lily, Viv and I regularly went off on non-Party business. He'd never asked about those days – and sometimes nights – that I disappeared to help look after Heather. When I'd finally told him, he'd already known that we bunked off – just not why.

"Yeah," Simon said now. "Saying f-all. Plus I didn't even get it till after they were gone."

"It's your own fault. You never check messages." I would leave it to Viv to enlighten him, if she ever did.

"Yeah, well," Simon said sheepishly. Then he brightened. "Good thing I didn't get Adam's. I'd have booked an hotel before I got Viv's message to tell me to ignore his." He fed more roti and curry into his mouth and chewed with a look of absolute delight on his face. "God this stuff is great!"

"Did she say when they'd be back?" I pushed the serving dish of curry in front of him.

"Nope. I'll expect them when I see them." He helped himself to more curry. "Oh, well." He grinned. "Maybe some long lost uncle died and left one of them a fortune. Hope they give some to LRS." That was the organization he worked for. "We could use a bit of a windfall."

Adam came back into the room. "What's the problem?" he asked as he sat down and started toying with his food again, tearing roti into tiny pieces, a frown creasing his forehead. "Funders not forthcoming?"

That set Simon off on a moan about the sorry state of NGO's, because international funders were giving money to the government, which was lining its own pockets. Adam didn't seem to be listening. When Simon had finally had enough of the curry, I got up and went to fetch the melktert I'd made for dessert, puzzling over Adam's attitude. Perhaps he was still thinking about the innocents involved – mainly Mel and Heather. I wished he'd stop fretting about it. It was over – for us, anyway. In the dining room, Simon was finally winding down his one-sided conversation. He looked up with relief when I entered. "What's the matter with him?" He jerked a thumb in Adam's direction.

"Just tired, I guess," I answered, handing him a slice of melktert. "It's all this work, cooking dinner for you. It's worn him out."

Simon grinned as he tucked into his melktert. I took away the remnants of Adam's food and put his favourite dessert in front of him. He pushed it away with a shake of his head. Surprised, I took it back and started eating it myself. It wasn't until we were all in the kitchen, Adam washing, Simon drying and me packing away, that Simon mentioned Canada again. "You know who's in Canada?"

The big glass bowl Adam was rinsing dropped into the sink. Soapy water splashed down his front. He took the tea towel Simon handed him and dabbed at his shirt. "Half of the coloured population who left before ninety four because they could pass for white and live like whiteys in Canada?" he asked sarcastically as he handed the towel back to Simon. "Plus half the white population who are scared of living under a black government?"

Simon chortled. "That too. But no," he resumed drying dishes. "I'll save you guessing. I meant Zac. Remember that vark?"

"Are we likely to forget?" I asked, rhetorically.

"No," He pushed his glasses up his nose with his forefinger. "I suppose not."

"All the *kak* he caused for us. Him and his bunch of loonies fucking up everything we worked for – I'm surprised you can even mention his name without choking."

His brows rose at my hostility. Simon had been the one on the CC who was most cautious about adopting the hardcore left politics of Zac's party and the new international they claimed to be setting up. For him, however, it had been all political, not personal. I didn't think he'd ever understand just how personal the differences between Zac's party and ours had been for me. "Well if you're still so pissed off with him and his lot," he said, "I sure don't want to be in his shoes if Viv and Lily bump into him in Canada. You know how she and Lily hate his guts. That thing he had with Lily, you know, bad memories and all that."

It was on the tip of my tongue to tell him that seeing Zac was exactly why they'd gone to Canada, but I was suddenly tired of talking about the issue. "I know you're called Simon," I said instead, "but try to remember you're the Simon with a PhD in maths, not your simple namesake. Canada's a massive country. They might never come within hundreds of miles of one another." I went into the sitting room, hoping that put paid to the discussion. Simon followed me, while Adam stayed to wipe surfaces. I sat down in an armchair, kicked out the footrest and leaned back. Simon went through the shelves of CDs and put some Nora Jones on. "Zac, hey," he mused, slumping onto the sofa. I didn't answer. He seemed to get the hint. He stretched his long thin legs out in front of him, hands folded contently across his little potbelly. He picked up a collection of Chomsky's essays from the small table at his elbow where Adam had laid it earlier. "Can I borrow this while I'm here?"

"Sure." I looked at the title. "In fact, have it. We've got another copy."

He started leafing through the book. "You know how I came across him?" he asked absently.

Adam joined us, wiping his hands down his jeans. He sat himself down on the arm of my chair. "Who? Chomsky? You never said you'd met!"

Simon laughed. "Nah. Not him. Zac." Neither of us answered. That didn't stop him telling us that he'd been doing some research on behalf of one of the unions which his organization sometimes worked for. He'd been looking into a company which had branches in South Africa and had recently moved its headquarters from the UK to Canada. He'd thought that odd, until he discovered that the CEO was based in Canada. "And guess who's heading up the company?" He responded to his own question before either of us could venture the obvious answer. "Yep. Good old Zac."

"I don't know why you're so surprised," I said. "I told the EC long ago, this boytjie – he's always on about sacrificing the personal to the political, giving one's all to the party, yahdeyahdah, but check out what the man's cover is. It just happens to be all the stuff we're all supposed to foreswear. The man lived well – plenty of time off, a social life, the works. And it's all 'cover'. So what does our revered EC leader, the guru Ben, say when I point out this little anomaly?" I sneered. "He accuses me of uncomradely pettiness towards poor comrade Zac, so self-sacrificing, willing to live the good life to protect his politics. Guess I would have ended up in Siberia if we'd been in the USSR."

"Do we have to talk about this?" Adam asked. "Haven't we got something better to discuss?"

"Why shouldn't ex-Trotskyists be CEOs of multinationals?" I wouldn't let go, now Simon had got me all wound up. "Ex-union secretaries are multimillionaires in the new South Africa. They wouldn't drink tea with the bosses in the old days, but these days they're happy to take shares in the companies they used to fight against and provide the company with some black faces in the interests of black economic empowerment."

"Chill out, Yazz," Simon said. "You're preaching to the converted. Sorry, OK? Didn't mean to spoil the evening and all that." Adam muttered a protest that he hadn't. I held my peace. An awkward silence reigned for a while until Simon went over to the small bag he'd deposited on the sideboard and took out a bottle of brandy. He held it up questioningly at me. I shook my head. He asked the same mute question of Adam. Adam held up thumb and forefinger, indicating a small measure, and went to the kitchen to fetch coke and glasses. "So what's with the new guest accommodation?" Simon said as he poured for them. "You got someone else in my usual room?" He dropped back onto the sofa.

Adam gave me a questioning glance. I shrugged. "Adam's turning the spare room into a nursery, Simon," I said. "I'm pregnant."

Simon's jaw dropped. He glanced at Adam then at me, his gaze travelling from my face to my stomach. I was wearing an oversized sweatshirt. "Serious? You okes are having a baby?" He burst out laughing when I pulled the sweatshirt tight to expose my growing bump, slapping the arm of the sofa to emphasize his mirth.

"Yeah, right, very funny," I said. "I should have sold the copyright."

"Sorry." Simon removed his glasses to wipe tears from his eyes. "I just had this vision of you pushing a pram." He started laughing again. I aimed a kick at his foot. He pulled it in, got up and came over to kiss me. "Congratulations. And you mate!" He slapped Adam's shoulder. "I'm glad you decided to go through with it this time."

"What do you mean, 'this time'?" I demanded. "We decided last time too. We'd have a big child to play with this one, if it wasn't for the fucking Party rules." Simon looked at me as if I was speaking in tongues.

Adam put a calming hand on my arm, stroking it, murmuring, "Let it go, Yazz, please. Don't work yourself up."

I shrugged his hand off. "Don't look all Mr. Innocent," I said to Simon. "The Rules, remember? No kids? I didn't exactly choose to have an abortion!"

"Hey, hang on a minute!" Simon held up both hands, palms outward, as if he was silencing a mass meeting. "What d'you mean you didn't choose? We've got an EC report saying you told the EC you wanted to have an abortion because you didn't want anything interfering with your political work."

I felt as though he'd kicked me in the gut. Adam said angrily. "For God's sake! Did you have to bring the issue up?"

Simon started to protest that he hadn't started this. I raised my head and cut him short, "Are you saying nobody at home voted for it? You didn't?"

Simon threw an appealing look at Adam, getting a black one in return. He ran his hand over his thinning, grey-streaked hair. "Yazz," he said pleadingly, "we got this news in an addendum to a report from Ben. Something like he hoped the commitment demonstrated by comrades in exile would be inspirational for comrades back home. That was it. We just thought, wow, you guys are really something, going through that over here, without any support except from the few comrades here in the UK."

I felt sick, but it had nothing to do with being pregnant. I took a deep breath and counted to twenty. "He gave us a lecture on how selfish we were, wanting to put aside the struggle to have a child when working class kids were dying every day back home," I said at last. "Ben cited chapter and verse from Zac's party, of how many of their comrades had either had abortions or been sterilized so kids wouldn't interfere with their work."

"I never took Ben for a liar," Simon said. He came over and squatted in front of me. "Yazz, do you think I'd have agreed to Ben leading the EC if I didn't trust him?" I snorted and pushed him away. Simon went

160

back to his seat on the sofa. He downed some of his drink before asking, "But tell me, why didn't either of *you* let us know?"

"How?" I asked. "The only line of communication between the EC and the Party back home was through Ben and Hannah. Our leader and his woman. He drafted the reports, she typed them. We never got to see them. Security? Remember how that got drummed into us? What was I supposed to do? Pick up a phone and call you?"

"Yeah, you're right." Simon thought for a while. "So why didn't you just have the kid, if you really wanted to? You were always so feisty, why didn't you stick up for yourself?"

"And get kicked out of the Party? Like Viv? She was your *girlfriend* and you kicked her out."

Simon sighed. "Viv had political differences with the party, not personal issues. And by the way, we didn't kick her out. She resigned. Then she decided, even though she disagreed with us in some respects, she agreed with the essentials. She asked to re-join, we agreed to let her in again. I mean, did you really think we'd kick you and Adam out? And lose a third of our fledgling EC that we'd dreamt for years of building?"

"That is such tripe," I said, ignoring Adam's attempts to shush me again. "Why did we bother having Party Rules then? For fun?"

Simon didn't answer. He sat on the sofa with his elbows on his thighs, his hands hanging down between them, bony wrists extending from the sleeves of his jumper. He studied the carpet between his feet. After a few moments I went and stood over him, my hands balled into fists. I felt murderous. I shoved his shoulder so that he fell back in his seat. "Was it all a joke?"

He struggled upright. "No," he said, looking straight at me. "They were there because we thought we had to have them." After a while, he said carefully, "Yazz. Try to remember how young we were. We were all in love with the struggle. Everybody talked about being ready to give their lives for the struggle, but we didn't have a clue how to wage the struggle until we started reading the literature. From that we

161

learnt we needed a party to wage the struggle properly. We learnt that we needed international support. We had no idea how to build a party. We had no idea of what the international left scene was like. So we read some more. We made some contacts." He raised his hands, palms upwards in a helpless gesture. "We thought that was how revolutionary parties were built. With rules and strict discipline. We didn't know any better. We didn't know that in reality nobody could live like that. We learnt the hard way that we would have lost a lot of cadres if we adhered to them strictly."

"You'd have had me," I said bitterly. "The only one who didn't know the rules were made on April Fool's Day."

"Many people made all sorts of sacrifices," he said. "Not because of the rules, but because they believed that was the only thing to do. We thought that included you. We admired you for that."

I could have screamed with rage. Instead, I stumbled to the window and flung it open. I leaned against the frame and breathed in the cold night air. I watched the moon duck in and out of clouds. I listened to the trees and shrubs dripping the last of the recent rain. "My own fault," I kept thinking. "He's saying it was all my own fault."

Adam came up behind me. "You'll catch your death." He pulled me in, shutting the window. He put an arm around my shoulder. "It's over. Don't let it go on getting to you. Come on, go to bed. I want to talk to Simon."

"We thought you were amongst the most committed comrades we had," Simon said quietly, as I turned from the window. "Me especially. I knew you'd broken the very same rule for Lily, yet you refused to break it for yourself. At least, that was what I thought till now."

I gasped. "What d'you mean I broke…….. Are you saying you knew about Lily's child? You knew back then? But how? I thought Viv said she never told anyone…."

He raised his eyebrows, looking a question at Adam. Adam sighed. He pulled me around to face him, both arms around me. "Yazz, I'll tell you, but you must promise to calm down. The baby –"

"I am calm, Adam," I said, icily. "I am very, very calm. This will be the calmest pregnancy ever, if you tell me what the fuck is going on!"

"Viv didn't tell Simon about Heather," he said. "I did."

I struggled free of his embrace.

"Why? Why would you do that?"

Simon started to say something, but Adam held up a hand to silence him. The other closed around my wrist, keeping me close. "Yazz," he said. "Just sit down and listen a minute, OK?" I sat. "When the CC decided to send you out after me," he said. "they chose four other people to make up the EC – including Lily. Lily was meant to come out at the same time as you." He sighed. "You came to me before I left SA, remember? Our last night back home? You were worried. You told me about the child. You didn't know what Lily was going to do about her. You asked me to get the CC to change its mind, to let Lily stay in SA."

"I didn't mean do it by telling them about Heather!" I said. "What was the point of me and Lily and Viv going through hell to keep her existence a secret, if I was going to ask you to blab it all to the fucking CC? What were you thinking?"

"I didn't tell the CC, Yazz," he said. "I told Simon. I obviously wasn't thinking. It was a bit hard to concentrate on Lily's problems when I was getting ready to leave my entire life behind. I'm sorry if that sounds selfish and sentimental rubbish but it's the truth. I was still on the run. I saw Simon once. The only thing I could think to do, was to tell him - in confidence, mind you – to see if he could come up with some acceptable reason for her not to be one of the exile group."

"And you didn't think to talk to me about it first?" I was angry now.

"When? I didn't see you again until the day I left," he protested. "And then it was just for a couple of minutes! The next time I saw you was in London!"

"You could have told me then!"

"Why? The first thing you told me was that the child was dead. Lily was coming out here, we'd have to keep a close eye on her. I didn't think that what I'd told Simon mattered any more. What good would it have done to tell you then?"

"And since then? Since I came back from Cape Town? Did you never think to tell me you'd blabbed something I told you in confidence to Simon?"

"This is why," he said. "I knew how upset you'd be."

"I am not upset," I said through gritted teeth. "I am perfectly fucking calm. I am even amused. See?" I stretched my lips into the parody of a smile. "I'm laughing. You know why? You tell Simon, Simon tells the CC, the CC tells Zac. It's like a fucking vicar's tea party, not an illegal revolutionary party. It's a fucking joke."

Simon leaned towards me, forearms on his thighs, hands clasped. "At the risk of offending you further, Yazz, I have to agree with Adam. I know it sounds defensive, but there was a state of emergency on. The unions were involved in strikes, the youth were caught up in boycotts, the townships were burning, comrades were being killed and arrested left right and centre. We – the CC, that is – we were running around all over the country, putting out fires. I didn't have time to address personal problems as carefully as I otherwise might have. So, when the issue of Lily leaving came up, I couldn't think of a single reason, aside from the truth, why they shouldn't send her out here. I told them. The decision was she'd still come over here. I would tell Zac, so that he could give her the assistance she needed with the child. After all, it was his kid. Sure, he didn't want the kid to be born, but come on, even he would let his own kid starve when he had plenty of money. So I told him."

"Do you know what *kak* you caused?" I asked.

"Why? I mean, the guy wasn't exactly jumping for joy. He'd paid for an abortion and here he was being asked to pay child support. But give the man his due, once he was over the shock of hearing he was a father, he did offer to help Lily any way he could. Then the laaitie mos died. Case closed."

"That was convenient."

"Shit, Yazz," He took his glasses off and wiped them on his T-shirt. "That's harsh."

"No, it's not, Simon. I said you caused a whole heap of *kak*. Do you want to know why Viv and Lily went to Canada? They went to get the *laaitie* who supposedly died."

Simon put his glasses back on and looked at Adam for confirmation. Adam nodded.

"Zac stole her. He probably got somebody to deliberately start a fire so he could steal the kid he never wanted. Do you want to know how many children died in that fire?"

"You're having me on, right?" Simon's face had gone gray under his tan.

"Adam will fill you in on the details," I said, glaring at my husband. "You'll want to know why Lily's going to tear your innards out and roast them when she finds out about this." I went to our room, closed the door, and lay down on the bed, listening to Adam's low monotone, interspersed with Simon's sharp interjections and exclamations. It seemed hours before I heard the front door open and shut, then footsteps going downstairs.

Adam came into our room. He sat on the bed. He reached out a hand to stroke my hair. "I'm sorry," he said.

I rolled away from him, sat up and switched on the light. "You're sorry?"

"What else can I say, Yazz?"

"I don't know, Adam," I said. "These lies – all these years - it's like I don't know you." He held a hand to his cheek as though I'd slapped him. "But it's not me you have to worry about, is it?" I switched off the light and turned my back.

After a long while, he said, "I'll sleep downstairs, if you like."

"Suit yourself."

For the remaining days that Simon was with us, I barely spoke to him or Adam. I stayed out to avoid eating with them in the evenings and went straight to our bedroom when I got in. Passing by my study or the sitting room, I'd hear them talking, playing music, rustling papers they were reading and I'd stomp past, flinging doors shut behind me to silence them and ruin their fun. Adam would come in to check on me. He didn't try to re-open the discussion. He just asked how I was. Getting no answer, he would hover for a while then go downstairs to sleep in his study. In the mornings, the pattern repeated itself, except that he went to work instead of to bed. I stayed in our room until after they'd both gone. The morning Simon was meant to leave, I went to my study, expecting to find it empty. Simon was writing at my desk. "Oh." I started to back out. "I thought you'd gone."

He held up a card. "Just leaving you this," he said. "Since it looks like you're too pissed off with me to say goodbye."

"I'm not pissed off," I said. "I don't know what I am, but not that."

"Adam is still sleeping downstairs. You're pissed off alright."

"That's his guilty conscience. I didn't ban him from the bedroom." He raised his eyebrows but didn't say anything. "What time's your plane?"

"Later." He came over to me and stretched out his arms to put his hands on my shoulders. He peered at me, short-sighted without his glasses, as serious as the night he'd told me there was nothing he could do about me and Adam having to leave our home. "We did good work,

Yazz," he said. "Try to remember that. We were a tiny group of very young individuals trying to find a way to beat a very tough system and trying to prevent a sell-out of the masses. The Party we formed to fight apartheid capitalism, the way we operated, it was the best we knew. We were so young, we didn't know any better. We were like David up against Goliath and all his friends. We did what the times and circumstances dictated. We fought the system. We contributed hugely to the downfall of apartheid. Try to forgive the mistakes we made along the way." He pulled me closer and kissed the top of my head. "Can't you put the bad bits of the past behind you? Can't you remember the good we achieved?"

I shrugged free. "I had better, hadn't I? Your plane might crash and I'd regret not forgiving you."

"Adam might go under a bus," he said. "You'd regret that a lot longer."

"As I said last night, it's not me and my regrets you have to worry about. It's Lily. What about what she's gone through?"

He raised his hands in a helpless gesture. "We did it with the best possible intentions, Yazz. I'll speak to her when we're all back home. I'll make her believe we were just looking out for her."

"Good luck with that," I said. "I know what Lily will say. 'The road to hell is paved with good intentions' – your good intentions, Lily's hell." I sat down at my desk, running my hand over the computer keyboard. "What if that child had been yours? Would you be willing to be persuaded of someone's good intentions under these circumstances?"

He reached over me for some books he'd left on my desk and shoved them into his suitcase. "I don't know," he said. "Good thing it couldn't have been mine then, isn't it?"

"Yeah? I seem to remember a party," I needled. "Lily's furious with Zac, ready to fuck anything with the right tools, even her best friend's burg, just to get back at him? You and her coming from your van outside?" He frowned. I watched his mind race over the years for the incident in question. He blanched. "Oops!" I said. "Touched a nerve there, have I? Don't worry. I'm sure Heather's not yours. My point was, she could so easily have been and would you be as understanding as you seem to expect Lily to be?"

He wouldn't meet my eyes. I left him to finish packing.

When he called up the stairs to announce that he was leaving, I went down and saw him off. I went for a long walk by the river. I spent time in the Tate Modern, then headed for Covent Garden, onto the British Library, not really looking at things, just thinking, trying to remember the good and forget the bad. In the late afternoon I came home and I cooked supper. I set the table and when Adam came home, greeted him and sat down to eat with him as though Simon had never visited. After the first few moments of uncertainty, looking at me as though fearing I had a fever, he fell in with what I was doing. He took it as a sign to come back into our bed that night. For the first few nights I stuck to my side of the bed, he to his. Then gravity caused us to roll together into the dent we'd made in the middle of the mattress after years of sleeping on it. Soon we were waking as we always had, with him curled spoon-fashion against my back. We were eating together. We were sleeping together. We were talking about baby, work, friends, the house, chores. It was almost as though Simon had never revealed that my husband kept important things from me.

Almost. Not quite. A no-go area had sprung up between us. Neither of us wondered aloud about the outcome of Viv and Lily's trip to Canada. For a while it preyed on my mind and I had no doubt it was on Adam's too. I waited for Viv to call. I left phone and email messages. There was no response. I contacted Simon. He'd not heard from her since she'd gone to Canada. I couldn't begin to imagine what had happened in Canada for Viv to go incommunicado. I had no doubt that she was off somewhere with Lily, dealing with the fallout from their trip. As the days went by I pushed Lily's affairs to the back of my mind. I needed to concentrate on what was happening in my own life. Viv would get in touch when she wanted to.

A fortnight after Simon had left, I was asleep when the doorbell rang. "What the hell?" I exclaimed, sitting bolt upright. The digital clock read 23:15. Adam wasn't in bed. He'd obviously slipped out for

168

something and forgotten his key. I sighed and slid from the bed, feeling about with my feet for my slippers. The bell rang again. "Alright, alright, I'm coming!" I muttered. As I passed the sitting room doorway, I heard light snoring. I pushed the door open. Adam had been reading the paper on the floor by the fire when I'd retired. He'd fallen asleep lying right there and said paper was spread over his face, rising and falling with each snore. The bell rang again, more insistently. "Adam!" I shook his shoulder. "Someone's at the door." Adam rolled onto his side, crumpling the newspaper beneath him, muttering. A woman's voice called. I went over to the window and moved the curtain slightly so that I could look out without being seen. The street lamp illuminated the top of a head covered in a woolly hat. Our long winter had not yet given way to spring. The woman stamped her feet and slapped her hands together. Then she turned her face up to my window and called again. Called my name. "At last!" I thought. Flinging the window up I called down to her: "Coming!"

"Whoozit?" Adam yawned, pulling himself up with the help of the coffee table.

"Viv," I answered. "I'll go down."

"Who? What? No, I'll go." He stretched and yawned. "Thought she was only coming for Easter. What's she doing here already?"

"What do you think?" I asked sarcastically. "Something to do with Lily and that trip to Canada, perhaps?"

He looked at his watch and groaned. "It's the middle of the night."

"Well hurry up if you're going! It's cold out there!"

He went out, leaving the door open. His footsteps thudded down the stairs. I followed him to the landing. Cold air blasted up as he opened the street door and I shivered in my pyjamas. "I'm not staying over, Adam," Viv said, her voice floating up to where I stood on the landing. "I'm sorry to have got you up. I just have to speak to Yazz rather urgently."

Adam had opened the door narrowly. His body blocked the doorway, one hand on the doorjamb, the other on the door as though he was about to shut the caller out. "She's actually in bed, Viv," he said. "It will have to wait till morning. She needs her rest."

"I know, Adam. I know." She sounded drained of her usual energy. "I wouldn't be here if it wasn't important. I'll only be a minute or two."

"Christ, Adam," I called. "What's wrong with you? Let her in!"

He stepped aside. Viv followed. "Be with you in one minute," I called out as they mounted the stairs. "I'll just put something on." In our bedroom I pulled a thick jumper over my pyjamas. When I joined them, Viv was standing in the middle of the sitting room like an unwelcome guest. I glared at Adam. "Sorry," I said to Viv. "You know. There's protective, there's over-protective, and then there's Adam. Come into the kitchen while I make tea. Have you eaten? Where's your stuff? And what do you mean you're not staying?"

She didn't answer my last question. "Don't be so hard on him," she said as she trailed after me. "He's only doing what he thinks he should be doing."

"What? Treating my oldest friend like a door-stepping Jehovah's Witness?" I filled the kettle and switched it on.

She smiled wanly. "Everyone gets a bit selfish when they're pregnant. Your pregnancy trumps everything else for him." She put her hands against the kettle to warm them up.

I waved a hand dismissively. "Anyway. Let's hear about Canada." I went to the bread bin and took out a few slices. I took some leftover chicken mayonnaise from the fridge and started making sandwiches. "You can't be bothered to answer my messages. I hear nothing from you in weeks. I expect you at Easter. It's not Easter, yet here you are, in the middle of the night without warning and, if you don't mind my saying so, looking like shit. What's up?"

"You say the nicest things." She pulled her hands from the swiftly heating kettle. "Could I pass on the tea and have something a bit stronger?"

I dropped teabags into cups for Adam and myself and poured water onto them as I answered. "Simon brought some brandy when he was here a couple of weeks ago. There's some left in the sideboard, in the sitting room. Make yourself a double and start talking."

She went off, returning with the brandy, a can of coke and a tumbler. She mixed herself a drink, sipped and rolled her eyes appreciatively. "That's better."

"Then let's hear about Canada – and why you've been awol for weeks."

Her answer was delayed by Adam's entry. "Is that all the luggage you have?" He pointed at the small backpack she'd slung down at her feet. "Or have your bags been nicked from our front doorstep? There's nothing out there!"

"I told you," she said. "I'm not staying. My bags are at an hotel near Russell Square." She paused. "With Lily." She slid onto a stool across the breakfast bar from me and took a sandwich. "And to answer your earlier question, Yazz, I haven't been in touch because I've been in Canada until now. It was just impossible to leave Lily alone for a minute."

I did a quick mental calculation. "Jesus! That's nearly a month! What the hell happened?"

"Nothing." She bit into her sandwich, chewed, swallowed, put the remainder back on the plate. "It was a big waste of time. There was nobody home when we got to Canada."

"And it took you this long to discover that?"

Viv drank some brandy. "Lily wouldn't go home. She was a bit upset."

171

"You mean she went totally apeshit. I don't blame her." I handed a cup to Adam and sipped at my own tea. "It must have been hell for you, though. "

"Not really," she said. "I gave her some Valium."

"Thought you didn't believe in little pills."

She shrugged. "Needs must when the devil drives. She dragged me around Canada like what you'd call a lunatic. We asked the neighbours. We went to all the branches of his firm. We went to Mel's faculty. We went to the kids' schools. Nobody knew where they'd gone or when they'd be back. So she decided we'd stake out the place day and night. Eventually the neighbours called the police. They escorted us to the police station. You can imagine what they thought of the story Lily told them. I had visions of them sectioning her. I thought we were going to be arrested and deported." She took up the sandwich again, finished it this time and washed it down with brandy and coke. "I gave her the Valium when they let us go," she said. "It was the only way to get her on the plane. She's sleeping it off as we speak."

"And you're in London because you told her Mel was studying here," I guessed. "So she thinks they fled here? She's going to rush all over this city looking for them? She's insane."

"Oh, she's not that," Viv said. "She's able to plan ahead quite logically. Listen. We booked our tickets with BA. We had a stop at Heathrow. I thought we were going to spend a few hours in the transit lounge en route home. I discovered when we arrived at Heathrow that she'd changed our itinerary. We're now scheduled to leave here tomorrow night. "

"That's even crazier. She can't hope to find them in a day! Supposing they're here at all, which I doubt."

"Again - not so crazy, to Lily's way of thinking. The reason I'm paying you a midnight visit is to warn you that it's *you* she's coming to see you tomorrow."

I groaned. "Thanks Viv. The warning's nice but it would have been even nicer if you'd let her be arrested in Canada and deported straight back to SA. Shit! She's probably developed a conspiracy theory, in which I've warned Mel and Zac to go into hiding with Heather, having been originally involved in a plot to kidnap the child…" I shook my head.

She sighed. "You're being absurd. She doesn't even know you've met with Mel. I didn't tell her that Mel's studying here. I didn't say a word about your having been in touch with Mel. I wasn't going to drag you into this again, in the circumstances." She gestured at my belly. "I simply told her that you'd shown me the letter and helped me to trace Heather to Canada. She accepted that without question. In fact, she's very grateful to you, considering that you've made it clear to her that you don't want to be involved in her affairs any longer."

I sipped my tea, thinking how hard it was for Viv, always standing between me and Lily, always trying to protect both of us. "So if she thinks I haven't seen Mel in years and if she's finally got that I don't want her in my life, what does she want with me? "

"She's desperate," Viv said. "She thinks that given that she's been proved right about Heather, given that you've been involved anyway, she can convince you to take one more step – tell her about possible places where Zac and Mel may have taken Heather."

I buried my face in my hands. "Jesus! Talk about clutching at straws!"

"As I said, she's desperate. Wouldn't you be, in her place?"

I didn't answer. There was no need.

"I'll let you get back to bed," she said, sliding from the stool. She brushed crumbs from her trousers. It was a slow, tired gesture. "Adam's right. You need your sleep. I simply wanted to tell you about Lily's plans so that you could be prepared. I'm sorry not to have been in touch to let you know what's happened. I've had my hands full with Lily. You know how it is." She turned to Adam. "Would you mind calling me a cab, please?"

173

Adam didn't move. "I'm not having Lily come round here and upset Yazz, Viv," he said, breaking the silence he'd observed throughout Viv's relating of events. "I'm sorry. I know she's suffered a lot. I can't tell you how bad I feel for causing it, but it's not going to help anyone if Yazz... I'm sorry, I don't mean to be nasty. You know how it is... I understand you're concerned about Lily, but I have to consider Yazz's condition. This business has placed enough stress on her as it is."

Viv held up a hand. "Alright, Adam. I appreciate what you're saying. I apologize for being inconsiderate towards Yazz." She didn't sound apologetic. She sounded miffed with Adam. "One doesn't think too clearly when one is rushing around from one strange country to another." She finished stiffly. "Yazz? You'd better go and seek asylum somewhere at the crack of dawn and stay away from your home until we leave. Our plane takes off at 9pm."

"Oh bollocks," I said. "I can cope with a few minutes of Lily. That's all it will take to tell her I don't know any more than she does. Besides, who's to say she won't stick around and hound me till I face up to her and convince her I don't know where they are? Let's just get it over with."

Viv glanced at Adam. "Why don't the two of you talk it over? Decide whether you think you should speak to Lily or not. We'll be here –" She flicked out her wrist to expose the watch under her sleeve. " – later today. If you're home, you're home and if you're not..." She shrugged.

"I'll call that cab," Adam said gruffly. He went to the sitting room for the phone.

"So," Viv said to me. "How was Simon?"

"Pissed with you for leaving SA without telling him. Didn't get your email or phone messages."

"There's a surprise," she said.

"About Simon and surprises," I said. "I should tell you something." I pushed the kitchen door shut. "Simon dropped a bit of a bombshell." I told her the gist of what Simon and Adam had told me. "You don't seem surprised," I commented when I'd finished.

"Oh I am. That is, I'm half-surprised. It wasn't you. It wasn't me. So it was either chance or Adam. Hence I am half-surprised." She looked thoughtful. "So that was what Adam meant when he said he'd caused Lily suffering."

"I thought you'd be livid."

"What would be the point of anger after all this time? They explained that they did it for good reason. They weren't to know what Zac would do. Besides, you're probably angry enough for both of us."

"Not as angry as Lily will be. Hopefully she'll be concentrating so hard on finding Heather, she'll forget to hassle about who was to blame for her loss."

"Indeed." Viv took her coat from the back of her chair and started to put it on. "I'll go and see where that cab is."

"Stay." I said. "We'll go to your hotel together tomorrow. Let's both have a good rest tonight. You can cook us a fortifying breakfast in the morning and then we'll deal with Lily."

"It's a nice offer," she smiled. "But best not." She poked her head round the door of the sitting room. "Adam? How long will the cab be?" The sound of a car pulling up below answered her. Moments later, someone leaned on the doorbell, followed by a pounding on the door and then a voice calling out. I didn't fancy having Viv go anywhere with some impatient fool. I turned to ask Adam to go down and tell the cabbie to never mind. Then I heard the flap of the letterbox lifting. A woman's voice called out for me and Adam to open up. We all froze. It was Lily.

Viv recovered first. "Stay here," she said. "Go to bed. I'll take her away with me." She went down the stairs, pulling on the woolly hat. I made no objection. I was suddenly overwhelmingly tired and didn't fancy dealing with Lily. Adam stayed with me. Viv opened the street door. "For goodness, sake, Lily!" she scolded. "Stop that noise. It's the middle of the night. People are sleeping. You're causing a disturbance." As she spoke, she stepped outside and tried to pull the door shut behind her. She wasn't quick enough for Lily. Viv stumbled inwards as Lily, a foot taller than she, put her hand above Viv's head and shoved the door open.

"I want to see Yazz!" she said, as the heavy door thudded against the wall.

Viv snatched at Lily's hand. "Yazz is tired. We'll come and speak to her at a civilized hour."

Lily struggled to free her wrist, craning her neck round to look up the stairs. "I want to see her now. You spoke to her. Why can't I?" She sounded like a child protesting unfair treatment, not an angry adult. I started to go down. Adam laid a hand on my arm and shook his head. Instead he went and stood at the foot of the stairs. "Adam!" Lily strained towards him, Viv hanging onto her hand like the owner of an untrained dog hanging onto its leash. "She won't let me speak to Yazz!"

"Yazz is sleeping," he said. "She'll speak to you tomorrow, alright?"

"No, it's not alright! Wake her up. It's important." Viv gave up the struggle and Lily moved towards Adam. She tried to peer round him. With his big body in the way and the light on the upstairs landing having timed itself out, she couldn't see me. "What's the big deal? She's usually up half the night." Adam didn't budge. "Please let me in, Adam," Lily coaxed. "I just want to see her for one little minute to ask her something."

I switched the landing light back on. "Let her up, Adam," I said. "She won't let any of us rest tonight. Plus nosy next door's probably got the cops on the way with all this row."

"I knew you were up," Lily crowed.

Adam turned his head to protest. I flapped a hand at him. "It's OK. I'm not made of crystal. She can't shatter me." Reluctantly he stepped aside. She bounded up the stairs, already talking. "Stop!" I held up a hand to reinforce the word. "Pipe down. You either behave or you leave, OK?"

"Fuck, Yazz, I only want to ask you where –"

"Inside, Lily." She shut up and followed me into the sitting room. "Sit," I said and she perched obediently on the edge of an armchair. Viv and Adam trooped in. Viv slumped down on the sofa. I took the chair across from Lily. Adam hovered near me. "Now, Lily," I said. "Viv told me that you think I know where Heather might be. I'll tell you what I told her. I don't know."

"You must have some idea where they went." She wrung her hands, twisting them into a gesture of prayer. "She's your friend. You knew him. You know where their families live. That's probably where they've taken her…to one of their – "

"For crying out loud, Lily!" I threw my hands wide. "I never knew anything about Mel's parents, really. When you meet people on campus you don't talk about your families. As for Zac, don't you think you know more about him than I do?" It was a low blow, but I was too tired to finesse a point.

She leapt up and started pacing back and forth across the room. "She was your friend. You were so tight with her on campus. She saved Adam for you. How can you not know anything?" She stopped in front of me, urging. "You must have been in touch with her. I know you. You'd never let go of a friend, of someone who…please Yazz, just try to think."

"Lily," I said, wearily. "Until a few weeks ago, I'd not seen hide nor hair of Mel since I asked her to help Adam. Look, this is getting us nowhere. You've heard all I can tell you. I'm sorry it's not what you wanted, but there you are. I'm off to bed. I really am shattered."

Lily sank down on the sofa next to Viv. There was an odd expression in her eyes. She probably didn't believe a word I'd said, but I was too tired to care. "Stay if you want to," I said to Viv. "Key for my study's on the hook in the kitchen. There should still be bedding downstairs in

177

the box under the sofa bed." I walked towards the door, gesturing with my head for Adam to follow me.

Behind me, Lily said. "A few weeks ago? You saw her a few weeks ago?" Her voice was barely above a whisper. Too late I realized that I'd just told Lily what Viv had been at pains not to. Lily's green eyes were almost black with fury. "You saw her a few weeks ago!" she cried. "You warned her! You lying two-timing bitch!" She came at me, outstretched hands curled into claws. "You warned her! That's why they were gone when we got to Canada!"

Adam moved swiftly between us, grasping Lily's arms. He thrust her, thrashing and screaming obscenities, firmly back to the sofa. Viv put her arms round Lily while Adam hovered over them. "That's nonsense, Lily," he said. "And you know it. Yazz has gone out of her way to help you, why would she do something like that?"

"Because she's friends with that bitch who stole my baby!" she spat. "That bitch is Yazz's fucking Mother Teresa, her big heroine. Yazz was probably the one who told them about Heather. She was in on this with them the whole time. Now she's helped them again."

Viv held onto Lily until she'd run out of invective and subsided into hysterical weeping against Viv's chest. Viv brushed her hair from her face with one hand as though she was a small child, talking soothingly.

"Lily," she said. "Listen to me, just listen." Lily hiccupped. Silent tears rained down her face. "It was my idea, Lily. Yazz was only trying to help." No response. Viv drew out one of the tissues she always kept up her sleeve and wiped Lily's face. "It was for Heather's sake, Lily. You can't simply appear in Heather's life without any warning. Somebody has to prepare her for that. I thought Mel was the only possible person, the appropriate person, to tell Heather about you. I told Yazz to meet with Mel and explain everything to her. Yazz didn't want to, but she agreed for both your and Heather's sakes. I'm sorry if it seems to have gone wrong, but it was me. I take full responsibility."

"Lily." I forced myself to speak as soothingly as I could, trying to pour my share of oil on troubled waters. "I'm sure Mel will be in touch with me, as soon as she's sure Heather's got over finding out that her father's a bastard, and is ready to meet you. It's a lot she's had to take in. So why don't you just go home to Cape Town? When Mel calls me to say Heather's ready to meet you, I'll call you. Now you should get some sleep. You've got a flight in a few hours."

"You said you don't know her any more." Lily raised reddened eyes. Her face was so swollen, it looked as though it had been stung by wasps. "How can you be sure she'll give Heather up? Why would she want to go against that bastard when she's probably living the life of Riley with him? Him and my daughter!" The hysterical weeping started again.

"Because she's like that," I replied. "She's not Mother Teresa, but she loves Heather. She'll want her to know the truth. Believe this or not, Mel knew nothing about Zac stealing Heather or about Heather's birth mother being alive, until I told her recently. She's looked after your daughter and loved her as though she was her own for all these years. Instead of ranting against her, you should be grateful to her for that." I stabbed a finger in her direction to emphasize the point. "But no, not you," I wagged my finger from side to side. "All you can think of is yourself. You want to barge into that child's happy life and grab her back to satisfy yourself. You're not thinking about Heather. You should be grateful that at least her *other mother* is!"

Lily gasped as though I'd punched her in the gut. She wrapped her arms round her middle, rocking back and forth, moaning. The look Viv gave me would have frozen Cape Town on New Year's Day at noon.

"I'm sorry," I said. "I guess I'm just tired. I didn't mean that the way it sounded. I know you love Heather more than anything in the world."

Adam looked from me to them to his watch. "Come." He stretched out his hand to me. "We're all tired and overwrought. Let's get you to bed. I'll bring you some hot milk and honey."

"You think I'm a bad mother." Lily pushed herself upright, brushing Viv's ministrations aside. "You think she loves my baby more than I do. Did you think so back then? Is that why you helped him to take my baby away?"

Adam snapped. "Christ, you're not listening are you? How many more times do we have to say it? Viv's told you. Yazz's told you. Now I'm telling you. Yazz had nothing to do with Zac taking Heather." I put out a hand to restrain him. I had a premonition of what he was about to say. He went on before I could stop him. "It was me. Alright? Me. If you're looking for someone to blame for Zac taking Heather, Lily, then blame me. I'm responsible. I told Simon and Simon told Zac. I won't bother to explain to you how and why it happened. You're too worked up and it would just sound like excuses. So now you know. I'm the one who caused it all. Not Yazz."

Lily fixed angry disbelieving eyes on Adam. "Don't go fucking with my head, Adam."

The anger left Adam as quickly as it had come. "Believe what you like, Lily," he said, quietly. "It's the truth. Now I'm going to see Yazz to bed, then I'll come back and you can stick a knife in me. I'll even fetch it for you myself."

Lily started laughing. At first it was just a small giggling sound. Then it grew louder and louder until tears were rolling down her cheeks again. "Oh my," she said, shaking her head from side to side. "Oh my oh my oh my!"

"Stop it, Lily!" said Viv. Lily went on laughing. Viv shook her slightly, but it didn't stop the wild laughter.

"Shit!" I said, aside to Adam. "That was helpful. Just when Viv got her calmed down. What did it matter what she thought of me?"

Adam ignored me. "I'm sorry, Lily. I really am. Simon and I never intended…"

Lily's hilarity ceased abruptly. "Fuck your good intentions, Adam!" she hissed. "You think that makes it alright? Who are you to fucking decide what's fucking right for me and my baby? What if she'd been yours, hey? Would you let someone stand there making mealy-mouthed excuses about good intentions when they've put you through hell?" She came over to him as she spoke, arm raised as if to strike him. He stood, head bowed, waiting for the blow. It didn't come.

He raised his head to look at her. "I'm sorry, Lily," he said. "I can imagine what you must feel."

"No you can't! You with no kids, forced to abort one kid, trying so hard for another one – you'll never have kids. You can't begin to imagine how I feel."

At the mention of my abortion, Adam's lips tightened. The hands hanging at his sides balled into fists when she mentioned our continued childless state. He looked at me. I shrugged and patted my stomach, implying who cares what poison she spews now that we have our baby well on its way?

Lily caught the gesture. She looked at my middle. Then she looked round the room at each of us and her face underwent a startling change. It was as if a fairy godmother had waved a wand, removing all traces of tears. Her eyes settled on Adam, wide and sparkling with malice, the red mouth twitching at the corners with cold amusement. Adam watched her as one watches a snake, waiting for its forked tongue to flick out. "The only way you can imagine how I feel is if she was yours. I mean, she could so easily have been yours. Couldn't she? How would you feel then? Imagine someone, some good friend with the best intentions let someone kidnap your only child, lets some stranger raise her while you think she's dead!"

I snorted. I'd stuck the same needle into Simon but it could only sting under certain conditions. Lily, in her anxiety to lash out at Adam, seemed to have forgotten that. Viv didn't find it amusing, though. Perhaps she too was thinking of Simon and the possibilities that existed there. "Enough, Lily!" Viv snapped. "We all know how angry you must be with Adam, but spare a thought for Yazz. She's been a good friend to you. She doesn't deserve to hear this rubbish!"

"Hey, I'm doing Yazz a favour." Lily turned innocent eyes on Viv. "He's just like every other bloke, Saint Adam. Him and Simon both. Yazz deserves to know that." Her eyes were back on Adam. He hunched his shoulders, head down, seeming to shrink beneath Lily's gaze as though it was a laser. Lily struck again. "I mean, you all only have my word that Heather is Zac's. I could just have been trying to

181

screw money out of him. She could be Simon's. She could be yours, Adam. Imagine," she mocked him. "Zac raising your only child. All because of your good intentions."

At that, Adam's head snapped up. He reached out and grabbed Lily by the shoulders, thrusting his face into hers. "What?" he asked her. "What is it that you're saying?" The large vein at his temple throbbed. It looked as though he would literally bite her head off. Lily stared back at him, unflinching.

"Come on, Adam," I said, moving forward to pull him away. "You can bear a bit of her bile. I think you're getting off lightly, after what you've told her, if all she hits you with is a bit of fantasy."

Adam ignored me. The muscle in his cheek jumped. Through clenched teeth he asked, "Whose is she?"

I gasped. The room tilted. I reached for a chair and sat down in it. "Let her go, Adam," said Viv, her cool voice coming from far away. She stood beside Adam and Lily, a tiny referee handling two heavyweights squaring up. Viv reached up to lift Adam's hands from Lily's shoulders. "She'll say anything to upset you, now she knows what you did." She dropped his hands and they hung limply at his sides. He stared over Viv's head at Lily. He appeared to be still waiting for her answer. Viv put a hand to Adam's chest and pushed. He took a step back. "Can't say I blame her," said Viv. She looked at me. "But that's all it is, just talk."

Lily sneered. "You're such a spoilsport, Viv. I had him going there for a minute."

Adam fell back, leaning against the wall and covering his face with his hands.

"Look at him," Lily jeered. "Nearly pissed his pants. He can dish it out, heaps of good intentions, but he just can't swallow them down." She looked at me with a triumphant gleam in her eyes. I remembered then, what I'd forgotten the night I'd seen her emerge with Simon from behind his van. I remembered that Adam had been trailing in their wake. He and Simon had gotten into the front of the van and

182

driven off. Neither man had come back into the house. I'd assumed he'd gone to talk to Simon about the error of his ways, and I'd tried to do the same with Lily. And what had she said to me, all that time ago? "Oh, chill out, Yazz. I wasn't fucking Simon. Not tonight, anyway." She'd had that same smirk on her face then, standing close enough for me to smell the sex on her. I'd wanted to smack her. Smack her for lying. Smack her for not caring who she hurt when she herself was hurting. Smack her for not seeing that someone else's misery wouldn't lessen hers. I'd walked away instead.

Now I went to her. Unlike Viv, I had a couple of inches on her. I reached for a handful of her hair and yanked it back to tilt her face to mine. I saw the fear in her eyes as I raised my free hand. It smacked into her cheek. "That," I said, "is for Viv." I swung my hand back and slapped her other cheek. "And that is for me." I slapped the first cheek again, really hard. "And that's for my baby." I let go of her. She sank to the carpet at my feet. "I reckon Adam's already had his share of you. Him and every man of every friend you ever had. Now get out of my house and get out of my life, you ungrateful treacherous bitch. Go and find your kid yourself."

I left the room. I went down to my study. I locked it behind me, took out the blankets I'd offered Viv and Lily and lay huddled in them on the sofa bed. Me and my baby, safe and warm. Safe from the madness upstairs.

CHAPTER EIGHT

Bright light pouring into the room woke me. My face and hands, exposed to the chill beyond the duvets, felt numb. I struggled for a moment to work out what I was doing on the sofa in my study. Then I remembered. I pulled the covers over my head and arms. I couldn't hide from the previous night's events. They played and replayed in my mind. Finally I gave up. Wrapping the duvet around myself, I padded to the kitchenette off the study to see if Simon had left any of the staples I usually kept for guests. The only coffee remaining in the cupboards was instant. There was no milk, of course. I looked at my watch. Seven a.m. Adam should be getting up and leaving for work soon. Meantime, I'd have to make do with black instant coffee. I boiled water and stirred in coffee granules and sugar. I went back to the sofa and waited for the sound of the door upstairs, the footsteps on the staircase, the unlocking and shutting of the street door. I wanted a shower and a change of clothes. The former I could get down here, but not the latter. Eight o'clock came and went. I decided that Adam must have left while I was asleep. I unlocked the door and went upstairs.

Adam was slumped in a chair at the kitchen table, asleep with his head on his arms. He was still wearing the jeans and pullover he'd had on the night before. It looked as though he'd fallen asleep just where he was. He didn't wake when I entered. I went to our bedroom and took fresh clothes from my wardrobe. I took my purse from my dresser. I looked into the kitchen again. Adam hadn't stirred. I left, banging the door as I snatched my coat from the hook on the landing. Behind me, I heard a thud, then a curse. Satisfied, I went back downstairs. I showered, changed my clothes and shoved my purse into my coat pocket. I went out. To keep my mind off the previous night's events, I concentrated on exactly what I was doing – walking along the pavement, crossing the road, choosing a café for breakfast, reading the menu carefully. I made myself eat the toasted bagel with cream cheese, orange juice, fruit salad, coffee that I ordered. When my phone rang, I switched it off. I paid the bill and set off towards the river. The food lay heavy in my stomach. By the time I got to Westminster Bridge, I was too tired and leaden limbed to go along the river towards Tower Bridge as I'd planned on doing. I walked down the steps to the riverside itself and sat on a bench to rest. Finally the cold drove me homeward. So much for this being Spring. It felt as though Winter would never end. At home, I crawled back under the covers of the unmade sofa-bed and slept. When I woke, it was dark outside. The curtains had been drawn. The lamp on my desk was on. I rose and went upstairs. Adam came out of the sitting room to meet me as I opened the front door of our flat.

"Can we talk?" he asked.

"I've got nothing to say." I pushed past him into the sitting room. "I'm going home."

"Home? You've just been!"

"So?" I went over to the fire and depressed the button to light the gas fire. Turning it up high, I sat in front of it on my haunches, holding out my hands to the false flames. "I want to see my mother," I said with my back to him. "I want some peace and quiet. It's been like fucking Piccadilly Circus here recently, people trafficking in and out of my life."

"If that's how you feel, then of course you should go," he said quietly. "Can I ask how long you're going for?" Ignoring the question, I got up and sat in an armchair on one side of the fireplace. Picking up the TV remote, I switched on the early evening news. Adam went over to the TV and switched it off on the set itself. He turned to face me. "I'm asking because if you stay too long they won't let you on the plane to come back." he said. He took the chair on the other side and leaned towards me. "*Are* you coming back?"

"I've no idea," I said, leaning back in my chair and shutting my eyes.

He cleared his throat, but his voice was hoarse when he said "You're saying this may be the end of everything we had? Just like that?"

"No, not just like that, Adam."

"Jesus Christ, Yazz! We've got a baby coming and you're thinking of leaving me over something which happened nearly twenty years ago? A drunken one night stand before we were even going together?"

"Oh please," I said. "I don't want to hear it. I want to go home. I want my mother." To my horror, my voice broke on the last words. I got up hastily and went to our bedroom. I shut the door, reached under the bed and pulled out a suitcase. Then I started to pack – random panties, bras which would probably soon not fit any longer, tracksuit bottoms and big t-shirts. I closed the case and took it out onto the landing.

"That doesn't look like much," Adam said.

"It's enough to tide me over when I get there," I said coldly, squashing the hope I'd heard in his voice, the cautious optimism in his eyes. "I can buy what I need for the rest of the time."

His shoulders slumped. "Won't you give me a chance?" he murmured.

"You've had your chances," I said harshly. "Years and years of them. You had a chance when Simon was here." I left the bag where it was, went downstairs to my study and started hunting online for a ticket home. I'd just made my booking when the phone rang. Without thinking, I picked it up, then wished I hadn't.

"Are you alright?" Viv's voice was barely audible above the background noise of wherever she was phoning from. An announcement about people keeping bags and personal belongings with them told me she was at the airport.

"You spend all day comforting poor little Lily, and now you've got what, five minutes to spare before boarding and you finally squeeze in some demonstration of concern for me?"

She sighed. "I've been trying all day to reach you, Yazz," she said. "I've even been round to your place. I waited. I went away. I went back and waited some more. I was around your place for most of the day. Then I had to get to the airport."

"Well, if you must know, I'm fine, OK? Fine. I'm so fine, in fact, that I'm going home soon."

There was silence on the line for a moment, except for the airport noises. Then she said, "Adam can't be too happy with that."

"He's not."

"I know you're furious with him," she said, "but do try to remember it was a long time ago. It was before your time with him."

"So he says."

"So does she."

"Fuck what *she* says. Anyway, does it matter when the hell it was?"

"You know it does," she said. "You may believe otherwise now, but even when we were young, everyone messed about. These days people pick one another up in pubs and clubs. They wake up the next day not knowing the names of the strangers in their beds. Are you going to be upset at everyone he had sex with before you?"

"Don't be obtuse. This wasn't a stranger. It was Lily. He should have told me. I didn't expect *her* to, but he could have told me. All these years and he never said a word. And there I was, thinking what a saint he was, being so caring about his wife's friend, so patient with all her shit, when all the time it was his ex he was concerned about. I suppose men get brownie points for caring about women after they've done with them, but I feel like a bloody fool."

"Why should he tell you? I thought you disapproved of people talking about their sexual encounters. Didn't you once say that it was like locker room kiss and tell? Have you told him about every person you ever had sex with? When you've calmed down you might to well to remember that he's never fussed about your sex life before him."

"It's hardly the same thing. I've never fucked his best friend. If I had, I'd have told him."

187

"And yet, you never mentioned the episode with Zac to Adam. Not really a friend, I admit, but still within the realm of things one should mention, don't you think? In these circumstances?"

"That is so low. Who the fuck's side are you on?"

I heard her taking a big breath. "I think that pointing out to you that you shouldn't forego a good relationship and the prospect of a happy family, for the sake of something which happened so long ago, qualifies as being on your side." In the background I heard the boarding call for the SAA flight to Cape Town. She paused to listen. "I have to go," she said. "One last thing. Remember, Lily didn't have a relationship with Adam, Yazz. She had ten minutes. You've had nearly twice as many years. Let it go at that." She paused. "When do you arrive in Cape Town? I could fetch you from the airport."

"Don't bother. I'll get my dad to fetch me." I hung up.

I slept in my own bed that night. At least, I tossed and turned in it all night. Adam didn't join me. Just before dawn I finally fell asleep. The smell of coffee woke me. There was a cup on my bedside table. Adam sat at the foot of the bed, his arms resting on his thighs, head dangling down. When I stirred, he straightened up and looked at me. "Would you stay if I asked you to?" He leaned towards me and took my hand. "Would you, if I begged you to please not leave me?"

I pulled my hand free and looked at my watch. It was close to mid-day. "You should be at work."

"I called in sick." He looked sick. His skin was grey and his eyes had dark circles round them. "I can't let you go." His voice caught in his throat. "I can't let our baby go. Please, Yazz. Please, please don't do this." He buried his face in his hands. His shoulders shook.

I wanted to reach out and hold him. I wanted him to hold me. He'd always been my refuge from bad things. With an effort, I reminded myself that he'd caused the bad thing. "I have to go, Adam. I need my home. I need my family."

He muttered," This is your home. I am your family."

188

I rolled to the other side of the bed, away from him. "Don't do this. Not now. I have to get ready. I'll miss my plane." I swung my feet to the floor, feeling around for my slippers. When I left the room, he was still sitting there, so I was surprised to find him shaved and dressed when I came out of the shower.

"Let me at least come to the airport with you," he pleaded.

"Only if you let this thing rest. I can't get my head round it now. I need time. I need space."

"Alright," he said. "Alright, if that's what you want."

The doorbell rang. "That'll be the taxi I ordered," I said. The words of the old song, sung in the sweet, unpretentious voice of a teenager at a fundraising concert for the youth movement, echoed in my ears: "All my bags are packed and I'm ready to go............I'm leaving, on a jet plane.....don't know when I'll be back again...."

He locked the door and followed me downstairs, carrying my bag. We were silent for the entire long ride. At the airport, seeing clusters of families with babies in arms or prams, it finally hit me that that might never be us. Adam looked at them too. He seemed to share my thoughts, because he turned and hugged me fiercely to him. "Travel safely, Yazz," he whispered into my hair. "Come home soon." Then he kissed me as he always did when we met or parted, long and hard, as though to make up for the time without.

I disengaged myself. 'Bye, Adam. I'll phone when I get there."

A long night of watching the trashiest movies I could find on the airlines listings ended when the plane finally landed at Cape Town International. The airport, like many places, had also been shorn of the name of the long dead Afrikaner politician which it had borne before. I allowed myself to be carried along with the crush of passengers headed for passport control. Over the booths indicating where we should queue was a sign: "South African Citizens – Welcome Home". I'd got a real kick out of it when I'd seen it, on my first trip home with Adam after the end of apartheid. He'd teased me because I fell for the

189

corniness of it. I handed my green and gold passport wordlessly to one of the smiling officials sitting under the sign. If I ever went back the other way, I'd produce my maroon passport on those distant shores. The one thing I always had, no matter which direction I went in and which of my two passports I used, was someone of my own to welcome me. This time, there was no-one. Tears stung my eyes. I hadn't called ahead to ask my dad to fetch me, as I'd told Viv I would. My parents would have been full of questions I just hadn't felt I could handle on the phone.

I went outside to a taxi rank. There wasn't much of a queue. Most local people had cars parked at the airport or someone collecting them. Most visitors had hired cars. There was little call for the handful of sedan taxis – as opposed to the minivan township taxis – which plied their trade at the airport. Within minutes I was on the N2. The long grey wall which shut the sprawling squatter camps from the sight of those coming to and from the airport, especially tourists, whizzed by. The driver provided a soundtrack as boring as the wall – what the weather had been, currently was, would be soon, surmising what the English weather was like. My intermittent monosyllabic responses didn't discourage him. He was probably used to his passengers being zombies after long flights. I drifted in and out of sleep, dimly aware when we turned off the motorway and passed by the old "coloured" townships of the Cape Flats, where people had been dumped after being forcibly removed from District Six in central Cape Town in the Sixties and Seventies. I was asleep when we came to the quiet long established upper working class cum middle class "coloured" area of the Cape Flats where my parents lived. I woke with a start when the car stopped and the driver turned off the engine. "Here we are, Miss," he said.

I peered blearily out of the window. We were indeed outside the big old house my dad had inherited from his parents. Grandfather had long ago bought as large a plot of land as he could afford in what had then been nearly the outskirts of the city. What my grandmother had called "daar buite" – literally "out there". It wasn't near the city centre, it wasn't near work or shops or anything anyone wanted to live near back then, but with the Group Areas Act constantly shrinking the areas where black people could live to make room for white residential areas and the expanding business of white South Africa, there wasn't much

190

choice. Eventually more people had come and then the shops and a few factories and industrial areas nearby. Then had come more forced removals from the city centre and elsewhere and the growth of the "notorious" council housing estates of the Cape Flats across the main road, which housed honest hard-working people willy-nilly alongside gangsters, drunks, dope-dealers.

The driver opened the backdoor of the car and helped me out. I stood waiting while he swung my suitcase onto the pavement then paid him and wheeled my suitcase to the driveway where the gates stood open. My dad's car was gone. Despite being retired for years, he still hadn't learnt to lie in. He was already up and out. My mother's car was at the end of the drive. It didn't necessarily mean that she was home but the smell of baking that wafted through the windows told me that. The noise made by the wheels of my suitcase brought her to the front door.

"Who...Yasmin?" she cried out, peeping through the bars of the security gate outside the door. She fiddled with the keys and the locks, babbling in consternation, "Darling, is something wrong? What are you doing here? Has something happened to Adam? Why didn't you call your daddy to fetch you?" She managed to get the out on the stoep by the time I lugged the case up from the drive to the front door.

"Mummy, mummy, stop! Nothing's wrong!" I silenced the clamour of questions which were about to erupt again with a hug and a kiss. "I didn't call daddy because I wanted to surprise you. Adam's fine -more than fine. Nothing's wrong, in fact everything's right, Mummy." I said. I freed myself from her and stepped away so she could see me full-length and patted my bump. "See? I came to tell you in person."

Her eyes went to my belly and remained fixed there for some time. When she raised them to mine, her eyes were filled with tears. "Hey, Ma, if I knew you were going to cry about it, I wouldn't have come!" Wordless for once, she cuffed me playfully then folded me into her arms again. "So where's the grandpa to be?" I asked, ushering her back indoors ahead of me.

"He's out," my mother said. "Visiting one of his girlfriends!" Since he'd retired, Dad had taken to checking up on some of the poor old ladies in the neighbourhood who lived on their own or with grown up children who were at work during the day. He ran errands for them, took them bits of food or cake, broke up the long lonely days with a bit of chat and a few laughs. Some of them were women he'd worked with, retired on a sparse factory pension or an even more meagre state pension. My mother's gifts of food was as welcome to them as my Dad's reminiscences of the good old, bad old, days.

"I don't suppose he's got a mobile phone," I said.

"You mean a cell? Of course he's got one. You never know when a car lets you down. You can't take a chance, getting stuck without a phone…." I didn't point out that they'd managed perfectly well, as had everyone else before the – very recent – advent of mobile phones. She would only have gone on about how the crime rate wasn't as bad then as it was now. "Wait a minute, I'll call him," she said. "When she'd done so, she turned to me, "You'd better go and lie down till he comes. I'll bring you something to eat and a cup of tea. I just baked some bread and cake, so I sent him to take some to old Mrs Abrahams."

"I'll sleep later, but I'll have some bread and tea now, thanks Mum. Just butter on the bread. Don't know when last I had freshly baked."

"Does your mother-in-law know about the baby?" my mother asked with elaborate casualness as she filled the kettle.

"No, Jealousy!" I said. "I'll go over there as soon as I get a cup of tea down my parched throat."

"You need to rest," she said. "The journey must have been terrible, in your condition. What was Adam thinking of, to let you travel alone?"

I rolled my eyes at her. "Don't fuss, Mummy. He couldn't get leave again. Who's going to support this one," I pointed at my stomach. "If he loses his job, taking off too much time?"

"Well, you'd better call him to say you've arrived safely," she sniffed. "I'm sure he must be worried." I nodded, feeling a hint of satisfaction as I saw the touch of tarnish on her beloved son-in-law's halo.

For the next few days, I was swept up by the excitement of the extended family –and friends, neighbours the entire community, it seemed - over the imminent arrival of the long-awaited baby. I became adept at a smiling, even jovial, fielding of questions about Adam's response to my pregnancy, Adam's absence from my side, Adam letting me travel on my own, all the same questions and comments my parents had already made, repeated ad nauseam. I listened patiently to advice and admonitions from old aunts and young cousins, all of whom seemed to have forgotten that I was a woman approaching middle age, not a giddy teenager or a first year bride. Each of course brought gifts. Those who could not bring them, sent them. My mother came into my room one day and stood looking round at the piles of baby garments on the dresser, the larger gifts arrayed around the room. "I know everyone means to be kind, but are these people mad? How are you going to take all this back with you on the plane?"

"Don't worry," I said. "Let them make themselves happy. We can set up a nursery in the spare room for when we visit here with the baby."

"That's a relief," she said, starting to pack things from the dresser into drawers.

"What?" I sat on the bed watching her. "That I'll be leaving a lot of this here? Or that I'll be sure to bring your grandchild to see you?"

"No." She shut a drawer and turned to face me. "It's a relief to hear you say 'we'. I was beginning to think it might just be you and the baby visiting. In fact, I was beginning to think you and the baby might be staying and we might not see Adam again."

I lowered my eyes. "What makes you think that?"

"Well, when I pick up the phone, Adam doesn't sound like his usual self. You don't sound like your usual self when you're on the phone to him. You talk to Adam like he's a stranger asking how you are. You don't sound like happy parents to be talking to each other."

I fiddled with a loose thread on the quilt covering my bed, twisting it round my finger to knot it off. "I suppose it's just the baby, Mummy. I mean, we're over the moon - I'm healthy, the baby's healthy, but there's my age and the birth coming and all that. You know how it is."

She came over and sat next to me, taking my hand. "Of course I know how it is, darling. Sometimes a baby coming can cause a strain between a couple, especially when it's just been the two of you for so long. No matter how much you want the baby, that can happen. And as you say, there are the other worries." She paused, stroking my hand with her free one. "But that doesn't explain the way you've been since you've come here. When there are people around, you're all smiles. Then you sit in your room or out in the garden moping. I'm your mother. I know you. It's more than what you've just told me." She paused again. "I don't mean to pry, tell me to mind my own business if you like, but have you and Adam had a fight?" The denial stuck in my throat. I felt tears welling and squeezed my eyes shut to keep them from rolling down my cheeks. She pulled me against her and then the tears really did flow. When I'd stopped, she took a hanky from her apron pocket and gave it to me. I wiped my eyes and blew my nose. "Come on," she said. "Let's have some tea and we can talk." I followed her to the kitchen and watched her put the kettle on. Only when we were seated across from each other at the big wooden table with a cup in front of each of us, did she ask, "I can't believe I'm thinking this about Adam, but… Is it another woman?"

I sighed. "Sort of."

"Is he, or isn't he?"

"He isn't – now. He had an affair with someone before we started going out together. He never told me about it."

My mother's brow creased into a puzzled frown. "*Before* you got married?"

"Yes."

"Nearly twenty years ago?"

"And you're upset about it *now?*" To my amazement, my mother started to laugh.

"What?" I asked. "My husband has an affair and my mother thinks it's a joke?" I felt my face heat up with anger.

She stopped laughing. "Sorry, sweetheart," she said, reaching across the table to take my hand. "I didn't mean to laugh at you, but it's funny, when you think about it. Here you are, supposed to be the modern woman of the world. You're always telling me I'm old-fashioned, but even I know these things happen all the time. People do have affairs before they get married. Even in my day they did, let alone these days. If you look at the TV, people hardly know each other before they sleep together." She paused. "Look, darling, it's not as though he did it while you were married." When I still didn't answer, she stroked my hand. "You keep telling me that people live together, even have children, without being married. If there's nothing wrong with that, according to you, then how can there be anything wrong with what Adam did?"

"She was a friend of mine!" I said sharply.

"If he left her for you," my mother said carefully. "Why are *you* upset? Isn't *she* the one to be upset?"

"It's not like that. They weren't going out. It was just once…you know…that they uhm…slept together."

She looked at me over the rim of her cup before taking a drink from it and putting it down again. "I think you know you're being silly."

"Excuse me?" I wasn't sure I'd heard her right.

My mother folded her arms across her chest. "You don't leave your husband because of some old girlfriend, especially one that he left for you! It's nonsense. Do you really want to make your baby grow up in a broken home for that?" She shook her head. "I'm just glad Adam is being so patient and understanding."

I stared at her. "*Adam*'s being patient and understanding!" I got up and pushed back my chair. "I should have known you'd take his side. You think the sun shines out of his backside. Well, I'm telling you Mum,

195

he's not the saint you think he is!" I stomped to my room and slammed the door. I flung myself on the bed. My mother didn't come after me. She hadn't when I was a teenager and went off in a fit of rage. The idea was to leave me alone to reflect on the event which had led to the tantrum and work out the rights and wrongs of it. She hadn't changed her policy.

It was my father who tapped on my door after half an hour to ask, "Are you alright, Cookie?" I had to smile. He hadn't changed either. "I'm fine Daddy. Come on in." He popped his head, now topped by steel grey hair rather than the salt and pepper I remembered from my youth, round the door, holding it ajar without stepping inside. "You sure?" I swung my legs to the floor and sat on the edge of my bed as he came into the room. He bent down to kiss my cheek. I reached up an arm and put it round him, inhaling the smell of cigarettes and cut grass that came from mowing the lawn, then rewarding himself with a fag. "Mummy's only trying to help, you know. We've been worried about you." He paused and added slowly. "And Adam, the baby coming…"

"Sorry Daddy. Didn't mean to upset you people." I got to my feet. "I'd better go and apologize to Mum." He followed me to the kitchen, where my mum was cutting up vegetables for soup. As he went past her, he patted her on her bottom. My mother blushed, dropped the knife and swiped at him in pretended annoyance. He deftly side-stepped and managed to somehow plant a peck on her cheek. My mother giggled like a girl.

"You two!" I chided. "Behave!" My dad went on out into the front garden, laughing like a naughty schoolboy.

My mum resumed her task. "That man!" she said. "I'll divorce him one day, see if I don't!" My mother had been threatening to divorce my father on the grounds of bottom patting, sneaky kissing and the like, ever since I could remember. I felt a lump in my throat. How I longed for what they had. I went and put my arms around her, propping my chin on her shoulder. "Sorry, Mum. I didn't mean to shout at you earlier. It's not your fault."

"It's *nobody's* fault, darling," she kissed my cheek. "Women get a bit odd at this time. That's why you're taking everything the wrong way."

196

She let me go and picked up her knife again. "It's that thing, what do they call it?"

"Hormones? I suppose so," I said, nibbling at a carrot. "Can I borrow your car, please Mum? I feel like going out for a bit."

"Where to?"

"Just for a walk on the beach," I said, reaching for her car keys on a cup hook in the dresser. "I'll walk on the Promenade, where there are loads of people, all willing to take care of a pregnant woman, should she have any problems." I put my arm around her and gave her a squeeze. "Good thing I like the beach, else I'd be sick of the same walk all the time. Don't know when last I went to Blouberg or Newlands or up the mountain."

My mother gave me a look. "Still, be careful. And don't be late for supper."

I looked at my watch. "Don't you mean lunch? It's mid-morning!"

"Once you're out, you forget the time!" Another refrain from my youth.

I'd backed the car to the end of the driveway when Viv's car drew up at the pavement. She'd called a couple of times since I'd come to Cape Town. I'd asked my mother to say I wasn't in or that I was tired and resting. "Down!" Viv commanded the two huge Alsatian dogs which rose up from the back seat of her car and started nosing at the slightly open window of the rear door closest to the pavement. The dogs lay back down. Viv got out and came round her car to me.

"You should have called," I said. "As you can see, I'm on my way out."

"I've called," she pointed out. "You don't take my calls. I thought it would be harder for you to refuse to speak to me if I simply dropped in." She leaned her elbows on my car's window frame. "You weren't very happy with me the last time we spoke. You turned down my offer of a lift from the airport. I assumed you were still angry with me. Is

197

that so, or is it just that you're enjoying being cosseted in the bosom of the family?"

"The cosseting thing, I suppose," I said. "You know how it goes."

"I had an idea that the bosom might become a trifle stifling," she said. "Which is why I risked having my head bitten off by coming to see you."

"Speaking of biting," I said, "When did you get the hounds? I thought you weren't going to get more nasty beasts after Sheba died."

"They are *not* nasty beasts," she said. "They are well-trained guard dogs. Their owner was a friend of mine. When he emigrated he didn't know what to do with them, so I adopted them." She turned and waved affectionately at the dogs. They went into a frenzy. "Would you like to accompany us on a walk? Perhaps we could have some of the world's second best chocolate cake afterwards?"

"Why not the best?"

"You'd have to wait for me to make it," she smiled. "And the dogs need a greater leg stretch than my yard can provide."

"Self-praise is no recommendation!" I made a rude noise. "A walk sounds great. Exactly what I was planning to do, in fact." She stepped back as I opened the car door. I used the door to lever myself to my feet. "However," I said. "Something tells me you didn't drive all the way out here just to relieve my boredom. What's the hidden agenda?"

"Does there have to be one?"

"Oh, yes, given what happened the last time we saw each other." I raised both eyebrows at her, waiting.

"You can be so suspicious, Yazz!"

"And you can be so devious, Viv!" I mimicked her tone. "Mainly where Lily's concerned. I'm telling you straight, if it's her you want to talk about, you might as well get back in your car and take your doggies for a wander by yourself. Ditto if it's Adam's case you've come to plead."

She sighed. "In that case, I'll just pop inside and say hello to your parents."

I glared at her back as she sauntered up the path which led from the driveway to the stoep. I didn't feel like a walk on my own, now she'd dangled the prospect of her company before me. If she'd agree to a conversational exclusion zone, we could have a great time out. All indications were that she wouldn't. I got out, locked the car and trudged into the house. Viv was sitting at the kitchen table, nibbling a *koeksister* from the plate my mother'd put in front of her. My mum had abandoned her vegetable peeling to put the kettle on. The conversation was already flowing. It looked like a full-scale visit had started. So much for popping in. "I thought your dogs needed walking!" I snapped at Viv. "They're probably boiling to death and going stir-crazy while you're here stuffing your face!"

"Then go and turn the windows of Viv's car down or let the dogs play in the yard," my mum said. She nodded in my direction and shook her head towards Viv, as though to apologize for my backwardness. Viv winked conspiratorially at my mother. They hadn't seen each other in years, but it could have been yesterday that Viv had last sat in that spot, eating cake, drinking tea, watching my mother cook, discussing recipes, cooking and baking techniques – and of course, me.

Years ago, I'd have teased Viv, "No wonder my mother doesn't moan when I sleep out at your place. You're like an old woman." Now I said resentfully, "They'll mess up the yard. Daddy's just cleaned the place."

My mother opened her mouth to respond but Viv silenced her with a wave of her hand. "Yazz is right, Mrs Patel." She got to her feet. "They do need a long walk. And they *will* mess up your yard. I won't have that cup of tea today, if you don't mind. I'll invite myself some other time?"

"You can have it when you bring Yasmin home." My mother stood, brushing her hands down the front of her apron. "And stay for supper if you like. There's plenty of food –"

"I'm not going with Viv," I said. "I don't feel like going out."

"Nonsense! A minute ago you were desperate for a walk and fresh air." My mother put her hands on her hips and clicked her tongue at me. "And now you've got company and Viv's got the dogs so I won't be worried about you driving and then walking somewhere alone – and you don't want to go!"

Viv's mouth quirked at my mother's scolding tone. "Oh, don't force her, Mrs Patel." She kissed my mother's cheek. "Give my regards to Mr. Patel."

"You go with Viv," my mother insisted. "Enjoy yourself with your friends before that baby comes. You won't have time after that, believe me. Besides, a walk will do you good, instead of sitting around the house all day. We won't have this nice weather much longer."

I gave up. "OK, OK. I'm going." I bent and kissed her. She reached up a hand to tuck some stray hair behind my ear.

I followed Viv to her car, slipped into the passenger seat and belted myself in. Then I reached into the glove compartment and took out a stack of CD's. When Viv started up the car, I put on Nina Simone Sings The Blues and lay my head back against the seat. For a while there was only the music and the snuffling of the dogs to be heard in the car. I drifted into a half-sleep on the music and the movement of the car. Whatever Viv wanted to talk about, she'd have to wait until I was good and ready.

Viv's voice jerked me awake, though it didn't rise much above the music. "Please don't sulk, Yazz. You didn't have to come just because your mother told you to. You're a grown woman. If you didn't want to come along, all you had to do was say so."

"And get more than the earful I already got?" I muttered without opening my eyes. "No thanks. You don't know how long my mother can keep a good moan going."

"Your mum seems well. She and your father must be delighted about the baby."

"Mmm." My eyes were still shut. "There I was, enjoying royal status and you had to get my head chopped off."

She laughed. "Sorry about that." Silence for another little while. I drifted again. "Presumably you haven't told them about your fight with Adam? Or is your mother just very good at hiding her concern for you?"

This time I opened my eyes. "Can't we just make aimless polite conversation? The weather's an ideal topic, since we're going for a walk. I mean, isn't the weather great for this time of year? If you'd rather not do aimless and polite, we could adapt the topic into a political discussion on global warming."

"I'll be aimless and polite after you've answered my question." She overtook the lorry in front of us and steered the car smoothly onto the off-ramp leading to the motorway. I put my head back again, humming along to the music.

She reached over and turned it off.

"Jesus fucking Christ!" I said. "That's my favourite track!" She gave me a quick sharp sideways glance. I sighed loudly. "If you must know, I *have* told my mother, OK?"

"Good," Viv said, leaning forward to turn the player back on.

"Aren't you going to ask me what she said?"

"What did she say?"

"My mother said that men will be boys, and being boys, they will be led by their dicks. According to my mother, that's the way it always

201

was, that's the way it will always be. Once my hormones stop messing about and I can see reason, I'll accept this wisdom. I'll kiss and make up with Adam and all will be right with the world." She swung the car neatly around a taxi which had stopped for passengers without bothering to indicate or pull to the side of the road. "I paraphrase, of course. 'Dick' in my mother's lexicon is the name of many of my cousins."

She laughed. "Your mother is a wise woman. I have my doubts about her reasoning, but I can't fault her conclusion."

"I thought you might. Well, now you're through being nosy, unless there's something else on your hidden agenda, let's talk about you. What have you been up to since you got home? How's work, how's play?"

"Work's fine. I haven't had much time for play lately, as you can imagine. "

I could imagine alright. How could she play when she had Lily in that state? Part of me was curious to find out what had happened after they left us, what the state of affairs was in relation to Heather. Just a tiny part though. Most of me just couldn't be bothered. "Poor you!" I genuinely felt sorry for her. It wasn't easy bearing the burden of Lily, even for someone as practiced at it as Viv.

"And how's Simon? Recovered from me *kakking* on him??

"Simon's fine too, though he's a bit concerned about you and Adam."

"*Now* he's concerned?" I ejected the Nina Simone and rifled through the CD's for something else to listen to. "The time for Simon to be concerned about me and Adam was long ago. I told him that in London. And do you know what he said?" Viv didn't answer. We were on De Waal Drive now. She concentrated on steering the car round its graceful curves. A hunk of mountain hung above us. Below us the city lay spread out with the bay beyond it. "Not guilty by reason of youth, ignorance and eagerness to wage the struggle regardless of what personal sacrifices had to be made. Not to mention the fact that we were complicit in causing our own problems. We joined the Party and we stayed in it because we wanted to be an active part of the struggle. We were convinced that it offered the only way to resolve the struggle. We never objected to anything it did, certainly not to Simon's knowledge. At the end of the day, why didn't we just buck the Party or leave it if we didn't like what it did. And by the way, *how* could we not like what it did when we were *part* of it? After all, the party wasn't some kind of monolith, it was a collection of individuals, including yours truly. Ergo, whatever *kak* happened to us was our own fault. Jesus! That bloody man. How can anyone that bright be so dim?"

"Then you should be pleased to know that you've turned on all his lights. What you said to him in London had a great impact on Simon. He felt even more responsible when I told him what happened subsequently. Simon really is concerned about you and Adam."

"So concerned he sent you instead of coming himself?" She shrugged. "Well, I don't know about Adam, but you can tell Simon *I'm* fine. Kakking on Simon really warmed the cockles of my heart. I felt even better after making him grovel for forgiveness and understanding. But if he thinks he needs more penance, he can come and lick my arse in person."

She shuddered. "I hope you wash your nether regions first!"

I found an old Gill Scott-Heron collection and put it in the player. "You and Simon bought me that on an LP for my 21st," I said. "Geez – what a crazy *jol* we had!"

"I remember." Viv said quietly. She gave me a sideways glance without turning her head. "I'm glad to see some memories of the old days can make you smile."

I turned the volume up. Then I leaned against the window and listened to *The Revolution Will Not Be Televised* while Viv brought us off the mountain and across dirty old Woodstock with its derelict buildings and air of decay and decrepitude, onto the N2. I'd thought she was headed for the old Docklands, now renamed The Waterfront, the first of the sprawling new shopping and entertainment complexes which had sprung up like boils on Cape Town's beautiful bum. Instead, she swung the car onto the motorway in the opposite direction.

When the track ended, I turned the volume back down and waited. There had to be more to come from her. Yes, she and Simon were my and Adam's best friends from the old days. I was sure that they were concerned about me and Adam, but I knew her well enough to know that wasn't the sole reason she was here. Viv said nothing. We passed the latest shopping mall, an even more vast monstrosity than the Waterfront, known as Century City. The silence remained unbroken. Viv left the motorway and slowed to a gentle cruise down the long road that led to Bloubergstrand. I glanced at her. Still, she kept her eyes on the road. Her face was a mask of concentration, as though we were in peak hour traffic, not cruising amongst a trickle of cars on the road to the beach on a weekday in Autumn.

I looked out the window. All that could be seen for mile after mile alongside the road was housing and more housing. On the other side of the road, the housing complexes were interspersed with shops, cafes and fast food places. Once one could see the lagoon and the sea from the road. A sheltered housing complex for well-heeled white retirees had been built on the shores of the lagoon just before I left to live in London, obscuring the view of the lagoon, the dunes and the sea beyond it. The "development" of the area had galloped along since then. The sea finally came into unbroken view. I turned down the window. The dogs, alerted by the smell and sensing that they were close to being released, were instantly aroused from the deep slumber they'd appeared to be in. They stood on the back seat, each with its nose stuck to one of the windows at the back.

Viv looked in her rear-view mirror. "Sit!" she commanded. They sat down obediently, one with his head on my shoulder, the other's head on Viv's shoulder, tongues lolling.

"Get this bloody animal off me!" I said, pushing at the dog dribbling down my front. "What do you train them to do – dribble strangers to death?"

"He's only being affectionate," she reached back to stroke the muzzle on her shoulder. She pulled into one of the beach parking areas, over the road from a complex of shops and restaurants. The minute she switched off the car, there was an explosion of paws, jaws, ears and noses, accompanied by deafening barking, as the dogs whirled about on the back seat with excitement. Viv got out of the car and opened the back door. The dogs scrambled out. The next minute they were across the car park and onto the dunes.

"Well, don't expect me to go chasing after them!" I said as I levered myself out of the car. I seemed to have grown alarmingly heavy since I'd come home. I wondered how much of it was baby and how much of it was just plain old fat.

"They'll be back when they've worked off their excess energy." Viv made no move to go after the dogs.

I stood leaning against the car bonnet while she busied herself gathering dog paraphernalia from the boot. Across the water I could see Table Mountain. This was the only convenient angle from which you could see the familiar table shape giving the famous mountain its name. Otherwise, you'd have to be out in the Bay on a boat or on the notorious Robben Island – Mandela's long time prison - to see the flat table top front-on. Today the mountain was covered with a cloth of clouds. It looked lovely, but with the wind from that direction, I knew that my mother's prediction of a pending change in the weather was probably correct. Soon the Cape of Good Hope would be the Cape of Storms. I could just about see the outline of the Island. These days it was a famous jailhouse monument, favourite haunt of tourists. It had also been restored to one of its earlier roles as a sanctuary for wildlife. Viv locked the car and came to join me. She had a plastic carrier bag in her hand containing bowls, balls, leashes, a water bottle. "Looking at the Island?"

"Just thinking what changes the place has undergone. It's been what - wildlife sanctuary, leper colony, political prison, now back to being wildlife sanctuary, plus tourist attraction and world heritage site? Much like its last inhabitants - paupers, freedom fighters, unionists, political prisoners to trillionnaires, ministers of state, bosses......"

She shrugged. "Places change, people move on."

"Except me?" I asked.

"I just wish," she said. "That you'd look over there and say something positive. Take pride in the fact that we contributed hugely towards the downfall of apartheid, though we were David up against Goliath. 'We' includes you. Take some of the credit for what we achieved – and take at least your fair share of the responsibility for the mistakes we made. Then move on. You're having a child. Don't let the rest of your life, the life you will share with her, be dogged by this bitterness you've allowed to build. The past is past. Bury it."

"There I was, thinking you loved me just the way I am. You know, like the song says."

She turned from the view and looked at me. "I do," she said. "Love you, that is." She pushed herself away from the bonnet with her bum and set off in the direction the dogs had taken. "So does Simon," she tossed over her shoulder. "And Adam, most of all."

I stared after her, trying to pick my jaw up from the ground. Sentimental statements were not what I was used to from Viv. Then again, I asked myself as I strode after her, did friends need to state how they felt about each other? She waited for me when she reached the path running alongside the low dunes above the beach. The wind tugged at the voluminous brown shorts that came down to her knees. It moulded her equally large-shirt against her ample breasts, made her short hair stand up around her head. We stood looking at each other for a moment. Then she turned and started slowly along the path. I trudged after her, feeling the loose gravel slip and slide beneath my feet.

"Hey," I said, tugging at her arm when I caught up with her. "Thanks for the declaration of love and all that, but I'm not the fucking TRC, OK? I don't just say forgive and forget and it's done." A couple of quad bikers roared down the dunes ahead of us, doing their best to destroy the delicate ecosystem of the dunes. I let their noise and fumes pass before I continued. "If you must know, when I kicked Simon's arse, it was like kicking the Party. He being on the CC and all that. It was cathartic. It's out of my system. I call that moving on." Sand blew off the dunes, stinging my legs through the thin trousers I wore under what my mother called a "maternity top". I sat down at the top of some wooden steps leading between the dunes to the beach and took off my sandals. Holding onto the rickety rail, we made our way down the harder sand of the beach. Viv kicked off her flip-flops and put it in the bag with the dog stuff. We walked closer to the water.

Viv raised her free hand up to shield her eyes and looked around. "Where are those dogs?" I looked about too. A number of surfers were taking advantage of the wind to ride the waves. In the distant sky, a colourful kite floated above a figure skimming across the water. No dogs. Viv put her fingers in her mouth and emitted a piercing whistle. The dogs came charging from behind some shrubs on the dunes further along, raced along the beach and skidded to a halt in front of us.

"You were going to raise a 'but'," I said as I watched her pat and scold the dogs.

"No but," she said. "It's a 'because'." She took the dogs' bowls and the bottle of water from her plastic bag and poured water for the dogs. They lapped furiously, spilling as much as they seemed to drink, before again taking off. Viv didn't try to stop them. She picked up the bowls, shook out the last of the water and returned them and the bottle to the carrier bag. "I'm glad to hear you've moved on, because I've a favour to ask you."

"The hidden agenda surfaces." I muttered, turning to walk in the direction the dogs had taken. She fell in beside me. "If the favour's to do with Lily, there's a limit to how far and how fast I can move on, you know."

"I thought once movement started the momentum would carry you along."

I strode along easily on the damp sand packed hard by the last high water, but my pace made her puff. I slowed slightly. Further along, the dogs frolicked in the shallows, chasing the remnants of surf fading back into the ocean, then running away when threatened by incoming swells. "Not as far as kissing and making up with her."

"I don't expect that."

"So what is it she wants that she's too much of a coward to come and ask me herself?"

"She hasn't sent me to ask you for anything," Viv said. "In fact, I've not heard from Lily since we arrived back in Cape Town. I'm really worried about her."

"What? That she's done herself in?" I snorted. "Not likely. She's probably just hiding somewhere, planning how to find and kill Zac and take Heather back. That's what I'd do in her place."

She stopped and faced me, frowning. "Lily's not at home. She doesn't answer calls or email. The other day I let myself into her house with my key. Her luggage from the trip hasn't been unpacked. Her passport is lying on the kitchen table, so she hasn't gone in pursuit of Heather......" She broke off. "Yazz, when we were in London, before you had the fight with her, you said that you'd let her know if Mel contacted you."

"She hasn't."

"Will you tell me when she does?"

"Why?" I dug one foot into the sand to steady myself and used the other to draw a doodle. "You've just said Lily's disappeared."

"I thought that Lily may be picking up my messages, even if she's not responding. If I leave her a message saying that Mel has contacted you, that you know where Heather is and you've told me, Lily will get in touch with me."

"Well, as I said, there's no news." I turned and continued walking, slowly so she could keep up.

"Have you tried contacting Mel?"

"I meant what I said to Lily in London. She can bloody well sort out this mess herself. If you want to stay involved, that's your business, but I'm out, OK?"

"I'm not asking you to do this for Lily, Yazz. I'm asking you to do it for me. *I'm* concerned about her. I'd like to know that she's alright,

208

because, like you, she's my friend. I don't enjoy seeing friends in trouble and not helping. You'd be doing this for me. You'd be giving me peace of mind, if you'd like to put it that way."

"What about my peace of mind? I'm your friend as much as Lily is but you can upset me to help her? That's alright, is it?"

"Don't be childish, Yazz. This isn't a competition for attention. Unlike you, Lily has no family. She has no-one but me. I was angry with her after her behaviour in London - towards you, as it happens - so now she won't come to me for help. I'd like to restore her confidence in me. I'd like to let her know that someone cares about her. I need something concrete to offer her, such as establishing contact with Mel."

"What if she's not checking her email or her phone messages? Listen, I haven't checked email since I left London. I switched off the mobile I used there and I think our home phone's answer machine's been too full for messages for a while now. I'm totally free of my normal life – only Adam knows how to contact me. People do go awol sometimes. Lily did, for years."

"She stayed in touch with me, as well you know."

"OK. You want to draw Lily out of the woodwork. Then what? You tell Lily where Mel and Heather are and Lily rushes over there and causes chaos in Mel and Heather's lives?"

Viv stopped. "Let's sit here a while. It's out of the wind." We'd come to a bend on the long beach, where some rocks provided shelter from the wind. She dropped down and sat hugging her knees, looking at the sand. Reluctant to get down and then have to haul myself up again, I leaned against the rocks, with my toes curled into the sand, looking out to sea. Viv said, "I have no intention of allowing Lily to do what you envisage. I merely want to get her to come to me so that I can sit her down and talk through with her what her next steps should be."

"And what do you think those are?"

"To meet with Mel and discuss things with her."

"And what makes you think Mel would agree to meet with Lily?"

She sat for a moment, doodling in the sand with a bit of dried up seaweed. "I know it's a lot to ask, but I thought that perhaps you could persuade her."

"And why would I want to do that?" I lifted a foot free of the sand, feeling it slide through my toes. Then I lifted the other free and dug them both in again. "I meant it when I'd told Lily to fuck off and sort out her own problems, Viv. You don't seem to get that."

"Oh, I understand, Yazz. I understand completely that you've finished with Lily. Whether, how and when Lily is reunited with Heather doesn't, however, concern Lily alone. Have you forgotten the other key players in this life drama? Mel and Heather?" I said nothing. She sighed.

Suddenly the dogs caught my attention. They'd been playing some way down from us. Now the dogs dashed away from the water to avoid a sudden surge. In their rush they knocked over a person who'd been standing in the shallows, looking out to sea. "Shit! Looks like your dogs are drowning someone." I pointed. The man was thrashing about wildly, trying to get to his feet. The dogs were nosing at him, barking and waving their tails excitedly, no doubt thinking it a great game.

Viv's gaze followed my finger. "Oh no!" She raised her hand to her mouth to whistle to the dogs. The dogs ignored her. She started to waddle hastily towards the trio. The man was in no danger in the shallows. He didn't need my help with Viv about to get in and rescue him. I'd do nobody any good, adding to the mêlée and getting wet for nothing, so I sat on the sand where Viv had dropped her plastic bag and flip-flops. As I watched, Viv managed to shoo the dogs off the man. The dogs emerged from the water, shaking themselves as she stepped into the sea and reached down to help their victim to his feet. Just as she'd got him up, another big wave knocked him back on his bottom. Viv, still holding onto his hand, was pulled on top of him. I was convulsed with laughter. It was only when they finally struggled free of the water and each other and stood shaking themselves like two more wet dogs, that I finally recognized the man.

"Amos!" I called out. With an effort, I managed to get to my feet. I'd forgotten that it was becoming increasingly hard to get up once I was down. The pair staggered towards me, burdened by the wind and water. "Amos!" I said again. "My god! What are you doing here?"

Amos sneezed, letting go of Viv to cup his face between his hands. Then he wiped his hands on his wet pants and rubbed at his eyes with both hands to clear them. He swung his head from side to side, peering at me. "Yazz? Is it you?"

"Of course it's me, Amos! Where the hell's your glasses? Don't tell me it's gone in the drink!"

"No, I-" he patted the breast pocket of his shirt then his back pocket, frowning. Then he smiled. "I left it in the car," he said. "Yes, it's in the car." He turned to Viv, who was standing with her arms wrapped around herself for warmth, her hair plastered to her face. "Sorry. I didn't mean to get you wet."

"You were only returning the favour," I said. "It was her dogs that knocked you down."

"Yazz," Viv said through chattering teeth. "I'd rather not be apportioning blame while we get pneumonia if that condition can be avoided. Go to my car, if you don't mind." She fumbled with the buttons of one of the pockets of her shorts for the keys. Her hands were too cold and wet to be any good. "There are some towels and clothes of mine and Simon's in my boot. Could you go ahead and get it?" I unbuttoned her pocket, took out the keys and told them to sit in the sun on the wall near the toilet block, while I fetched dry things. When Amos and Viv had gone off towards the beach toilets to change, I went across the road to a takeaway café and bought three coffees. The girl who served me put them in a shallow a cardboard box in lieu of a tray. I gathered up plenty of sugar and headed back to the car park. Viv sat waiting for me in the car. She took her cup, sipped, made a face and helped herself to sugar and a stirrer from my makeshift tray. Amos emerged from the men's side of the toilet block some time later.

211

It was a good thing Simon favoured baggy clothes. They just about made it over Amos's stomach and backside.

I handed him a cup of coffee. "I thought you'd left the country," I said as he lifted the lid of his coffee cup and, like Viv, laced it heavily with sugar.

"I came home to sort some things out," he said. "Tomorrow I'm off again." He turned to Viv, his eyes anxious. "How will I get Simon's stuff back to you?" Viv waved a dismissive hand. Amos gulped his coffee down quickly. "I must go," he said. "I was just leaving when-" He nodded vaguely in the direction of the dogs, who were now lying next to the car, out of the wind. Amos didn't make a move to go though. He shifted his feet about, crushed the styrofoam cup in his hands, turned red, cleared his throat and finally asked. "I wonder, Yazz, would you mind helping me find my car? I think I left it in the next car park."

"Jesus, Amos," I said. "If you're that short-sighted, you shouldn't be driving and you need a guide dog." Amos turned a deeper shade of red. "I'll walk you to your car, OK? But first you and I have a bit of catching up to do. I would have updated you earlier, if I'd known you were back in civilization." Amos tossed a quick glance in Viv's direction, then turned to me with a question in his eyes. If he had gone any redder, Amos would have combusted.

"It's OK," I reassured him. "Viv knows all about that letter of Sandy's. A whole helluva lot's happened since you gave it to me. Talk about bloody Pandora's Box! Come on. We'll both walk you to your car while I fill you in." Viv locked her car. We walked along the pavement, one of us on each side of Amos while I informed him of the salient facts. "So basically, Sandy was right. Heather's alive. Lily knows about Heather. Zac and his wife know that she knows. I'm handing over the final sorting out to Viv because," I patted my stomach. "of this."

Amos's eyes widened. "Oh. Are you-? Really? You're going to-"

"What? You thought I was just fat? No, Amos, I am having a baby. And yes, I'm a bit old, so I don't feeling like stressing myself if I can

212

help it, which is why I've pulled Viv in. She's better at this stuff than I am anyway. I know you said Sandy wanted me to do it, but she would have understood that, under the circumstances, I've had to delegate. I've in any case delegated it to the very person Sandy herself would have chosen, if she'd had time to think it through." We were at his car now. He patted his pockets for his keys much as he had for his glasses. "If you're looking for your keys, Amos," I said. "I think you're more likely to find them in your own clothes. He nodded, lay the bundle he'd been carrying under his arm on the bonnet of his car and pulled from his jeans a huge bunch of keys. I was amazed that it could fit into his pocket. He started sorting through the keys. "Here, let me," I said. I inserted what looked like the right car key into the door and unlocked the car. Amos reached into the glove compartment and took out his glasses.

When he'd settled them on his nose, he turned to both of us. "I'm on email," he said, as though it was something I hadn't considered. Which of course, I hadn't. I'd just assumed that wherever he'd gone, he would be uncontactable by modern means of communication. "Everywhere has internet and email these days you know." He knelt on the seat and popped the glove compartment again. This time he extracted a slip of paper and a pen. He scribbled an email address on it. He looked from one to the other of us uncertainly, the piece of paper wavering in the middle between me and Viv. Then he held it out to me. "Good-bye Yazz. Let me know when it's all sorted out." His eyes flicked to Viv. "Thanks Viv." He squeezed behind the wheel of his car and wound the window down. He frowned at me. "You're sure it will be alright?"

I leaned into the window and kissed him. "'Course I am, Amos. And I will let you know when it's all settled. Travel safely." Watching him drive off, I shivered suddenly. The intermittent clouds sent scudding overhead by the wind had piled up sufficiently to pose a threat to the sunshine. Autumn seemed to have arrived at last. I turned to Viv. "That chocolate cake we came for? Can we do it another time? I'm feeling a bit bushed. Plus it's getting chilly suddenly." She looked at me with a worried frown but I waved away her concern before she could mouth it. "It's nothing. We pregnant women just need a bit of a nap in the afternoons, that's all. I'll be right as rain after half an hour's kip."

We'd reached her car. I sank into the passenger seat, while Viv put the carrier bag of dog things in the boot with her wet stuff. She roused the dogs and leashed them, tying the leashes to the car doors as she brushed the dogs down. I lay my head against the window, closing my eyes, listening to her soothing murmurings to them. When Viv finally got into the car, she reached over me and tugged at my seatbelt. She adjusted it and clicked it into place. Then she tied her own, started up the car and drove in silence. She was probably quiet so that I could rest. I was quiet because I really was tired and also because of the encounter with Amos. Meeting him had reminded me of how and why I'd got involved in this business in the first place. It had been for Sandy's sake. She'd died confident that, if Lily had been wronged, I would set that wrong to rights. I had blithely told Amos that I'd delegated that task to Viv, but I hadn't equipped her to deal with it.

I opened my eyes, wrestled my bumbag free and took out my purse. "Here," I extracted Mel's card from my purse and put it on the dashboard. "All Mel's contact details. Do with it what you will." She didn't ask what had changed my mind. She didn't thank me. The look she gave me, warm and comforting, was enough. I settled into the seat and joined the dogs in slumberland.

CHAPTER NINE

"Hey, Sleeping Beauty!" Viv woke me with a hand on my shoulder. "We're here."

I rubbed my eyes, yawning. "Looks like there's nobody home," Viv said.

"Can't be," I looked at the front door. The security door was locked across it. The blinds were half drawn. No cars stood on the driveway. "Old girl made me promise to be home for supper. She never mentioned they were going out. She'd have told me to take keys." I got out of the car. "Wait here. Let me check around the back." My mother sometimes pulled her car into the garage and locked up the front of the house if she was working round the back or sneaking a nap. As I put my hand on the garden gate, someone called my name, followed by a "Cooee!" I turned towards the sound.

My parents' neighbour – a woman I called Aunty Ida because I'd grown up in front of her - was waving from her stoep. "They had to go out," she called. "Wait there!" She hurried indoors. There was the sound of a child crying and Aunty Ida scolding. She came back out with one of the many grandchildren she cared for whilst the child's parents worked, straddled on her hip. One of her arms cradled the child's bottom, the other held out the keys to me. "Your mummy couldn't reach you on your cell," Aunty Ida said to me, "So she asked me to keep an eye out for you. She left you a note on the table." I remembered then that I'd put my mobile into the glove compartment of my mother's car, which I'd intended to go out in before Viv came along. I thanked the woman and stroked the child's cheek. We exchanged a few pleasantries. I declined the usual offer of tea, pointing to Viv waiting for me. If I'd said I was tired and needed a rest, she'd have offered to come and make the tea for me and tuck me up, despite probably having a dozen chores.

I waved the keys in Viv's direction and called out, "Safe. No probs!" Instead of hooting to show she'd heard and then driving off, she pulled the car into the driveway. I unlocked and went in. My parents' note

215

explained that a cousin had had an accident. He wasn't hurt, but badly shaken. They'd gone to offer comfort and company. The food was cooked, so why didn't Viv and I enjoy it by ourselves since they were likely to eat at my cousin's? "You want to stay for supper?" I showed the note to Viv. "You're invited." I lifted the lid of a pot. "Mum probably took the soup with her. This looks like chicken curry." I lifted another lid. "Basmati rice. Probably salad in the fridge." I replaced the lid and stifled another yawn.

"I've got to see to the dogs," Viv said. "Then I'm going to the Kubrick retrospective at the Peninsula Film Soc."

"PFS? God, does that still exist?"

"Would you like to come with me? You could stay overnight at my place."

"My mother will throw a blue fit," I said. "But what the hell. Get some tupperwares out of the cupboard and dish up some food for us to take along while I pack a toothbrush and knickers." I suited action to words. By the time she'd packed up the food, I was ready with the overnight bag I'd used as hand luggage. "Let's go. I'll just give them a call." I looked up my cousin's phone number. I told her not to call my mother to the phone but simply tell her that I was going out and staying over with Viv. There was bound to be at least one obstetrician and midwife where we were going, not that I was likely to need either for some time. I hung up before my cousin could draw breath.

The movie on offer that night was "2001: A Space Odyssey". Viv had first taken me and Lily to see it during freshers' week, decades ago. We'd both fallen in love with the movie. Viv and I stayed for a bit of the discussion afterwards, then headed back to her place.

Viv went to her computer as soon as we were in. It was as if memories stirred by the movie were urging her on to find Lily. "Here," I said when I saw the disappointment on her face as she turned to me after scanning her inbox. "Let me." Viv raised her eyebrows, but she rolled her chair back and got up. I took her place. "I know I said you should handle this affair from now on," I said as I logged her off and logged myself on. "But sending an email to Mel can't hurt me. Whatever

216

damage this whole affair was going to do to me, it's done." I stared at my inbox. "Well, check this out!" There was a message from Mel. It had been sent and re-sent half a dozen times. In fact it had been sent daily since I'd left London, which was the last time I'd checked my email. I clicked to open the message and read: "I need to speak to you. Please get in touch."

"The good lord has heard your prayers, Viv. Mel wants to see me."

Reading over my shoulder, Viv murmured, her brow creased in a heavy frown. "Quite desperately, it appears. That email's been sent a few times." She straightened up.

"She probably tried to call as well. She doesn't have the number of the pay as you go I've been using since I got here." I paused. "Why do you think Mel wants to speak to me so urgently? You reckon Lily's caught up with them?"

"I doubt it, Yazz. She'd have said. I told you earlier. The reason why I'm worried about Lily is that all her luggage and her passport are at her place. She must still be in South Africa. Unless Mel and Heather are in South Africa, Lily can't have found them. What would she be travelling on?"

"I see what you mean." I drummed my fingers on the edge of the computer table. "So why does Mel want to see me so urgently?"

"I'm not clairvoyant, Yazz," Viv snapped.

"OK, keep your hair on. I was thinking out loud, really."

"Sorry, I didn't mean to bark at you. I only meant that Mel's your friend, not mine. You were the one who discussed this with her. You're in a better position to work out why she wants to see you. In any event, why speculate, when you can simply give her this number and tell her to call you here? Or at your parents'?" She pulled up another chair and sat down next to me.

I swivelled back to face the screen and typed a response to the last of Mel's emails. "It'll have to be on the phone. I'm not in London. I'm in

Cape Town, with my parents." I gave her the number and pushed "send". Viv got up, murmuring something about making hot drinks. I followed. "So," I said as I watched her pour milk into a saucepan and set it to heat. "Your worries about Lily will soon be over. When I speak to Mel, I'll find out where she is and you can use the info as Lily-bait."

"I'm inclined to wait," she said, setting out mugs. "We should find out what Mel's plans are before we make any of our own."

I noticed that she was talking as though I was an integral part of this affair again, but I didn't object. I reached into the cupboard where she kept her canisters and took down the tin of cocoa. As I lowered my hand, my elbow caught a photo which stood on a side shelf of the old-fashioned dresser. I bent to pick it up. The glass of the plain wooden frame was intact. I brushed my hand across it and looked at the three young women pictured in an almost idyllic setting. Sunshine, blue sky, rolling green hills, faint outlines of far-off blue mountains surrounding a grinning trio. Viv, small and already chubby in her baggy shorts and trademark checked shirt, stood between me - still gawky and not quite filling my halter-necked cropped top and jeans cut-offs - and Lily, looking wonderful in a tight t-shirt and the tiniest denim shorts in creation. We looked happy as only a group of young people with nothing to do except hang out together enjoying life, could look. The picture caught more than that. It depicted the relationship we already had - Viv as mediator between me and Lily, always falling out, always making up. Somewhat like an older sister refereeing squabbles between younger siblings. Neither Lily nor I ever really fell out with Viv. I wondered now, looking at this picture whether that was the bond amongst us. Sisters. Both Viv and Lily were only children. So, in a manner of speaking, was I, since my sister Farieda had been long grown up when I was born.

Viv interrupted my musings by taking the picture from me and restoring it to its place. She made the cocoa and pushed a mug towards me. I folded my hands around its warmth and took it to bed with me. I lay that night in the enveloping softness of the bed I always slept in when I visited Viv, thinking. I'd come this far. There couldn't be much more before to the road before we hit the end. I might as well complete the journey.

I got onto Viv's computer first thing next morning, while she was feeding the dogs and taking them for a quick early morning walk on a nearby field. I had no email from Mel. I picked up my mobile and sent a text to her. It gave Mel basically the same information I'd sent the night before. Both the swiftness and the content of the answer shocked me. "She must have got hold of Adam after all," I said aloud. "He might have mentioned she'd phoned and that he'd told her I was here!" Then I remembered that I'd not been home to take his call the previous night. I'd been out the night before that too, when he'd called. If Mel had been in touch with him, he'd had no opportunity to tell me. I re-read the two sentences of Mel's reply. When I heard Viv return with the dogs, I went outside. "There's something you have to see." I held my phone out to her.

Viv let the dogs off their leashes. "And there I was, hoping you were making breakfast!" She took the phone from me and squinted to read the message: "I know where you are. I'll see you soon." Viv looked up at me. "Does that mean she's already on her way here?"

"Or at least making preparations to come."

We went inside and got together a breakfast of coffee and muesli with milk. "Now all you have to do is find Lily and dig out a bit of chalk," I said. She gave me a quizzical look. "The *Caucasian Chalk Circle*. You'll need to draw a circle and put Heather in the middle."

"I don't think we need a circle," Viv said. I noted the "we" once again. "Everything you've told me about Mel's relationship with Heather makes me think that she wants to work out what's best for Heather. I think she wants to prepare the ground for Heather being reunited with Lily. I doubt very much that she wants a tug of love."

"War," I corrected. "You mean a 'tug of war'. With regard to Heather, any tug by Lily is one of war."

Viv didn't answer. She pushed back her chair and went to get ready for work. I cleared the table and fetched my things. As we drove away from her house, she said, "If you're not doing anything special today I could drop you in town on my way to work. There are a couple of

219

exhibitions on that you may be interested in." The night had made good on yesterday's threat of a change in weather. This morning could have been a London Winter's day. Cold, grey and dreary. In fact it could have been a London day in any season, I'd thought when I'd opened the curtains of Viv's guest room that morning. My parents weren't much for going out in weather like this. It would mean a day cooped up at home, perhaps enlivened by visitors.

"Sounds like a good idea," I said. Viv dropped me off at what my dad called "The Grand Parade" – a big tarmacked area which my dad remembered for the speeches Mandela and the like used to deliver there when Dad was a boy and used to bunk off school to go and listen. I remembered it for the fruit stalls, the colourful cabins along one side that sold equally colourful milkshakes and soft drinks and the Wednesday markets that took over half of what had essentially become a large city centre car park. I wandered about for a while, doing what I liked most when I was at a loose end –looking at people, listening to their talk. The end of apartheid had seen the massive growth of squatter camps in and around South Africa's major cities. It had also seen the rapid Africanization of those cities which had once had pretensions to being a mislaid part of Europe. The grand old Post Office I wandered through was now a crowded indoor market. All manner of goods were called out in dozens of languages, not all of them from South of the Limpopo. St. George's Mall, once a pedestrianized area where mainly rich white people could sit in the sun, served by poor blacks from the townships, was now a colourful, lively tourist trap of stalls selling everything from ebony and ivory carvings to painted ostrich eggs. I laughingly dismissed offers by stallholders – mistaking me for a tourist until they heard my local accent – to sell me these trinkets at outrageous prices. They chaffed back good-naturedly.

I was just about to head towards an exhibition in the old City Hall, a grand colonial building along one side of the Parade, when my phone sang out the first bars of "To Be Young, Gifted and Black." I didn't even have to look at the caller ID as I answered it. "Hi, Mummy. Yes, I'm fine. Yes, I slept well. Yes, I *did* have breakfast."   I turned the corner off busy Darling Street into a side street alongside the City Hall so that I could hear her better.

"I wasn't going to ask any of that," she sniffed.

"Why? Because you know that Viv's an old woman, just like you? I'm pregnant, not sick or a child."

She "gmffed" before she said, "I wanted to tell you you've got a visitor."

"I can't have one, Mummy. I'm not home."

"I told her you must be on your way, Yasmin. So she said she'd wait."

"I'm *not* on my way home, Mummy. I'm in town! Tell whoever it is to come back some other time - and to phone first!"

"What are you doing in town? I thought Viv was dropping you off here on her way to work! That's why I told your visitor it's alright to wait. How was I supposed to know that you're going traipsing around?"

"In my condition? I know, Mum. Well, unless it's the Queen of Sheba or the Empress of China, I'm not rushing home. Even if it is one of them or the Queen of England, tell her I'm a socialist. I don't drop everything for royalty." I stepped aside to avoid being splashed by a car hitting a puddle. I wasn't quick enough. My shoes and pants took a drenching. I waved a fist in futile fury after the roadhog as he roared round the corner.

"If you're going to be rude, be rude to the person's face, Yasmin," my mother's cross voice said in my ear. "Don't expect me to do your dirty work. I'll take the phone to her."

I looked down at my sodden shoes and my mud-splattered pants and sighed. Walking around an exhibition in wet things didn't take my fancy. "Never mind, I'll come home right now," I said to my mother. We had a brief argument about whether I should wait somewhere for my dad to fetch me or take the bus. I finished it by insisting that I was right at the bus stop and there was a bus waiting, whereas it would take my dad some time to reach me. Surely the less time I kept our very important guest waiting, the better. I shut off the phone and walked back across the parade to the bank of bus stops at the far side opposite the station. To my surprise, there really was a bus waiting. I joined the back of the queue but found myself ushered to the front by my fellow passengers. A young hawker with a stall by the bus stop who'd taken it upon himself to help the old and infirm onto the bus, insisted on lifting me onto the step of the bus too. This was typical Cape Town, I thought, as I lay my head against the window of the bus and drifted off on the chatter around me.

The rental car parked outside my parents' place mystified me. I knew nobody who rented cars in Cape Town. Out of town visitors who hadn't driven from wherever in the country they lived, usually borrowed cars from friends or relatives. If they were on business, they had company car loans. On the other hand, these days if you had the right kind of job, it probably came with first class flight, five star hotel and a rented car. The picture this conjured up wasn't of someone I was keen to meet. Some might accuse me of succumbing to the "politics of envy" that damning description of anyone who raised objections to gravytraining, but as I approached my parents' front door, I was glad I'd made my visitor wait. Then I felt a twinge of guilt. Times had changed. Some poor out of town cousin without a car might have scraped together money to hire one to come and pay respects to the cousin from overseas, namely me. I'd barely formed the latter thought when my mother opened the door.

"There you are, Yasmin!" she said through the security gate. "Thank goodness." She looked me over anxiously. "Are you alright?" I offered verbal reassurance to confirm what her eyes told her as she opened the gate and let me in. "Daddy took his car to the garage for the gearbox when you said you didn't need him, but you took so long, I was just going to ask your friend if she would mind waiting alone while I go to see where you are."

I didn't even bother to quibble with the logic of her going looking for me in a car, when I was on a bus coming in the opposite direction in crazy Cape Town traffic. "I need to change." I pointed to my clothes. They'd dried on the journey but were still a mess. I moved past my mother down the passage towards my room. "Can't let our visitor see me like this."

222

"I don't mind," A familiar voice said. "Hello, Yazz."

"Mel?" I blinked at the figure in the lounge doorway, her face thrown into shadow by the light from the windows in the room behind her. "Mel! What are you…?"

"Surprise!" she said. There was none of the excitement in her voice with which the word is usually spoken, but her teeth gleamed in a momentary smile. "I'd have thought you'd be used to those by now. I hear you've had a little accident. Come on. Let's have a look at you." I followed her back into the lounge. She patted my bump then put her arms round me. "Well done! You look great!"

I sank down into my mother's old rocking chair and hooked out the footstool beneath it. "Thanks." I couldn't return the compliment. She'd taken a seat in an armchair opposite me. In the light from the windows, her face was pale and worn. In the time since I'd seen her in Pedro's, the apples in her cheeks and the roses on her lips had died. The blue eyes had lost their clarity and sparkle. There were new lines at their corners. My mother usually allowed visitors to smoke in the house – not that she had much choice, she would have been thought rude otherwise – and the lounge reeked of smoke, despite both windows being open. The ashtray on the coffee table was overflowing, though Mel couldn't have been waiting for more than an hour or so. The tea in her cup looked cold. My mother's *koeksisters* sat untouched on a plate in the middle of the coffee table. "How'd you get here so quickly?" I asked. "Did you take the Concorde from Canada?"

She shook her head. "We left there a couple of days ago. We'd just arrived in Cape Town when I got your text. I said I'd see you soon, remember? I came straight over."

"How'd you know I was here?"

"Pure fluke. Your answer phone in London isn't taking messages. I sent texts to your cell phone and got no joy there either. I thought, if you're not answering your phones or your email, you must be away. I called that college where you told me you worked to find out when you'd be back. They said you were on maternity leave. I took a chance

223

that you might visit your folks before the baby comes, so I called here and your dad confirmed my guess."

"Dad never said a word to me."

"There was nothing to say. I literally asked if you were in Cape Town and if you were staying here and hung up when he said yes."

"Why didn't you want my mother to tell me it was you waiting?"

"I didn't want you telling your friend Lily we're here, until I'd had a chance to speak to you." She reached out a hand to her cigarettes. Then pulled it back.

"Let's go out back," I said. "You can smoke there without guilt-tripping yourself about the baby. She'll be perfectly safe." I patted my belly. "Give me a mo." I cleared the tea things and ashtray away. Mel picked up her bag and her fags and lighter and followed me down the passage to my room and the sitting room beyond it.

I opened the French windows and we stepped into the small walled garden. The sun had come through the clouds again. The garden was guaranteed to trap sunshine, no matter how little of it there was around on any given day. I took cushions from indoor chairs and tossed them onto the wrought iron outdoor ones around the garden table. "I wouldn't have told Lily you were here," I said as she sat down and lit up, blowing the smoke carefully away from me. "We're not on speaking terms. Lily and I had a huge fight recently."

"About me?"

I shrugged. "Lily knows Heather's alive."

Mel tapped ash from her cigarette. Her face remained expressionless.

"Lily knows where your family lives. She's been out there. When she didn't find you, Lily stopped off in London to ask me whether I knew where you were. I couldn't help her so she accused me of warning you to run off with Heather and hide her from Lily."

Mel puffed at her cigarette. "I don't blame her for going off the rails. I'd go mad if I were in her place." She shook her head. "First my husband steals her daughter and then I cost Lily a life-long friendship. How much more misery are we going to inflict on that poor woman?"

"Don't take on board Zac's guilt, Mel. None of this is your fault. As for Lily, I don't know about my friendship with her being life-long. Lily and I hadn't seen each other in years until this came up and she needed my help."

"If you have a good relationship with someone, Yazz, the time between seeing each other doesn't matter. You and Lily were so close on campus. Now you're caught in the middle between us. I'm sorry."

"If I'm in the middle, Mel, you didn't ask me to get involved. I chose to. So, how can I help?"

"I don't know if you can. It depends how bad your fight with Lily was."

"Never mind the fight. Tell me anyway."

"I haven't yet told Heather about Lily," she said slowly. "I wanted you to arrange for me to meet with Lily so that we could discuss how best to tell Heather." She paused and looked down abjectly at her hands. "I'm didn't know you were pregnant or I wouldn't have bothered you with this. "

"Yes, you would have. Or at least, I'd expect you to. When I needed you, you were there for me. Do you really think that I'd let you down?"

She glanced up at me and I saw relief replace the misery and despair in her eyes.

"Before we go any further, isn't there one person you've forgotten to mention? Zac? Isn't he involved in all of this? Should he be the one talking to Lily? Talking to Heather?"

She took a last drag from her cigarette and ground it out, sat for a moment studying her hands spread out on the table. "I've left Zac. Or rather, I've thrown him out." She looked at me and laughed mirthlessly. "Couldn't let him have the house. The kids and I need it."

I stared at her in disbelief. "And he actually left? Just like that?"

"Of course not just like that," she mimicked. "As they say in the movies, I made him an offer he couldn't refuse." She shook another cigarette from the pack and lit it. "This is the deal. He fucks off out of my life. In return, I don't tell the kids the whole truth about what a shit he is and I don't make public all the things he's done. That way, he doesn't end up with the kids, especially Heather, hating and despising him." She studied the tip of her cigarette. "I've also, of course, got to allow him access to the kids. I can't explain cutting him out of their lives altogether unless I tell them the full story."

"And you trust him?" I leaned towards her and put a hand on her free one. "Mel, this man went to immense – some might say totally unbelievable – lengths to steal one of his kids and then he just up and lets you hold onto that one plus two more?" I clasped her hand and shook it slightly. She looked at me. "How can you trust him to keep his side of the bargain?" I asked. "What if he-"

"Don't worry." She cut me off. She withdrew her hand from mine and waved it dismissively. "He can't pull the same stunt he pulled with Heather. For one thing, the boys aren't toddlers who can be spirited away and spun some fairytale. Heather's a grown girl. For another, the boys are at boarding school and the teachers have been told that we're in the middle of a divorce and they are not to let the boys out with Zac. Heather's here with me. Last but not least, Zac doesn't have the kind of resources he had when he took Heather." Her lips thinned in a grim parody of a smile. "I'm taking his money – almost all of it. I'll just about leave him enough to live on. And as I said, if he wants to go on seeing the kids now and then, he has to stick to the deal."

I laughed. "Jesus! And I thought it was Lily who was going to grind Zac's balls into mincemeat and feed them back to him on toast."

She didn't join in my laughter. "Lily and I have a lot in common. Enough, I hope, for her to help me with the kids."

I waited. She tapped the two fingers holding the cigarette on the table. "My side of the bargain with Zac is that I don't tell the kids the whole truth. That won't help him very much if *Lily* tells Heather the whole truth."

"So it's not just for the sake of preparing Heather that you want to see Lily?" I asked. She wouldn't look at me. "You also want to ask her to go along with some lesser version of the truth?" Still she kept her face averted. "Why would she do that, Mel?"

"I hope," she said, meeting my gaze at last. "Because she loves Heather more than she hates Zac." She paused. "You said that Lily I have a lot in common," she said. "You're right. It's not merely that we both want to kill Zac. Lily and I share something far more important. That's our love for Heather." Another pause. "I told you before, Yazz. No matter what else Zac is, he's a decent father to our kids. They all love him. It would devastate them if they knew just how bad he's been. I can't hurt my kids by telling them all the things their father's done." Her blue eyes filled with tears. Mel blinked fiercely, wiped at an errant tear with the back of her free hand. "I'm hoping," she said. "That Lily loves Heather too much to tell her the whole truth about her beloved father."

I thought about that for while, then I asked, "And how is Lily supposed to explain her disappearance from Heather's life, her resurrection from the dead, or whatever? The story Zac tried to sell you is hardly likely to make Heather want any sort of relationship with Lily at all. It's certainly not calculated to have Heather fall into her arms, as Lily doubtless envisages."

Mel didn't answer. She got up and walked over to a lemon tree that grew in the corner of the small garden, plucked a few leaves and rubbed them between her fingers. The smell rose in the air, challenging the smoke from the cigarette she held in her other hand. She tossed the latter under the tree and ground it into the soil with her shoe. I said more gently, "Come on, Mel. You can't really expect Lily to play the villain in this drama. Especially not when Zac's perfect for the role. And not when the claptrap he tried to sell you is guaranteed to put Heather off Lily forever."

Mel came back to the table. She took a tissue from her bag and blew her nose. "Please, Yazz," she sniffed. "Give me some credit for commonsense. You're not saying anything I don't know." She wadded the tissue and threw it in the ashtray. Then she looked hard at me. "Lily will have to do something she won't like. We all have to. I don't want to meet Lily. She's suffered terribly and the man who's caused all this is my husband, the father of my children. Meeting Lily will make me feel guilty and ashamed. I've had all the wonderful times with Heather that should have been Lily's. If Lily disliked me years ago for no reason, she must hate my guts now she has reason. Last but not least, I'm jealous and I'm scared when I think about reuniting my daughter with her birth mother." She lit another cigarette. "But in spite of all this, I'm *going* to meet Lily." She blew out smoke. "I'm going to meet her because between the two of us, we have to work out something which will have *neither* of my daughter's birth parents emerge as anything but loving." She smiled bleakly. "No villains in this piece."

I was contemplating how to respond to that, when my mother appeared in the doorway to say that she and my dad were going out. They'd lock up the front of the house and just wanted to make sure I had my keys so I could get out – or answer the door for that matter – in their absence, though she didn't really want me answering the door when I was home alone. I offered the reassurances she wanted and then she turned to Mel. "I don't know if you'll still be here when we get back, so I'll say 'bye now. Nice seeing you again."

"It was nice seeing you too, Mrs. P. Thanks for the cake and tea."

"You didn't eat a thing!" my mother exclaimed.

"Sorry, Mrs. P.," Mel said. "I wasn't very hungry. Never mind, I'll take some with me." Satisfied, my mother left.

Mel looked at me. "All you have to do is arrange for me to meet Lily," she said. "That's it. You don't have to tell her everything I've just told you. Simply tell Lily that I want to discuss with her how to make the

228

reintroduction of Lily into Heather's life as painless as possible for Heather. Lily and I will take it from there, once we meet."

I looked at my watch, surprised to find that it was already lunchtime. "I'll call Viv. Lily may not bother to respond to me," I said. "But she'll listen to Viv. I hope. You remember Viv?"

"Viv," Mel said thoughtfully. "Yes, I do remember her. She's the other person you hung out with a lot. Short black hair? Dumpy like me? She's nice. Bit tight-arsed, I remember, but nice."

I laughed. "I don't think anyone would ever call you dumpy, Mel. Not anyone male, anyway. Viv might be considered a bit round in the wrong places, but not you. As for Viv being tight-arsed...let me simply utter a judicious 'ahem!' and blush."

A smile trembled on Mel's lips.

"Let me get my phone." I started to get up.

"Use mine." Mel turned and opened the bag she'd hung by its strap on the back of her chair.

I took the phone she held out to me. I dialled. Viv's phone went to voicemail. I left a message for her to call me urgently, then shut off the phone and handed it back to Mel.

She returned the phone to her bag. "It will be nice to talk to Viv again, regardless of the circumstances." She stubbed out her cigarette and rose. "I have to go. I left Heather sleeping off her jetlag. She'll wake and wonder where I am."

"Heather's grown up. Nothing's going to happen to her. You make it sound as though you've left a toddler on her own in danger of kidnapping or murder." The words were out before I realized what I'd said. Too late, I clapped my hand to my mouth.

Mel eyed me with the first real amusement I'd seen since I'd met her in Pedro's. "Wait until that one's born," she said. "You'll understand that they're never too old for you to stop being anxious about them. You even worry about them worrying about you, like I am now."

I took her to her car the back way, through the arch in the fourth wall of the little garden into the area where my dad had built a *braai* spot when we were kids. We rounded the corner of the house and had to duck beneath sheets my mother had left to flap dry in the wind, the wash line stuck up high on a curved stick in the old-fashioned way. Mel turned to me as I ushered her ahead of me through the side gate leading to the stoep and front garden. "I know I said you needn't do anything except arrange for me to meet Lily," she said. "But suddenly I wish you could come with me. For moral support and all that." She laughed a small nervous sound. "I'm just being silly. I know you've got your own life, your own plans," she said. "You're probably wanting to get back to Adam, being pregnant and all that." Her eyes begged me to contradict her.

I hesitated, not wanting to tell her that I had no plans yet to go back to London. "It depends," I said. "We'll have to see how soon Viv tracks Lily down." I laughed lamely. "I could be lying in a maternity ward by the time Lily puts in an appearance. You never know with her."

"But if you can?"

"Sure. Didn't I say I'd do anything I can to help you?"

When she'd left I sat on the stoep. From over the road came the sound of Aunty Ida's grandchild crying and her scolding. The hum of traffic in the surrounding streets had increased, indicating the first of the afternoon school runs, when the youngest children were collected by parents and taxis from primary schools. In a year or two, it would be my toddler crying and me scolding. A few years more and I'd be doing the school run. Where though? Here? In London? My thoughts turned to Adam. I missed talking things through with him. We were meant to be sharing these months of anticipation and planning before the baby came. We were supposed to be nesting, not sorting out other people's lives. I was overcome with longing for my own life, my own home, most of all, for Adam. I got out the phone book and started calling airlines. With holidays coming, nobody had any seats available in the next week or two. Disappointed, I put down the phone. Then I cheered up. My mother was sure to know of some relative or other with connections in an airline or travel agency. There was always a way, here in South Africa. I went back to the garden and tried to read one of my mother's thrillers. The sound of the phone ringing in the front room roused me just as I was about to reveal all ahead of Poirot. It was Viv, as I'd half-expected.

"You're not going to believe this," I said. "But Mel's here already. When she said she was on her way, she didn't mean on her way from overseas. She meant on her way here to my home from somewhere within Cape Town."

"She's with you now?"

"Well, she was sitting with me in my garden when I called you. Now she's at some friend's place she's borrowed for the duration of her stay. I wrote the address down somewhere. And I called you from her phone, so you've got the number."

"Is Heather with her?"

"Yep. Mel wants to see Lily before Lily meets Heather, which is what you wanted too, for the two mothers to meet and plan how to tell Heather? Yes? It's either great minds thinking alike or fools seldom differing. So, now all you have to do is find Lily and make the arrangements."

"How was Mel?"

I told her the gist of what Mel had told me. "So, as you can imagine, her life's a bit *kak* right now. She's hanging in there, though, for her kids. For Heather."

"I'll send messages to Lily again."

"Mel wants me to go with her to meet Lily. Moral support and all that."

"What did you say?" Viv asked, as if she didn't already know the answer.

231

"What the fuck could I say? Jesus Christ!" I exploded. "So much for coming here in search of peace and quiet."

"Dare I point out," she said, "That now the drama's moved to Cape Town, you could have both peace and quiet in your own home?"

"You mean, pack up here and run away again? I'm sick of running away from problems other people cause in my life. Why can't I go where I please and stay where I want?"

"If that's how you feel, why don't you take charge of your life?"

"How? Every time I tell someone I don't want to be involved, they just insist on drawing me in! Sandy, Amos, Lily, Mel, you, now Mel again!"

"Just keep using that phrase you're so fond of. Tell all of us to fuck off."

I laughed. Only Viv could pronounce the phrase as politely as that. "OK. Fuck off then." I paused. "You might as well know. I *am* thinking about going home. I was checking for flights earlier. Happy now?"

"Delirious. Let's make the most of the time while you're still here. I'll contact you closer to the weekend. Before that, if Lily gets in touch."

"Oh, that's right. It's Easter weekend coming up. I thought you'd be on leave. You were supposed to come over to me in London. "

"I changed my arrangements, remember? I can't take off again, barring the actual weekend. I'm free from around Thursday noon. I could pick you up."

"Until then? You'll just be home every evening, waiting by the phone for Lily?"

"I have a life of my own too, Yazz. But as you say, that will include waiting for Lily to get in touch. One doesn't have to wait at the phone any longer, by the way. You may recall the invention of cell phones? I believe you even carry one."

I rang off and called a cousin of mine who I'd just remembered worked for an airline. She wasn't doing that any longer. These days she was into yoga and massage. I took up her invitation to come over for a visit and session. For two hours, I was able to wipe Lily and Mel and their troubles from my mind. When it was over, my cousin fed me some kind of vitamin smoothie for pregnant women. I returned to my parents' home totally relaxed. When Adam called, I was able to talk properly to him for the first time since I'd come to South Africa. It wasn't simply a "yes, no and I'm fine" dialogue, but a real conversation about what I'd been doing, what he'd been doing, friends and family. I was surprised at the ease with which I related to him the basics of Mel's visit. However, I did refrain from mentioning my continued involvement. Things felt too normal between us for me to toss a stone into our peaceful pond again. I'd come to Cape Town for normality. That had been disturbed. Now I was reaching back to Adam for that normality.

"When are you coming home?" he finished the conversation with the usual question.

"Soon," I answered as I always did. Then, instead of the usual "Don't push me," I added casually. "I was just looking for flights today. There's nothing available. I'll let you know when something comes up." The minutes of silence that greeted my words were far more eloquent than Adam's surprised, "I'll fetch you," which followed.

Viv picked me up after work on Maundy Thursday for an afternoon of hanging out at her place. We were to go out to dinner with friends at Simon's house. She smoothed over my mother's concerns about my going out so much at night "in my condition" by promising to make me nap during the course of the afternoon, feed me well and bring me back to hers in time for a good night's rest. My mother handed Viv a container of pickled fish and another of homemade hot cross buns. That was to ensure I ate before going out to dinner. It also showed that, Muslim or not, she could make good Christian fare, as long as it wasn't pork. Viv said the food would come in handy over the long weekend. I rolled my eyes at her arse-licking.

233

The security gates set in the high wall surrounding Viv's house stood wide open when we arrived. There was no sign of the dogs. Parked up against the back stoep was Lily's yellow Toyota. There was no-one in it. Viv pulled her car up next to Lily's. I braced myself for Lily to dash out of the house, yank open Viv's car and demand to know at once what news Viv had of Heather. The door didn't open. We got out of the car. Viv whistled for the dogs. From the shed came the sound of wild barking. Viv shut the gates and went to release and comfort the dogs. I stood on the stoep waiting. Finally Viv joined me and pushed open the kitchen door.

Lily sat at the table. In front of her was a bottle of gin, a carton of orange juice and a glass of orange coloured liquid. She looked up when we came in. Her eyes were blank, her expression unreadable. "There you are at last," she said. "So. You have news for me." Her voice was flat, as though she was deliberately forcing herself to suppress any show of excitement. If she had her hopes up, she wasn't going to show us.

"Where have you been, Lily?" Viv asked.

Lily shrugged. "Around."

"I've been trying to contact you for ages." Viv scolded like my mother, standing in the middle of the kitchen, hands on her hips. I shut the door and stood leaning against it, looking at Lily. She ignored my presence.

"I had things to do, people to see." Lily said in the weird monotone with which she had greeted our entry. "More important than assuaging your guilt for being pissed off at me." She toyed with her glass. "So, do you have news for real, or did you just want to see me to make yourself happy I'm alive and well?"

"I do have real news about Heather, Lily," Viv filled up the kettle and plugged it in. "Let me just get us all a hot drink. Then we can talk about it." She put teabags into cups and leaned against the kitchen counter waiting for the kettle to boil.

234

"I don't want a hot drink. I've got gin," Lily said. "If you have something to tell me, say it. If you don't, I'll go."

"I know where Heather is," Viv said.

The words galvanized Lily out of her chair. "Then what the fuck are we still doing here?" She grabbed Viv's arms, all her earlier languor vanished. "Let's go. We've got arrangements to make."

Viv disengaged herself from Lily's grip. "Stop, Lily! For goodness sake. We're not charging off anywhere until we've talked about a few things. So calm down!"

Lily looked as though she was going to hit Viv. Viv stood her ground. "Sit down, Lily. Let's talk."

Lily's arms slumped to her sides. The animation drained out of her. "Why are you *doing* this to me? You *don't* know anything do you? You just got my hopes up for nothing again." Her voice wobbled on the verge of angry tears. She struggled her jacket free from the back of her chair, fumbled for her keys on the table and started for the door. As if seeing me for the first time, she looked me up and down, then smiled slightly. "So," she said. "You're going to have your child after all."

I didn't move. "Yes." I said simply.

"And you still won't help me find mine." Her voice cracked with bitterness. "Do you really hate me that much?"

"Life's too short," I said. "I've got too much to do with what's left of mine to waste any of it on hating you." I put a protective hand on my bump. "I *have* found Heather. If you'll sit down and listen to Viv, you could have your daughter with you long before I have mine. But if you want to leave…" I stepped aside and opened the door.

Lily looked hard at me. Then she turned, flung her jacket over the back of her chair and resumed her seat at the table. She crossed her legs and folded her arms, waiting. I shut the door and took the cup of tea Viv handed me. I perched on a chair in the corner of the kitchen.

"Mel's been in touch with Yazz," Viv said. "She'd like to meet with you to discuss how best to re-introduce you into Heather's life."

"What's to discuss?" Lily asked. "All she has to do is hand over my little girl to me."

"That's precisely the point, Lily," Viv said. "Heather's not a little girl any longer. She's a grown woman. And she's not a parcel. She can't just be handed over like that."

Lily laughed harshly. "Like I don't know that, Viv. I don't know that I've missed all the years of my little girl growing up," she said sarcastically.

Viv weighed her next words carefully. "Which is why you need to speak to the woman who *did* spend those years with Heather, Lily," she said. "Mel can ease your way back into Heather's life as painlessly as possible. She wants to ensure that you forge a positive relationship with Heather."

"Either I'm crazy or you've got early onset Alzheimer's Viv," Lily snapped. Viv didn't respond. "I seem to remember we've been here before," Lily went on. "You've *already* given me the speech about not expecting all the love Heather had for me as a toddler to come rushing back in an instant when she meets me. I've *already* been told that children joyously falling into the arms of long lost parents only happens in the movies."

She turned to me. "I suppose this is your doing."

"No, but if you'll shut up I can tell you what Mel is asking for," I said. To my surprise, she shut up. Without mentioning where the conversation had taken place, I gave Lily more or less the same summary that I'd given Viv of the conversation I'd had with Mel. I'd not quite finished when Lily began to shake with silent laughter. I stopped abruptly, looking at Viv.

"I'm sure that Mel will be relieved that you find her proposal humorous, Lily." Viv cut caustically across Lily's laughter.

"Sorry," Lily spluttered, wiping a finger along each eye to clear apparent tears of mirth. "You don't know how funny this is." She turned to me. "Tell that woman, your friend, there's nothing to discuss," she said. "It's all academic. Or at least it will be," she glanced slyly at Viv. "Once I know where they are."

"What does that mean, Lily?" Viv asked. Lily merely shook her head. "Ah well," Viv said. "I suppose laughter is a better basis for discussion than hostility."

Lily sobered up abruptly. "There'll be hostility here right now, Viv, if you don't tell me where my daughter is. Do I have to choke it out of you?" She put her hands flat on the table and used them to push to her feet. "I've got travel arrangements to make. In case you don't know, it's Easter holidays. I'll have to *sukkel* to get a ticket."

Viv looked up calmly at Lily. "There are no travel arrangements to make, Lily," Viv said. "And no tickets to buy unless you intend travelling by public transport across the city. Mel and Heather are in Cape Town."

Lily sank down onto her chair and stared at Viv. "She's here? Heather's in Cape Town?" She waved her hands around helplessly, bewildered. "In South Africa?" she tossed the question to me. I nodded. She turned to Viv. "Why didn't you say right away? Viv, why didn't you? My daughter's right here in Cape Town! Why don't you take me to her?"

"I wanted you to listen to Mel's proposition first, Lily," Viv said gently.

"Where is she?" Lily's voice was a plaintive wail. "Where?"

Viv put a hand on hers. "I don't have the precise address, Lily. I have to call Mel to set up a meeting between you and her. Then you can discuss with Mel when and how you'll meet Heather."

Lily said slowly, "She won't let me see Heather straight away? I still have to see this Mel woman and negotiate with her?" Viv nodded. Lily was suddenly silent, looking dazed, as if the reality that she was soon to meet her daughter had only just hit home. "OK, Viv," Lily said finally. "Call her. Tell her I'll meet her where she wants, when she wants, as long as she lets me have my daughter."

Viv went to look for her mobile. I sat for a moment, watching Lily drumming her fingernails on the top of the table, tapping her foot impatiently. I snorted. "Count yourself lucky that it's Mel you're talking to about your daughter," I said. "I was the one who had to talk to Zac, if you can call it talking to someone when all you're getting is threats and abuse."

"Well," Lily said. "You won't have to worry about *that* for much longer."

Viv came back into the room. "Mel's somewhere without a mobile phone signal," she said. "I'll try again later." She sat down. "What will Yazz not have to worry about for much longer, Lily?"

"Lily's just offered to thump Zac if he ever threatens me again," I said lightly.

"It's more than thumping I've got planned for him," Lily said. "Once I know where the bastard is to be found." She picked up the glass of gin and orange and drained it. "Anyone for another drink?" Without waiting for an answer, she fetched two more glasses. From the fridge she took a bottle of fizzy water and mixed some with juice for me. She mixed gin and orange for herself and Viv. "Cheers!" she said. "Here's to one piece of shit about to be flushed down the toilet."

Viv sipped at her drink. "So now will you tell us where you've been hiding, Lily?"

Lily gulped gin. "Did you think to look at your calendar?" Lily asked. Viv's eyes went to the calendar pinned up behind the closed kitchen door. The picture above the month of April was an innocuous Autumn scene of fallen leaves beneath a grey sky. Viv wasn't picky about calendars. She just used whatever local tradesmen gave away free or what she could grab off the nearest supermarket shelf. Though it was well into the month, the usual red circles to remind her of important dates, scrawled messages to herself and so on were absent. The page was blank except for the printed information the calendar had come with. "Oh," Lily said. "I see you haven't marked it this year. Was that because you know that Heather's not dead? Other people died too, you know. Just because I don't have anyone to mourn for doesn't make the date meaningless."

"I use the calendar on my computer," Viv said, "I'm sorry. You're right. With all that's happened recently, ironically I forgot the date of the fire which started all of this."

"Actually, it was me fucking Zac that started it all," Lily said. "Which is also how it's about to end. For him anyway." She laughed and drank more gin.

"I would have thought you'd had enough of fucking Zac," I said.

"There's fucking and fucking," Lily retorted.

"I tend to agree with Yazz," Viv said. "We can do without the fucking of Zac." She paused to sip some more gin, then leaned back and said thoughtfully, "So you've been to the annual commemoration for people who lost family members in the fire... I don't remember that it's ever taken this amount of time, or that it has required participants to be incommunicado during the event."

"Ah," Lily responded. "But that's because we never had so much to plan and discuss before."

"You told them about Heather," Viv stated.

"Of course I did," Lily said. "I owed it to them, don't you think? Truth and reconciliation and all that?" She glanced slyly out of the corner of her eyes at Viv. "I don't know about the reconciliation part though. They were pretty the *moeren*." She put her hand to her mouth to stifle a giggle. "I must say it would have been a real pleasure to actually be there to see that *vark* get what's coming to him. However." She moved her chair back from the table and stood up. "I'd much rather

239

spend time with my daughter. So how about trying that number again, Viv?" She looked at her watch. "It's still early. If you contact that woman in time, I could have my daughter sleeping beside me tonight."

"Lily," Viv asked quietly. "What exactly did you say to those poor people? Did you tell them that Zac started the fire?"

"I did," Lily acknowledged. She stamped her foot impatiently. "Never mind the bastard, Viv. Make that call again."

"In a minute, Lily," Viv answered. "Let's just talk about Zac for that minute, alright?" Without waiting for Lily's reply, she went on, "You don't *know* that he was responsible for the fire." Viv talked patiently, a teacher explaining a difficult problem to a student. "Nobody knows *for a fact* how it started. Zac may simply have taken advantage of a given situation. A terrible thing to do, yes, benefiting from another's agony, but not as bad as causing the suffering."

"Oh, please!" Lily waved a hand in disgust. "Let him pull that one on them. I'm sure they'll fall for it," she sneered.

"Well, let's hope that Zac has the good sense to steer clear of South Africa," Viv sighed.

"Oh, he can run, but as they say in the movies, he can't hide. They'll get him," Lily said confidently. "This is the new South Africa, you know. It's been good to a lot of those poor people as you call them. Between them they've got the resources to get to him, once I tell them where he is. Which," She looked expectantly at Viv. "Should be sometime soon. Make that call, Viv. I need that address. I promised I'd let people know where he is."

"Lily, you haven't been listening properly have you?" Viv's voice took on an edge. "Yazz and I know where *Mel* is. At least we know that she and Heather are in Cape Town. We don't have the precise address. We certainly have no idea where Zac is. Did you miss the bit where Yazz said that Mel's left Zac? Even Mel doesn't know where he is."

"She knows where her children are, doesn't she?" Lily spread her hands palms upwards. "So? Where his children are, he'll be around sooner or later, now he's reinvented himself as the loving father." She gave a little giggle. "I hope they still know how to make a necklace."

"His *children*? A necklace?" Viv stared at Lily in horror. I was speechless. "*His* children?" Viv hissed. "Two of them are also Mel's children! Lily! One of them is yours! Have you thought about the possible consequences of what you've done? If these people want an eye for an eye do you know what they could do to Zac's children? Innocent children?"

"Don't be ridiculous." Lily tried to scoff but her voice trembled slightly with uncertainty. "They wouldn't hurt my child."

There was a moment of silence. I waited for Lily to realize what she'd just said, but she didn't show any signs of it. "Perhaps not *your* child, Lily," I said harshly. "But Mel's? It's alright if they hurt Mel's boys?"

"These are human beings, not animals like him," Lily snarled. "They care about children. None of them would dream of harming a child. Not after what they suffered."

Viv closed her eyes and took a deep breath. "Lily, we've all lived through times when people got over-enthusiastic about punishing the guilty and the innocents got caught up. We know that sometimes the innocents were actually punished for the acts of the guilty. Don't pretend you've forgotten how the children of collaborators suffered in one way or another."

"You're not making that call to Mel, Viv," I said. "No way. This woman is a fucking lunatic."

Neither of them took any notice of me. Viv seemed to still be waiting for a response from Lily. Lily simply stared back defiantly at her, arms folded across her chest.

Finally Viv said, "Sit down, Lily." Lily hesitated. "Go on," Viv insisted. "Sit, because I want you to listen to me very carefully. I won't say this again."

Lily sat.

"Lily," Viv said. "I could ask you to promise me on your life, on Heather's life, that you won't tell these people where Zac's family is." She paused. "Sadly, your promises are often like the proverbial piecrust, so instead *I* will make *you* a promise."

She now had Lily's full attention. Her voice hardened. "My promise to you is this. If any harm should come to any member of Zac's family because of information you've divulged to the families of those fire victims, I shall personally tell Heather that you are responsible. I shall tell her that nobody can prove that Zac set the fire in which Heather supposedly died, but that I know *for a fact,* that you sent people to hurt Heather's family."

There was silence in the room. Even from outside there was no sound, as if the whole world was listening to Viv. "Think about that, Lily – and remember that I never break promises to you. Heather will loathe you. She's nearly an adult in law. She will cut you out of her life forever."

Lily's face was a picture of warring emotions – disbelief, denial, fury, hatred, defiance and finally acceptance. "You didn't have to threaten me," she said sulkily. "You know I wouldn't let anyone hurt someone else's child."

"No, Lily," Viv said coldly. "I'm afraid I don't. When it comes to issues related to Zac, sometimes I think that I don't know you at all. I had no idea what you were capable of when you wanted him. I have even less idea what you're capable of now that you hate him." She reached for her phone. "I'll make that call." Viv left the kitchen, phone in hand.

Lily got up and paced around the room. I put the kettle on. By the time I'd poured water on a bag of chamomile tea, Viv had returned to the kitchen. Lily stopped pacing.

"Mel will meet you in the restaurant in the Gardens tomorrow at noon, Lily," Viv said. "I told her you'd be there."

242

"You mean I've got to wait till tomorrow?"

"Mel's taken Heather out somewhere tonight. Not everyone's life is dictated by your timetable, Lily," Viv said sharply.

Amazingly, Lily smiled. "OK." Even more amazingly, she said, "So, you two are going out tonight. Is it alright if I come too?"

"No, Lily," Viv said. "It is *not* alright."

Lily's smile broadened. "Keep your knickers on. I get that you're pissed with me. Go to your party without me, if that makes you happy. I'll just stay here by myself."

"No, you won't Lily," Viv said. "Go home. Think about tomorrow."

"I don't want to sleep alone tonight!" Lily protested. "Plus, if I'm here we can go to Heather – I mean, to Mel - together tomorrow."

"I won't be going with you to meet Mel tomorrow," Viv said. She didn't mention that I'd be at the meeting between Lily and Mel.

Lily's eyes widened with shock. "But I thought ... I need... I can't go on my own!"

"Yes you can Lily. As you're always telling me, you don't need me. You're all grown up now. You're the mother of a nearly adult daughter. Behave like one. You need time tonight to think through what happens tomorrow. You have to sort out your future with your daughter and the important people in her life."

Lily looked as though she would burst into tears. "Please Viv. I really don't want to spend the night alone. I don't want to go-"

Viv cut in wearily. "I'm not really concerned with what you want right now, Lily." She went to the kitchen door and opened it. "Please leave."

"Hell," Lily muttered. "Some friend you are, throwing me out, just when I need you, when I'm *begging* you –" She broke off when Viv didn't budge from the open doorway. Lily snatched up her jacket and grabbed her car keys.

When she got to the door, Viv held out her hand. "I'd like my keys back if you don't mind, Lily."

I gasped and heard an echoing intake of breath from Lily. She and I had had keys to Viv's place since way back. For obvious reason, mine had never been updated to keep pace with the changes in Viv's locks over the years. I had no doubt that like Lily I'd possess a current set if I lived in Cape Town. Viv had never asked either of us to hand back her keys. Unlike any of Viv's boyfriends, even Simon, neither Lily nor I had ever been denied access to Viv's place. Lily gave Viv a long searching look. Viv stared straight back at her, still holding out her hand. At last Lily dropped her eyes. Without a word, she took Viv's keys off her keyring. She slapped them into Viv's open palm. Then Lily stepped past Viv onto the back stoep. I heard the slam of her car door, but it was some time before I heard her car start up, heard her back out and drive off. Viv stood there until she was gone. She didn't go outside to shut the gates. She came back to the kitchen and dropped into her chair and drained her drink. I went outside and locked up. When I returned, she was staring into space, her face a mask of misery.

I went to put my arm around her. "Cheer up. You know Lily. It's probably more talk than anything else. I very much doubt whether a group of ex-squatters can get at someone like Zac, half a world away. And as Lily said, these people have lost their own kids. They won't harm someone else's."

"It's the thought that counts," she said despairingly. "Or rather, the lack of it. Could Lily not see what might happen to Mel's children? Or did she simply not care? Is this what suffering does to people? Does it make them want to inflict pain on others? Does it make them careless of or impervious to the hurt of another?"

It was the kind of naïve questions I expected of Lily, not of Viv. I let it go. Everyone was entitled to ask a silly question or two now and again. We retired to our respective rooms. Neither reading nor the chamomile tea, or even doing some of the yoga breathing I'd learnt had the slightest effect in relaxing me.

Viv still looked thoroughly miserable when Simon arrived. He took one look at us and asked whether we'd had a fight. We assured him everything was fine between us. "It's the other one then, is it?" he asked. Neither of us answered. We went to dinner. We made conversation. We even laughed and joked. By the end of the evening both Viv and I had bounced back sufficiently from our bruising encounter with Lily's careless disregard for others to give Simon cause to congratulate himself for cheering us up.

"You really aren't coming along tomorrow?" I asked Viv as we parted for bed.

"There's no need, Yazz. Only Mel and Lily can determine what their relationship with each other and with Heather will be. What is there for me to do?"

"They may need a neutral observer or an international peacekeeper type of figure."

"You'll be there."

"I won't be as good in the role as you will. You've had years of practice with me and Lily."

Viv shrugged. "You could simply introduce them and leave. I doubt Mel will need your support. I think I've issued enough threats to ensure Lily behaves."

I was sitting over breakfast next morning when my phone sang out. I looked at the screen, expecting my mother. It was Mel. "Can you come over now?" she asked. "As soon as you can?" Thrown off balance by both the question and the distraught sound of her voice, I didn't answer at once. "If you can't, it's OK," she said. "I just-"

"No," I said. "No, of course I can come, but has something happened? You sound strange."

"Yes," she said. "Something's happened. I'd rather tell you when I see you. Come to the house. Bring Lily." She gave me the address again and rang off.

"Mel's been on the phone," I said to Viv when she came in from seeing to the dogs. "She sounded totally weird. Wants me to come over there now. Something's happened. She wouldn't say what. Just to bring Lily and come straight over to where Mel's staying. It must have something to do with Heather. Do you suppose Lily-"

"There's no point in speculating," she said briefly. "I'll get ready and drive you over. Call Lily about the altered arrangements."

"There's no need for you to come. Lily can pick me up. We may as well go together."

Viv agreed with surprising readiness. "Call me if you need to be fetched. You may not want to wait for Lily to bring you back."

With startling speed for someone who wasn't a morning person, Viv whipped away the breakfast things and hit the shower. Lily sounded as strained as Mel had when I called her. I had no doubt that she'd been up all night. I suppressed the twinge of guilt I felt for letting her stew through the night on her own. She didn't protest or ask questions when I said Mel had moved the meeting up to right now. When I told Lily to pick me up, she agreed meekly, almost gratefully. I thought she was under the impression that I was substituting for Viv as her support. Viv had left by the time Lily arrived. Lily didn't get out of her car, but peered expectantly through her windows at the yard. Her face fell when she saw no-one but me. She was probably still hoping that it would be Viv coming with her, not me. The smile she gave me when she pushed open the passenger door for me was anxious. The first thing she said as we set off, to my surprise, wasn't about Mel or about Heather. "Yazz," she asked humbly. "Viv's really pissed off with me, isn't she?"

I remembered Viv's face at breakfast, tired, unsmiling, downcast. "Pissed off isn't how I'd describe it, Lily," I said brutally. "Disillusioned, disappointed, shocked and a few other things besides."

"I'm sorry. I never meant any of those things I said last night. I know she's been trying to help me with all this. She's always there for me. I was just a bit… you know…. It's been hard for me. I lose it sometimes. I thought Viv could handle it."

"Even Viv has her limits, Lily," I answered. "but I'd have thought that how Viv feels is the last thing on your mind. It usually is."

"Heather's the most important person in my life right now, Yazz," she said quietly. "But you know what I've been thinking the whole night?"

The question was meant to be rhetorical, but I answered it anyway. "Not interested Lily. Just shut up and drive, will you?" I gave her the name of the suburb we were going to, an area overlooking the city.

Again, she obeyed with that surprising docility. There were relatively few cars on the road early on the morning of Good Friday, but for a while Lily focused all her attention on it as though it was peak hour traffic she was manoeuvring the car through. She was obviously thinking about more than her driving, because she said after a while, "Listen Yazz, Viv's important to me. You know that. I've lived without Heather for all these years, but Viv's been in my life since way before I had Heather. Even when Viv was out of the Party and when I was in exile, she was still there for me."

"And your point is?" I expected her to moan about being deserted by Viv on such an important occasion in her life, but Lily surprised me.

"How am I ever going to make things right with her?" she asked. "You and me, we fall out, Viv knocks out heads together and we make up. She gets pissed off with us and we say sorry and it's all over. This time it's different, isn't it? She's never going to forget what I said."

"True," I said. "Viv never forgets anything. What you mean is, she might hold it against your forever. You might have a point there. As I said, even Viv has her limits – and god knows you can try a person's limits, Lily, even someone like Viv's."

She was silent for another while. Then she said, "I know it's a lot to ask, but can you help me? Explain to her I didn't mean what I said? She'll believe you."

"We'll see," I said. "Just remember what you promised her, OK? That will go a long way to making things right." Lily didn't answer. She drove in silence the rest of the way.

When she pulled up at the address Mel had given me, she said to me. "You get out and go up. I have to find parking."

I turned to her, surprised to see that she was crying. I sighed. "Here," I took a pack of tissues from my bag. "Wipe your face, for god's sake. Get your act together and at least try to look pleased that you'll soon be seeing your long lost daughter." She turned the rear-view mirror so she could see in it. "You're right," she said. "I look a sight. I'll put on some makeup. Go on up. I'll come in a minute." I hesitated. "It's alright, Yazz. I'm not likely to run off am I? Go on now."

I rang the bell and Mel buzzed me into the foyer. I paused apprehensively in front of the lift. Lily's conversation had prevented me from dwelling on the possible reasons for Mel's distressed call that morning. Now I wondered what awaited me. The lift arrived. The door opened and a woman stepped out. She held the lift door for me, waiting. I thanked her and got in, taking a deep breath before pushing the button for the top floor. Two flats faced each other. One had the usual security gate, locked and barred, covering its door. The one I wanted was the one with the door open. Mel hadn't been back in South Africa long enough to acquire the national paranoia about crime. I knocked and walked in. Mel stood in the centre of the large sparsely furnished lounge. Her arms were wrapped around her body. One hand held the habitual cigarette. Smoke from it wreathed her body.

I walked swiftly over to her, my hands outstretched. "Mel! What's happened?"

She dropped her cigarette into an ashtray and took my hands. Hers were cold. Her face was pale, her eyes expressionless. "Zac's dead," she said flatly.

248

Her voice was so low I didn't think I'd heard her correctly. "What?" I asked. "I thought you said-"

"I did. Zac's dead."

"How can that be?"

She dropped my hands and turned to face the window, her back to me. "I don't know the details. There were some people from the police here this morning. Just before I called you. The Canadian police asked them to find me. All they told me was that his car went off the road a couple of days ago. He was-" She shuddered. "He burned to death inside the car, Yazz."

I shivered, as though an icy wind were blowing through the room. "Fuck!" I heard my own voice come from far off. "I don't believe this!"

"I didn't either." She lit another cigarette. "It seemed like someone's perverted idea of a joke." There was a twisted parody of a smile on her face. "But I checked. It's true. It seems this is the good lord's idea of poetic justice."

"What is?" The voice from the doorway was Lily's. I stared at her, aghast. "A man let me in," she said, obviously mistaking her unexpected appearance as the reason for my shock. She looked at Mel. "Where's Heather?" she demanded.

"Lily," Mel said. "I'm glad you've come." Her cordial words of welcome were at odds with her bleak tone. The disparity must have got through to Lily, because she paused before repeating her question more quietly. "Heather's out with a friend," Mel said. "I sent her away so that I could talk to you." She shut her eyes. Her composure seemed to waver, but she steadied herself with a drag on her cigarette. "Then the police came." She paused. "I was so glad Heather wasn't here." Her voice trembled as she asked the plaintive question: "How am I going to tell her?"

Lily turned to me in bewilderment. "Police? What's she on about? The police came here for Heather?"

"Zac's dead, Lily," I said, feeling the unreality of it even as I said the words. "He died in a car crash a few days ago. Mel only learnt this morning that he burnt to death in his car."

Lily raised a hand to her mouth. "Dead! He can't be!"

"He is," I asserted, looking hard at her. "Burnt to death."

"Well, don't look at *me*!" she cried, eyes bulging with shock and fear. "It *wasn't* me, Yazz! Don't *look* at me like that. Don't! I didn't-" Her voice rose to near hysteria. "You have to tell Viv! It wasn't me! Tell her she can't-"

"Shut up, Lily!" I got up and shook her hard. "This isn't about you! Christ, can't you see that? Your daughter has to be told she's lost a father and gained a second mother. Mel's going to need your help breaking the news to her. Stop thinking about yourself for once and try to get your head around that!" I shook her again hard, but I didn't let her go. Mel stepped between us and pushed me away from Lily.

"Yazz, stop it!" she cried, blinking at me in astonishment. "What are you doing? Why are you shouting at her? Can't you see she's had a shock?" She turned to Lily. "Come. Sit down." She drew Lily down on the sofa beside her. Lily let herself be led like a child, pleading eyes still on me.

Mel cupped Lily's face and turned it to her. "It's never crossed anyone's mind that you killed Zac, Lily," Mel said. "You may have wished it," she stroked Lily's face. "And who can blame you? There's no use in feeling guilty about that." She tucked a stray lock of Lily's hair behind her ear in a gesture so simple that I wondered how often she'd sat like that, tucking Heather's hair into place, comforting her. "The fact is, Lily," Mel said. "That Yazz is right. I do need your help. I have to tell my boys that their dad is dead. I have to tell Heather a lot more than that. How much grief our daughter has to bear, only you can decide." Lily said nothing. She simply sat there, eyes downcast.

Mel sighed and got up. She went outside to the balcony and picked up a photo album from the table where it lay as though in readiness for perusal. For a moment she hesitated, then she came back to Lily. "I brought this to show you," she said. "I was going to go through it with you, to show you what it's been like for Heather, being part of our family." She held the album out to Lily. "Now I don't think I could bear it."

For a long time Lily looked at the brightly coloured album cover, neatly labelled, "Heather Yasmin Vivienne Smith". Lily ran a finger over the name, murmuring it over and over. Then she started going through the album, slowly, methodically, studying each one carefully. "She looks happy," Lily murmured. "I always wanted her to be happy. My little Heather. She was such good little girl." She looked at me. "Wasn't she Yazz? You remember!"

I nodded. "I do, Lily," I said.

"Thank you," she said to Mel. "You did that." She flipped back to a group photo of Mel and Zac with all three of their children. Lily stared wistfully at it. "Your perfect family," she said, without an ounce of rancour or envy. She looked at Mel again. "I'm sorry," she said.

They stared wordlessly at each other for a long moment. Finally Mel said, "Heather's gone up Table Mountain. We could go right now to fetch her if you like. We could take the Cable Car and meet her at the top."

"No," Lily sighed. "Let her enjoy herself. She's got enough bad news coming. We need to think about what we'll tell her about me. Yazz said you had a plan." They both turned to look at me as though her mention of my name reminded them of my presence.

Mel came over to me. "I think Lily and I will be alright now." She stood on tiptoe and I bent my head for her kiss. "Thanks for bringing her, Yazz. Thanks for everything."

"Thanks for everything, Yazz," Lily echoed Mel's words. Her eyes were back on the album.

I moved away from Mel towards her "'Bye Lily," I said to her bowed head. "Good luck."

Lily stood and put out a hand to my belly. "I'm sorry," she said. "For everything. If I could…" The baby kicked under her hand. Lily smiled. "I'll come and see you when you have the baby," she whispered. "Me and Heather." There was a small beat before she added. "And Mel."

I sighed and hugged her. Lily had called Mel by name, not "that woman." She'd spoken their names as though they were a unit. That was enough for me. At least that was what I told myself. In reality, I'd like to have been a flea on the carpet of that room for the next few hours, if minimalist décor had included a carpet, but I left them there.

I called Viv and asked her to pick me up in town. Walking down the long slope into the city centre, I fancied I saw a blonde girl in a coffee shop window. When I turned to look, of course it wasn't Heather. It was just some other young woman, out for a coffee and a laugh with her mates. I hoped that wherever Heather was, she would stay for a long time, laughing. There was a lot a crying ahead of her before she'd laugh again. At the bottom of the Company Gardens I turned towards the steps of St. George's Cathedral. Here on these steps a long time ago, I'd been amongst the beaten and teargassed students who'd protested against apartheid. Here Lily had been too, and Viv, though we'd not known one another then, or how that youthful passion against injustice would unite us and then divide us. A stone's throw away, the house of parliament lay silent, its post-apartheid occupants on holiday. A lone protestor called for righting of wrongs, unaware that there was nobody there to hear him or to care what it was that he wanted.

Viv's car swung round the curve which joined Adderley Street to Wale Street. I got up, dusted myself down and walked over to her. "Let's join the masses at Sea Point for some ice cream," I said. Only Viv could be patient enough to wait until we'd got the ice-cream and sat watching the waves crash against the sea wall, for my account of what had happened with Mel and Lily.

"That's that then," Viv said when I'd finished.

"Lily says to tell you that Zac's death had nothing to do with her. She was quite desperate for me to make that absolutely clear to you. I think she's afraid that you'll rock this new boat she's decided to sail on.

Sorry. That's unfair. She also wanted me to let you know she loves you and wants you to forgive her."

Viv laughed. "So now, what about you? Have you found a ticket back to London yet? I only ask because I need to invite people to your farewell party. Or would you rather have a baby shower?"

I rolled my eyes. "Christ! Not you too. I didn't even think you knew what that was. Hell! A baby shower? At my age? Do you know anyone who's even pregnant at my age, let alone having baby showers!"

"Half of the women in the developing world are still having children at your age and beyond that, Yazz!" she said huffily. "Admittedly they wouldn't be having their first children, so they would already have things accumulated from previous pregnancies. You, however….." She let the words hang in the air.

"I don't have enough stuff? Have you seen my sister's old room? It's packed to the bloody rafters. I could open a branch of Mothercare, assuming I could find the money to hire a ship to take it all over to the UK! Thanks but no thanks. Baby shower!" Then I saw she was grinning. "Cow!" I slapped her shoulder. "You were having me on."

Viv's phone rang. When she answered it, I asked, "Lily? That was quick!" Viv shook her head and waved me on. I strolled ahead of her and waited a short distance away.

"I'm afraid we've come to the end of our outing," she said when she caught up with me. "I'll have to drop you off at home."

"Oh? Hot date?"

"You could say that," she said serenely. "In fact, I absolutely know that you would call this a hot date."

"Oh, wow. We aren't shy are we? Does Simon know?"

"He knows."

"I thought open relationships were a casualty of the drive to safe sex."

"I haven't the slightest idea what you're talking about, Yazz. Shall we go?"

We'd reached her car. I threw up my hands. "Alright, alright. Can't say I'm happy to be blown off because you're horny – sorry, poor choice of words – but I guess I'm ready for my nap. It's been a bloody long day." I got into the car. As usual, the movement lulled me to sleep. Which was just as well because when I got back to my parents' house, once again, I had a surprise visitor. I called Viv later to tell her I no longer needed to worry about all the baby stuff getting to London. My luggage allowance had doubled.

"Did Adam come with hand luggage only?" she asked.

"You knew?"

"You simply assumed that it was *I* who had the hot date, Yazz."

"And you weren't going to disabuse me of the notion."

In the end, even two luggage allowances weren't enough for all that the baby stuff. We took from South Africa what clothes and toys we thought our daughter would need and gave the rest to the antenatal section of the clinic Sandy used to work in. It took some working at, but we were able to take back to London also something our daughter would need more than clothes and toys – a firm unit of two parents. Last, we took from South Africa names suggested by Viv for our daughter. Amina Harriet Josephine. Amina had been a Queen of Nigeria, resisting colonial invasion. Harriet Tubman had fought against slavery. Josephine Baker had been a wonderful singer. Those names had been shortened to Ami, Harry and Jo to hide the gender of later bearers - three modern day freedom loving women - from the security police in apartheid South Africa.

Ami, Harry and Jo were once code names for Party comrades Yasmin, Vivienne and Lily.

Lightning Source UK Ltd.
Milton Keynes UK
UKHW011944281120
374281UK00001B/19